THE BEGINNING
OF WISDOM

Also by C. J. Brightley

A Long-Forgotten Song:
Things Unseen
The Dragon's Tongue

Erdemen Honor:
The King's Sword
A Cold Wind
Honor's Heir

Fairy King
A Fairy King
A Fairy Promise

THE BEGINNING OF WISDOM

A LONG-FORGOTTEN SONG
BOOK III

C. J. BRIGHTLEY

Egia, LLC

THE BEGINNING OF WISDOM. Copyright 2016 by C. J. Brightley. All rights reserved. No part of this book may be used or reproduced in any manner whatsoever without written permission except in the case of brief quotations embodied in critical articles and reviews. For information contact info@cjbrightley.com.

ISBN 978-1533154040

Published in the United Sates of America by Egia, LLC.

www.cjbrightley.com

Cover art by Vuk Kostic

For Daddy

ACKNOWLEDGEMENTS

My lovely beta readers Sarah, Jeff, Kathy, Ferran, Beth, Courtney, Adriel, and Laura were incredibly helpful and generous with their time. My husband Stephen was incredibly patient while I obsessed over this book. Most of all, my father deserves undying gratitude. He is as clever as Edwin but a steadfast servant of El.

CHAPTER 1

THE STEADY COLD DRIZZLE of the winter night drenched the asphalt, washing bits of paper and trash toward the drain near the intersection. Streetlights glared muted yellow into the darkness reflecting off the glass storefronts and white concrete and marble of the historic buildings. Colonel Paul Grenidor hunched his shoulders further and kept walking, eyes on the pavement before him.

"You survived."

Edwin's sudden presence didn't surprise him, and despite the tension in his shoulders, he found his heart didn't pound as it had earlier. He was too tired, emotions too torn, to recoil in fear.

"Yes."

"Yet you did not kill the vampire. Interesting." Edwin's voice was smooth and untroubled, and Grenidor finally glanced at him. Raindrops slipped down the sides of Edwin's face, but he appeared not to notice, though he met Grenidor's eyes for a tense heartbeat.

Grenidor looked back down.

Edwin's quick steps betrayed his irritation, and finally, he said, "You seem to have lost the talisman I gave you. The bull figurine."

"The idol." Grenidor's voice was flat.

"Call it whatever you like. Yes, *idol* is perhaps more descriptive. It is a symbol." Edwin's voice was tight with anger. "You thought you could rid yourself of your obligations, your commitments, by misplacing the symbol of our cooperation." The water running off Edwin's shoulders began to steam.

"I bought it." The irrelevant protest came without thought.

Edwin chuckled, the sound like a razor cutting through silk. "When you did so, it was only a little wooden statue made by children in a far-away land. I gave it meaning." His voice had changed, no longer reassuringly human, like that of a middle-aged man. Now it was deeper, reverberating off the brick of the surrounding buildings. Grenidor could feel the vibrations through the soles of his shoes.

"How it was lost is irrelevant. I have replaced it. There is a duplicate, indistinguishable from the original, in your apartment. Let it serve as a reminder of our partnership." Edwin glanced sideways at Grenidor. "In itself, it is powerless, a mere piece of stained wood. But symbols, Colonel... symbols are important." He smiled, the yellow lamplight glinting off his teeth. "I should also remind you that Feichin is still dangerous. Not as dangerous as I am, yet far more dangerous than you imagine. Do not be complacent about either of us." Then he was gone.

Block after block, Grenidor wandered, hands stuffed in his pockets. The rain slid inside his collar, and he shivered, but he didn't turn towards home. Not yet. He had too much to think about, and his apartment was hardly a warm, inviting place. Might as well do his thinking out in the street, where the weather matched his mood.

I left the transport cage behind. There is no way they won't notice that. And that Feichin is missing. He couldn't muster up the fear that discovery of his actions seemed to merit.

A shadow appeared at his side, and this time, he jumped. *The boy. M8.* Grenidor would have fled, but the boy reached out and caught his sleeve in one strong hand. He shook his head, then carefully let go of Grenidor, eyes cautious. *Waiting for me to bolt like a frightened rabbit.* Something stayed his steps. If the boy wanted to hurt him, he could have already.

The boy gestured toward a dark alley. Grenidor hesitated and then nodded. *Whatever he does to me, I deserve.* He took a deep breath and followed the Fae child into the alley and around a corner, well away from any prying eyes or surveillance. In the rain, Grenidor could barely see the faint pale oval of the boy's face, and he stopped.

The boy reached out to pull him farther, his fingers cold and strangely gentle on Grenidor's wrist. He stopped to open a door, ushered Grenidor inside, and closed it behind him.

Grenidor stood, tense and silent, in the pitch dark, until a light appeared, a gently glowing blue-green orb that settled near the ceiling.

"What is that?" he asked. *This is it. He wants to be sure I remember him before he kills me. Killing me on the street, without knowing who did it or why, wouldn't be the same.*

The boy pulled out a notebook and scribbled in it. *It is light since you cannot see in the darkness. Is it bright enough?*

Grenidor swallowed. "Yes. Thank you. What do you want?"

Do you remember me? The boy looked up at him, blue eyes wide and serious.

"M8, yes."

My name is Niall. Lord Owen is my uncle. The boy's gaze held his, and Grenidor felt his face flush.

"Niall. I'm… I guess you know me."

Yes. The boy took a deep breath and let it out slowly. *There is a shadow over you. We call them the dark ones. Feichin said it spoke to him, too.*

"A shadow?"

Dr. Bartok meant to speak with you about it. He has more wisdom than I do about how El relates to humans. But you… left. The boy looked up with a question in his eyes.

"I… yes." Grenidor's throat felt tight. He hadn't fled because he was afraid of Feichin or Owen.

Edwin hadn't been there, at least, not in any form that Grenidor could sense. Probably not at all, since he'd been so adamant about Grenidor killing Feichin before the meeting. But he'd been inside Grenidor's head, a deep, secret whisper that played on Grenidor's fear and his loathing of the vampires. It whispered, "Shoot! Shoot now!" while Owen was talking. It rose, frantic and furious,

12

screaming in his mind until Grenidor could barely catch his breath from fear of what Feichin would do.

Another voice whispered inside, telling him to drop the gun and beg for mercy... for forgiveness.

Edwin had no power over him other than what Grenidor himself had given him. Owen would forgive him, had *already* forgiven him. And if Owen spoke the words of the Slavemaster... the other side might also forgive him.

Thoughts of his crimes, his deeds over the last year, rose in his mind. Torture of the Fae. Lies. Deception. The call to Fletcher about the Christians. The blood on the bullets; somehow he felt that was at least as bad, perhaps worse, than anything else.

Human sacrifice. I asked, and Edwin didn't disagree with the phrase. I let it happen anyway.

Actually, I commanded it.

How could the other side forgive him, after all he'd done?

How could he forgive himself?

He was too far gone. Even Feichin was better than Grenidor. Feichin had been provoked beyond endurance while Grenidor had acted in cold calculation.

The hatred he felt for the vampires was nothing compared to the hatred he felt for himself.

Even so, he had not shot. Killing Feichin would be committing himself to Edwin's side, and that, he'd realized, was not something he could live with. Not now, anyway. He'd thrown the gun away to remove the temptation, even as his finger tightened on the trigger. It relieved him for a moment, and then the weight of shame crushed him.

minutes
- low

"...disgusting inside..." He realized he'd been mumbling aloud, trying to explain himself to Niall. To justify himself, as if there could be any justification for what he'd done. Some of it doubtless made no sense.

The boy reached out to touch his arm. *If you are ashamed, that is good. It means you understand the weight of rebellion. The weight of justice. You cannot be saved until you acknowledge that you need to be saved. But, as Feichin has proven, shame does not have to be the end.*

"Why are you here?" Grenidor's voice felt raspy in his throat.

For you. Niall tilted his head. *Feichin forgave you, and he was forgiven. Humans cannot sense it, though you could see the difference in his actions. We Fae can sense...* the boy hesitated and glanced off into the darkness for a moment, his face thoughtful. *Perhaps you would call it a state of grace. We exist under a covenant that is different than yours; we are given the means to be obedient, although we can choose rebellion. We had thought rebellion was final and absolute. Now we know it can be forgiven, the same way human sin is forgiven. We cannot sense sin in humans, but we can sense it in Fae. When Lord Owen spoke to Feichin, Feichin nodded. In that moment, he committed himself to El again, and in that moment, we could no longer sense his sin. It was as if it had never happened. He is as pure—no, purer—than any infant. You saw it only when he said, "I forgive you." That was important, but the critical decision was made when he nodded to Lord Owen.*

Dr. Bartok meant to tell you how to accept the grace that is offered to you, but you left too quickly. I came because... he paused again, and Grenidor realized the boy was trembling.

"Are you afraid of me?" Grenidor asked.

Niall looked up to meet his eyes. *A little. But I am much more afraid of the shadow. I cannot see it, but I know it has a hold over you. It is powerful and dangerous. But it held Feichin, and Feichin is now free. You can also be free.*

"It isn't as simple as that." Grenidor sighed heavily.

Are you afraid of me?

"A little."

You don't need to be. I wish to help you. I forgave you before, and I followed you because I wished to help you... but I was still angry with you. Now that I have heard you, I am no longer even angry. You need help.

"You're not angry with me? You should hate me. Because..." Grenidor gestured helplessly. "You can't even talk." He wanted to look at the boy's face, but his gaze kept sliding away, unwilling to meet those clear blue eyes.

Anger is permitted. Hatred is not. All the same, my anger has faded. Now I am only concerned for you. The boy's hand shook, and he scribbled, *I wish I had learned more from Dr. Bartok. I am not wise enough.*

Grenidor's heart twisted, but he said only, "I need to get home."

I will walk with you, if you permit me.

The light faded, and he led Grenidor out to the street. Niall was silent at his side, slipping through the shadowed streets. The wind gusted, driving the rain sideways for a moment, and Grenidor hunched further into his coat. Niall seemed oblivious to the cold, but he clutched the notebook under his shirt, trying to keep it from getting soaked.

The doorman held the door for him, and Grenidor stepped inside, half-expecting Niall to disappear. But he followed Grenidor all the way into the elevator, a wordless shadow by his elbow.

Grenidor pushed the button for his floor and the elevator began to rise. "Are you going to follow me to bed?" he asked.

Are you afraid of your dreams?

"That's not any of your business." Grenidor couldn't muster any anger in his voice.

At this hour, the halls were deserted, and Grenidor saw no one as he led the way down the hall to his door and unlocked it. The boy hesitated, then asked, *May I enter? There is something in your room. Something… wrong. May I come inside?*

"I guess. I don't have an extra bed." As soon as he spoke, Grenidor recalled the legend that vampires could not enter without permission. Even Edwin had waited for an invitation. Maybe all these magical beings needed invitations or permission to enter dwellings or make themselves known. Too late now, though.

I will leave when you ask. The boy stepped inside, gaze flicking over the room to fix on the door to Grenidor's bedroom. *It is in that room. With your permission, I will go first.*

"If you want to." Grenidor followed him, hand dropping to his holster before he realized it was empty. "Yes. Please."

Niall stopped in the doorway, then crept forward, tense and silent. He pointed to the little statue with one finger and raised his eyebrows at Grenidor.

"It's just a token. A souvenir."

It is evil. Burn it. Niall was trembling, breath coming fast. *May I? Please. It should be destroyed.*

"Um…" Grenidor hesitated. "I…"

Edwin spoke from the front door. "Is there some sort of problem, Colonel?"

Sudden terror flooded him, as much for Niall as for himself.

"No. I'm fine." Grenidor looked back to see Edwin squinting at him. "Why are you here?" He was momentarily grateful for his drained emotional state. It kept his voice steady, not betraying the panic that fluttered within his belly.

"I felt… danger. Someone is here with you. One of the Slavemaster's minions."

Grenidor glanced at Niall, who only now looked back up at him.

Is something wrong? To whom are you speaking?

"Can you see him?" Grenidor gestured toward Edwin, who took a half step closer.

Niall glanced toward the door and around the room, then back to Grenidor. He shook his head, his face reflecting only innocent confusion. *Do you see something?*

"Yes." Grenidor glanced between them. Then, "Do you see him?" he asked Edwin.

Edwin's face was partially turned away, but he glanced toward Grenidor just long enough to meet his eyes. "I see a blank spot. I cannot see him. Move back. He's dangerous. Don't listen to him. Whatever he says, he lies. He twists truth into something unrecognizable. He is trying to trick you, as I warned you."

Challenging Edwin hadn't worked out well yet. His voice hissed with hatred… but it also held an undertone of caution, something held back as if

17

he wasn't quite sure who was in the room with Grenidor. Besides, if Edwin couldn't see or hear Fae...

"How do you know?"

Niall's pale lips were set in concentration, and he flicked his fingers at the wooden figure. Flames burst from the tabletop and surrounded the bull. Niall stared at it, watching the flames burn higher. The reflection danced in his eyes.

Grenidor stood transfixed, watching the wood turn to embers and then to ash in a matter of moments. The tabletop was unmarred, save the little pile of ash.

Edwin had not answered his question, and Grenidor didn't repeat it.

Niall turned to him, eyes hard. *That is better. But there is still a shadow in the room, both in you and...somewhere else. I cannot banish it for you. It is a decision you must make on your own.*

Grenidor glanced at Edwin, who squinted toward them as if staring into the sun.

"He's lying, Grenidor. The Slavemaster's minions cannot be trusted. Don't let him get too close to you."

Be careful, Colonel Grenidor. No one can hope to manipulate the dark ones, nor defeat them alone. It is better to plead for El's mercy. He will claim His own victory.

Grenidor hesitated, his gaze flicking between Edwin and Niall. Edwin seemed somehow less dangerous in Niall's presence. Less arrogant, at least, perhaps even a little nervous. *I'm more afraid of Edwin than Niall. If I were smart, I'd keep him here. I don't think he plans to kill me in my sleep, and Edwin's keeping his distance. But no; Edwin is dangerous, and*

Niall is a child. I've done enough to him, harmed him more than enough already. To keep him here, in danger, because I'm afraid to be alone with Edwin, is cowardly. I'm not ready to sink so low yet. Besides, it might just provoke Edwin. I don't want to see him enraged.

"I'll keep that in mind. I'm tired. Are you done?"

As you wish. Niall tucked his notebook under his arm, gave him a silent half-bow, and strode toward the door. Grenidor sucked in his breath. The boy's movements were so quick, and Edwin so unprepared, that Edwin barely slipped out of his way as Niall brushed past his elbow. The boy appeared completely oblivious to Edwin's presence, neither seeing nor hearing him. But Edwin hissed in pain as the boy's shoulder passed close by him. He stumbled back a half-step, raising his hands over his face; then he straightened to smile at Grenidor. Niall closed the door behind himself with an almost inaudible click.

Grenidor tried to replay the movement in his mind. *Edwin flinched back as if he'd been burned. But Niall didn't do anything to him, didn't even see him. What does that mean?*

Edwin stared at him a moment, eyes narrowed, then glanced at the ashes on the top of the table as if seeing them for the first time. An image flickered behind Grenidor's eyelids, a winged serpent raising its head to strike, vast and deadly, glittering scales and golden eyes narrowed in fury. Edwin checked himself and glanced around as if to reassure himself that Niall had left.

"You play a dangerous game, Grenidor." Then he was gone.

GRENIDOR COULD NOT SLEEP for hours. He lay in the darkness, thoughts churning, and wondered why he was still alive.

He'd begun, out of habit, by considering the tactical knowledge he'd gained about Edwin and the Fae from the encounter. Edwin hadn't appeared to notice the burned remains of the idol until after M8—Niall, had left. Evidently, it was in the blank area around Niall. But Edwin had seen Grenidor the whole time, so he was outside the blank spot. *Or maybe he can see me all the time since I'm in his service, or at least, I don't belong to the Slavemaster. But he didn't look like he was looking at a blank spot. It was more like he just couldn't look directly at Niall, like I couldn't keep my eyes open and look directly into a spotlight. Or the sun.*

He sighed. The thoughts were only a way to keep from thinking about the really important issues. The ones that truly frightened him.

Edwin was powerful. He lied, but he probably did have the ability to grant Grenidor the physical favors he'd promised. Power. Followers, perhaps even worshippers. He was also not lying about his ability to ruin Grenidor; he might do it even if Grenidor went along with his plans. He probably wouldn't as long as Grenidor was useful, but then Grenidor couldn't deceive himself into thinking he was indispensable. In fact, Edwin's own assessment of the meeting implied that he would have been willing, even preferred, to have Grenidor die killing Feichin and Owen. If he could manipulate Grenidor so easily, he probably had others under his thumb, as well. He would have replacements ready.

Edwin was probably lying about the Conflict, what he wanted, what the other side wanted... everything.

Including the Slavemaster.

Perhaps I could have told myself that I was deceived before. Not anymore. Owen and his side are better than I am. Edwin, for all his promises and all his power, is evil.

I didn't know I believed in evil, but now I do. It's more than ugliness. More than being repulsive. More than my stomach curdling when I think about him. He can be attractive, but he's always evil.

I wish I had never spoken to him.

Even the vampire told me he was evil, and I would be better not talking to him... and he was evil himself, and he hated me personally. Yet, I think he told the truth. So... how evil is Edwin?

I wish he would disappear, that the Slavemaster would kill him or eliminate him or send him back wherever he came from. But if he disappeared, my fate is... well, it wouldn't be pretty. The best I could hope for is a trial and quick execution. Assuming everything ends at death. But Edwin has pretty clearly said that death isn't the end; I'm afraid he hasn't been lying about that. At least not completely.

Perhaps death is fair, but I didn't mean to be in the wrong.

But I was. Oh, how I was and am. Liar. Torturer. Murderer.

There is no way the Slavemaster could possibly want me now. There is no hope for me.

There is no way the Slavemaster could possibly accept me now, even if I did try to turn to his side. Edwin isn't even pretending I can choose to be on neither side. Independence isn't an option.

C. J. BRIGHTLEY

Even though I keep telling myself I was tricked into choosing the wrong side, I think the things that count most against me were things I did with my eyes open.

I was never completely fooled. I just wanted to be.

I am evil. *I can't pretend to myself that I'm not.*

I just wish I weren't.

CHAPTER 2

THE FAE STUDIED FEICHIN, their eyes wide and wondering. Ardghal glanced cautiously over his shoulder at the little bull figurine, then murmured to Owen, his voice an indistinct whisper of wind in distant leaves.

Bartok strode to the idol and stomped on it. The wood cracked; one thick leg broke off and rolled across the concrete. The bull's miniature horns dislodged from their holes.

"You broke it." Ardghal's eyes widened.

Bartok's lip curled in disgust. "It's a piece of wood. It has no power but what we give it."

The idol was forgotten when Petro appeared without warning. He strode into their midst with an air of purpose, the Fae shifting away from him like water fleeing from oil.

Petro knelt directly in front of Owen and Feichin and studied their faces, his green eyes glowing. His clothes shifted in a breeze Aria did not feel, the fabric (*is it fabric?*) such a brilliant white that she could scarcely bear to look at him. His face was almost as bright, the metallic sheen highlighting the inhuman coldness of his expression.

"You have changed." Petro's voice was low, a rumble that reminded Aria of distant thunder or a coming earthquake. The words were a statement, not a question, but Feichin glanced at Owen as if wondering what sort of reply was expected.

"Yes. He has." Owen put a hand on Feichin's shoulder, the gesture protective and reassuring. He stared back at Petro, his brilliant blue irises ringed in white. Feichin seemed to be frozen in terror, unaware that Owen's fingers dug into his shoulder.

Even Owen, despite his courage, was terrified.

Aria wondered what they perceived that she did not.

His broad shoulders dwarfing the Fae in front of him, Petro shifted to study their faces from every angle. Owen and Feichin did not move, only watching him from the corners of their eyes as he circled them again. He glanced between them as if comparing them in some way.

"Why do you keep looking at them? What are you trying to figure out?" Aria's heart stuttered when Petro glanced at her, the hairs on her arms suddenly at attention. His glowing eyes had the dangerous look of heat lightening.

Petro turned his gaze back to Owen and Feichin, ignoring Aria. For long seconds he said nothing, and Aria had begun to think he would not speak at all. Then he said, "You pity humans for the wrong reason. You lament their short lives

24

as if they are mayflies and you are long-lived. To me, you are all mayflies, living for mere moments.

"Yet your short lives are critical and precious, and I am only now beginning to understand why. There is no end, as you have imagined it. *That* is why you should pity some humans.

"I had not fully appreciated the magnificence of the covenant under which El offers grace to your kind. I wish to partake of the benefits, but I did not understand, what the covenant meant. I am beginning to see more clearly how we are different."

"We… who? You and humans? You and Fae?" Aria asked.

"Your distinction between Fae and humans is artificially wide."

Owen blinked. "We are not even the same species. We only now have begun to understand that we can be saved as humans can."

"You call yourselves Fae, and them human, as if the differences between you are more significant than they are. You live under different covenants, and you magnify your superficial differences because you lack perspective. You see yourselves and each other as through a clouded glass.

"You were allowed to touch El's power for reasons I do not comprehend. He has His own purposes, and they are good. But with that power came temptations, and so He wrote rules on your hearts. The rules protect others, who have no such power, and they protect you. They keep you innocent, as children and as animals, for you obey without question. Obedience is worship, and worship is obedience. You are brought to worship as children before the sin that infects you is held against you. As children, you approach, and as children, you are accepted, with faith you do not understand. You are given grace. You can rebel, and you know this, but you are given the strength and inclination to obey. Most remain obedient, and when you die, your obedience is counted as righteousness."

Aria frowned and spoke first, though everyone but Petro looked confused. She asked, "So... they're without sin?"

"No. But El made it easy for them to understand and avoid rebellion. The lines are clearly marked and their hearts are drawn toward obedience. He has chosen to give them a generous covenant.

"A tree cannot be a good tree or a bad tree; it can only be a tree. It can conceive of nothing else but to be a tree. If it falls and kills a man, the tree has not sinned. It has only acted in accordance with its own nature and the forces that have played upon it. Fae are not trees, but they are closer to trees than humans are.

"Humans... their covenant is different. Newer. They approach El with sinful hearts, born into rebellion, and throw themselves on his mercy. They ask for the one they sin against to pay the penalty for them, and he does. It is appalling and beautiful. It is difficult for them, and they struggle with rebellion until their dying breath. Many never accept grace."

Aria felt an uncomfortable twinge of conviction. Guilt. Shame. If God had *really* died for her, then she didn't have the right to reject grace, did she?

Petro turned his eyes on her again and tilted his head to the side as if he were reading her thoughts on her face.

"What?" she asked when he continued staring at her.

"You tell yourself you are waiting for a miracle to prove El's grace to you. Yet the difficulty you face is not lack of proof. You—humans—are reluctant to commit yourselves to El. Indeed, you are disinclined even to carefully consider the question, for you know that if you consider, you risk deciding. You fear that accepting what is offered means giving up what you have. This is… illuminating."

She blinked. "I…"

Petro's gaze snapped upward and then he knelt, both knees to the floor, hands in his lap and head down. Aria blinked at a momentary impression of vast wings folding up behind him.

There was silence, taut and alive with the tension of something important hidden from their perception.

Petro's voice rumbled, making a sound that might have been a language but was nothing she could understand. It was revealed to her that he was speaking, though.

He looked back at them, though he did not rise. His size seemed changeable; though he was kneeling, his eyes were a foot or so above the top of Aria's head.

He vanished.

"WHAT HAPPENED JUST THEN?" Bartok murmured to Aria.

The Fae huddled around Feichin and Owen, offering strength through their song.

Aria glanced up at Bartok. "Can you see them?"

"Not anymore."

"Petro came." Aria shivered, unsure whether it was fear or relief or merely chill that made her skin tingle. "He said a lot of things that I need to think about." Her voice trailed away.

She relayed most of Petro's words to him later, over hot water masquerading as tea. He listened and nodded, his long, thin fingers wrapped around the warm thermos.

"So he vanished?"

"Like he wasn't meant to be saying those things to us. But... wouldn't God be able to stop him if he was going to say too much?"

Bartok shifted, his eyebrows drawing downward. "Of course, God *could*. But he didn't. I'm not sure that the *why* is particularly important, either."

The silence was comfortable, despite the questions whirling in Aria's mind. "What do you—"

"I was—"

They both stopped and then grinned. "Go ahead," Bartok prompted her.

"What do you remember of life before the Revolution?" she asked. "I don't remember much."

Bartok looked down at his hands. "School, mostly. Pre-med was rather intense. I've often thought I should have been paying better attention. I was focused on my little world and missed the changes that set up the Revolution. People vanished sometimes. I think some of them went underground; others were disappeared by the government."

Aria rubbed the back of her neck, imagining the tiny wire in her brain. "Do you think I'm still brainwashed?"

Bartok snorted. "Not in the least. Not in any way that matters. You're questioning, aren't you? You're wondering. You're learning. You're not just passing by, blithely confident that you understand it all."

The weak tea scent tickled Aria's nostrils, and she inhaled, closing her eyes. "Do you ever think about people you used to know?"

He sighed. "I do. I wonder about them. I pray for them. I wish I'd been bolder. I wish I'd told them about God."

The edge in his voice caught her, and she glanced at him. "I didn't imagine you had anything to regret."

He raised his eyebrows. "Being a Christian doesn't mean you don't have regrets. It just means that you're forgiven. Wallowing in regret doesn't honor the blood Christ shed for me."

Aria looked down, running her finger over the edge of her thermos. "Do you have an answer for everything?"

Bartok tilted his head. "Do I come across that way? I don't mean to."

"No, but... you never seem as flustered as I feel. Or frightened or lost or anything." Aria sighed heavily. "Is that you, or is that Christ in you?"

"It's definitely not me." He smiled ruefully. "And I'm pretty terrified, to be honest. I don't relish the thought of being tortured or executed as a political rebel or a Christian. But I gave my life to God years ago. I keep reminding myself that although circumstances have changed, God has not. I don't want to turn away simply because I forgot who made me."

MOST OF THE FAE dispersed in the tunnels. Owen remained some distance from the camp, sitting silently with his legs crossed and his elbows on his knees, looking across the human camp as if lost in thought. Feichin slept a short distance from him, and Aithne kept a silent vigil near her father.

Bartok had gone to sleep, but Aria still felt restless. She approached Owen, barely able to make out his figure in the shadows. It was past midnight, and the train station, while always dark, seemed even more desolate now with the few distant lanterns turned down as low as they could go.

Aria sat by Owen without a word, resting her elbows on her knees. It was impossible to guess how long she sat. Once she thought she heard Owen singing, but then she thought perhaps she had imagined it.

The darkness made her momentarily bold. "Do you feel anything for me?" The question was blunt, but then she'd already told him she loved him. *Can't get much more blunt than that.*

"You mean romantically?" he asked, his voice careful, as if he hadn't anticipated the question and wanted to be sure he understood what she meant.

"Well, yes. I mean… I don't expect you to, but I thought I'd ask. Not that there's much time to pursue anything. I should probably stop talking now."

She could hear the smile in his voice. "I am grateful for your care for me. Unasked-for kindness is exceedingly rare in my experience, and what you have given is worth much."

That wasn't really an answer. Maybe that's my answer. He doesn't want to hurt me by saying 'no', but the answer is no.

She stifled a sigh.

Owen shifted so that she knew he faced her, though she couldn't see him. Then a soft light suffused the air between them.

He studied her face and inclined his head toward her in a slight, regal bow. "I have many responsibilities, and they weigh more heavily on me now than at any previous time. I am not at liberty to consider my own romantic inclinations, whatever they may be. I have the utmost respect for you, as well as deep gratitude for what you have done for my family, for my people, and for me."

She felt tears pricking at her eyes, and blinked angrily, no longer meeting his gaze. Now wasn't the time to cry; he was as kind and honorable as she could possibly have imagined.

He sighed softly. "I am sorry I cannot give you an answer more pleasing. Yet I am not confident that any other answer would result in less pain for you, and I have no wish to cause you pain." He reached out to brush one cold finger over her cheek, wiping away the tear that had escaped her eye. "I—we, Fae—have misunderstood so many things about love that any answer I gave you would be fraught with misunderstanding."

"I know." She swallowed the lump in her throat and forced a smile. "Thanks." *For being honest. As if he could be anything other than honest.*

He smiled, and even in the soft light, she saw the kindness in his eyes. "I thank you." He hesitated and then reached out to brush the backs of his fingers across her cheek. The light faded.

FEICHIN ATE AGAIN only six hours later, a testament to the hunger that still tormented him. Eli had given him new clothes from their meager supplies, which hung on his skeletal frame.

Aria sat some distance away with Gabriel, Eli, and Bartok, going through the papers Owen had retrieved from the imperial facilities. Aria had trouble focusing on the papers, her attention inexorably drawn to the Fae.

Her wariness battled with pity when she saw Feichin's hand shaking as he raised a piece of meat to his mouth. Owen stayed close by him, closer than Aithne, who loved him but kept her distance after her initial welcome. Owen was warmer than the others, not especially demonstrative, but more concerned, more sympathetic, and more gentle with others' pain.

Perhaps that's why he's Ailill's heir. The thought came suddenly, and she turned it over in her mind. *Yes, I think so. Niall understood that, too, even if the others don't. Niall chose to act on the love Owen demonstrates, and to Grenidor of all people. Love for a man he has every reason to hate.*

Owen put a hand on Feichin's shoulder and sang, the music almost inaudible to her ears, though it wove around her soul. Silver threads in the air, gossamer thin, strong enough to banish her fear and weariness for a few short minutes. *Green grass, open meadows, a mountain brook leaping through the rocks. Light dancing on water, reflected glory of the sun above.*

She closed her eyes, letting the music touch her like sun on her shoulders, then looked up to see the other Fae smiling, their faces shining with joy like that filling her own heart. Gabriel, Eli, and Bartok appeared unaffected; they continued studying the papers before them.

"Doesn't it make you feel better?" she asked impulsively.

Gabriel looked up. "What?"

"The song. Doesn't it make you feel better?"

"What song?" Gabriel blinked at her blankly.

Aria opened her mouth, then closed it again. She shook her head. "Never mind."

Gabriel gave her a strange look, then shrugged and went back to reading. Bartok held her gaze for a moment and then glanced over his shoulder toward the Fae. He gave her a faint smile and went back to reading.

Owen is singing so quietly and so far from me that I should not be able to hear him. Yet I do. I am not even sure whether I hear him more with my ears or with my heart.

The realization that she could hear Owen as the Fae could, rather than remaining oblivious to his song, filled Aria with unexpected joy.

Feichin bowed his head. "I thank you, Lord Owen."

Owen smiled; then he sighed with weariness he could no longer conceal. "Thank El." He rested his forehead against Feichin's bony shoulder, barely able to keep his eyes open.

"What is wrong?" Feichin asked.

Owen gave a soft grunt, a friendly non-answer. He sighed again and then slipped forward, losing consciousness in slow motion.

Feichin twisted to catch him before his face hit the floor. Cillian caught him too, and the two of them turned him over so that he lay supine, eyes closed.

Feichin looked at Cillian with a question on his face.

"He is weak and in pain. He is healing, but he was close to death. Tortured beyond what I thought even Grenidor would do. We believe he still has getlaril in his body; it is being eliminated, but slowly." Cillian placed a hand on Feichin's shoulder. "But he is also strong, stronger than I. I wanted to kill Grenidor, and it would have been permitted. He forbade it." Cillian gave Feichin a faint, solemn smile. "You also are stronger than I. I don't know that I could have forgiven Grenidor if I were you."

Feichin sighed softly. "It is not my strength." His eyes followed Niamh, who paced slowly behind Cillian, only her tense shoulders betraying her frustration.

Feichin studied Owen's face for some moments, then pulled up the hem of Owen's shirt to reveal bruises still covering Owen's torso, purple and blue now as they healed. The dark blood spots of the bullet wounds had turned into livid red scars, still sunken and tender. "This is better?"

"Much," Cillian said.

Feichin nodded thoughtfully. Aria thought his eyes seemed more gentle than before. He said, "I know it troubles you that Niall is risking himself. But there is hope for Grenidor."

"Is there?" Niamh asked, halting to kneel beside them. "Do you think he will change his mind?"

"On his own? No, but. I would not have either. El pursued me, and I was saved. I have no standing to say that Grenidor is too lost to be saved." Feichin took a deep, shuddering breath, steadying his voice. "I don't think he has entirely committed to the dark one's plans. The dark one wanted him to kill me before this meeting, and he resisted. Perhaps not from mercy. Perhaps it was not any motive he would even be able to name. But he was pushed, and he resisted. That tells me El has not ceased pursuing him."

"I agree," Niamh said. Cillian nodded as well.

Owen sucked in a breath and his eyes fluttered open. "Sorry," he muttered, and started to sit up, then bit back a groan.

"Rest, Lord Owen." Feichin smiled, his eyes filling with tears. "I trusted you, because, well, you are Lord Owen. But I did not think you truly understood the pressure and the pain, the desperation. How much I endured, and why I turned. But now I think you know, and you merely did not fall, as I did. Rest, and we will sing for you."

Owen allowed Cillian and Niamh to help him sit up again, and he leaned forward to rest his elbows on his knees, letting his head hang down between his shoulders. "You give me too much credit. I did lie, not out of anger, but out of desperation and weakness. Perhaps some would see it as more understandable than other sins, but we know lies are forbidden. I would have fallen, only I prayed for forgiveness and El took mercy on me. As he did on you. I am no better than you are." He

35

raised his head to hold Feichin's gaze. "Forgiven is forgiven. That is all that matters."

THE SCENT OF HOT CHICKEN and rice soup drew Aria back to the human encampment. It was almost, but not quite, the scent of the soup her mother had made so often during winter when Aria was young. *It's reassuring, even though I know she's gone.*

She sat next to Bartok, feeling his quiet presence as a comfort. He smiled at her before bowing his head and closing his eyes. Aria took the opportunity to study his face. His hair was a bit shaggy, and his lean cheeks were darkened by a three-day beard. She hadn't noticed those tiny crinkles by his eyes before, nor the small, faded triangular scar just in front of his left ear.

They ate in silence for several minutes, listening to the others chat. On one side, Evrial was explaining some quirk about old Army logistics to someone and grumbling about how it was different now anyway. A little closer, Dominic and Benjamin were regaling Geoffrey with some story about a past mission.

"How'd you get that scar?" Aria asked.

Bartok blinked at her. "What scar?"

"By your ear. I just noticed it."

Bartok looked confused for a moment and raised his hand to the spot. "Oh, I fell out a window." He grinned at her expression. "I was eight. I had my bed lofted with my desk underneath, and my friend Pete and I liked to climb up and then swing down pretending we were paratroopers. I swung a bit too enthusiastically and tumbled out the window. Gave my parents a scare."

Aria snorted. "I bet so. How far was it?"

"Third floor! I landed on our neighbor's car more or less on my feet and broke my ankle. That's why I went into medicine. The scar was from something on my desk that I hit on the way out the window. Or possibly the window frame."

"You're lucky. That could have gone much worse."

"I prefer to think of it as being given grace." Bartok smiled tolerantly at her slightly skeptical look. "What is luck, anyway? Something going unexpectedly right?" His smile broadened. "As if God didn't make the rules of the universe?"

Aria shrugged half-heartedly, and Bartok's expression softened. "What's wrong?"

"I'm... There's so much to think about," she mumbled, no longer looking at him. He wasn't worried or concerned, and his confidence suddenly irritated her. *It's not fair,* she thought. *Why isn't he worried or afraid? If God exists... if he's good... why won't he intervene now? Why does it feel like we're on our own?*

Animatedly waving a hand, Dominic hit Aria's canteen, sending it tumbling. Aria caught it before it spilled.

"Nice catch," Dominic said. "Sorry about that. I didn't realize you had super reflexes."

"Um... I got lucky."

Dominic cocked an eyebrow. "I doubt it. Goes along with the hotshot marksmanship." He gave her an apologetic smile and turned back to Benjamin and Geoffrey.

Bartok studied Aria's face. "Yeah. Nice catch."

Aria forced a smile, but her heart was thudding in her chest. Bartok changed the subject, and she tried to put it behind her.

I shouldn't have been able to catch the canteen. Maybe someone else would have, but not me. Not even if I was expecting it. I'm not that fast or coordinated.

"Could you have caught that canteen, Bartok?"

He shrugged. "Probably not." His eyes held hers. "Someone with *really* good reflexes might be able to do it. Maybe. If they were lucky."

"I don't think I should have been able to catch it," she breathed, her words almost inaudible.

Bartok shifted, and she thought for an instant he meant to put his hand over hers. *He'll feel my hand shaking*, she thought wildly. He drew back without touching her. *Would it have been so bad if he had? It would be comforting. I could use some comfort.*

She didn't reach for him.

"You wouldn't have been able to... before?" Bartok murmured, his words for her alone.

Aria shook her head. *I'm not sure how I feel about having super reflexes. Maybe I was just lucky.*

FEICHIN DROPPED TO SIT beside her, the movement sudden and startling. Aria squeaked in terror and jerked away, trying to scramble to her feet. His hand shot out and he grasped her wrist, his grip cold and hard as steel.

"Stay. I mean you no harm." He held her wrist until she nodded reluctantly. Then he let her go.

She sat cautiously at the very limit of arm's reach, her heart thudding. *He killed a man with his teeth.* Without hatred twisting his expression into a grimace, she could see the model-perfect lines of his cheekbones, nose, and jaw. He should have been as beautiful as Owen. But he was still so thin the lantern light cast ghoulish shadows across his hollow cheeks and under his eyes. His irises were a pale silvery blue, lighter than Owen's, and they gleamed in the shadows.

"I mean you no harm," he repeated. "I was what you would call a vampire. I am no longer. I am not exactly as I was before, but I am not a monster to be feared either."

Aria tried to keep her voice steady. "I saw what they did to you. I can't blame you for being angry."

He inclined his head in an oddly regal gesture. "My anger was not my rebellion. My rebellion against El was in my hatred and judgment." He took a deep breath. "But I did not come to you to frighten you. I wished to speak with you about your status as a Fae raised human. Will you speak with me?"

Aria studied him. Her vision was sharper; even in the flickering light, she saw him clearly. The old cotton shirt he had been given hung on him; the points of his bones protruded so sharply that just looking at him made her want to wince in sympathy.

"Are you hungry?" she whispered.

He seemed startled by the question. "Are you asking if I desire human blood, or does my appearance frighten you?"

"Um… both, I think."

"We are carnivores. I enjoy the same food as Lord Owen and the other Fae when it is available. I do not desire human blood especially, but when I was a vampire…" he hesitated, watching her face. "When I was a vampire, I desired human blood and flesh above all other foods. The taste was much like that of any other animal, but the humanity of it both satisfied and fueled my hatred. I no longer hate; therefore, I no longer desire to hurt humans. I ate only a few hours ago, some of the meat that Ardghal procured, so I am satisfied for now.

"If my appearance disturbs you, I may be able to change it. It is easy to change a Fae's appearance to humans, but the technique does not work on Fae. Given your ability to see through our concealment efforts, I cannot promise that the attempt will be effective."

"Change your appearance?"

"We do not do it often; it is a form of lying and therefore to be avoided. Nevertheless, Fae who have not fallen are permitted to use a version of the technique to hide, so we all have some practice. If you are aware of the change and consent to it for your own… comfort… it is not rebellion. Shall I try it?"

She swallowed. *How can I ask him to conceal the physical evidence of the torture he endured so that I don't have to be made uncomfortable by looking at it?* "No. I… I'm sorry I even thought about it."

He inclined his head again.

"I didn't… I'm sorry, but I didn't expect you to be so articulate or so thoughtful. I thought you were different." She realized belatedly how insulting the words were.

Feichin let out a huff of breath, as if she'd punched him in the stomach. "Please do not believe that the entirety of my life is shown on those

40

videos." His voice was low, with the hint of sobs behind the carefully enunciated words. "I'm three hundred and twenty-one years old. I was captive for a little over two years. For the sake of a moment's anger, I threw away centuries of obedience and joy to indulge a hideous temptation. I am more deeply aware of that horror than you can imagine, and I thank El that I am no longer that vampire. But you should know that I was Fae before I turned, and I am Fae again, of a sort."

Aria caught her breath. "I'm sorry," she whispered again.

He stared at her for a tense moment, then nodded. When he spoke again, his voice had the sense of deliberately putting away the insult. "Thank you. First, I heard from Lord Owen the crime that was committed against you, that you were born Fae, stolen from your parents, and raised human.

"From what Cillian told me, Lord Owen seems slightly more human than other Fae, though no less pure. I seem more human than he is, though still fully Fae. They can sense that I have been brought back into fellowship with El, and there is no lingering stench of rebellion on me. You, though born Fae, appear to be fully human; we cannot sense rebellion or obedience on you, just as we cannot sense the state of a human heart. Dr. Bartok and Colonel Grenidor are not noticeably different to us, aside from their words and actions, which any human might observe.

"In considering this, I have a unique perspective, one that is perhaps unprecedented. To my knowledge, no turned Fae, or vampire as humans call them, has ever been forgiven before; Fae have never known it was a possibility. Turned Fae have rejected the covenant under which we commune with El and have taken themselves outside it. Humans also are outside it, and reach El as Lord Owen explained to me, by turning away from rebellion and begging for grace. This human covenant is also, apparently, available to us.

"You also are outside the covenant of Fae, but not the way a turned Fae is. With turned Fae, there is a stench of rebellion; it is repulsive and horrible beyond ... beyond my ability to describe it." He shuddered involuntarily, clenching his fists and breathing quickly, as if trying to quell overwhelming nausea. "I've met turned Fae before. It is horrifying; their very existence is obscene. Becoming one myself was like choosing, in a moment of weakness, to become, *to revel in becoming*, the pile of excrement you wouldn't want to get on your shoe.

"Humans, however, are opaque to us. We have no way to sense their rebellion. Yet we know they can commune with El.

"You also must be able to. As both Fae and human, you have the ability; you must only approach El. I doubt you can approach him as a Fae, but you must be able to as a human, for that way is open to both human and Fae. Do you commune with El?

Aria blinked, considering the question. "You're asking if I'm a Christian?"

Feichin tilted his head. "Is that what it is called in English? Do you trust in El's grace, as Lord Owen explained it to me?"

Aria swallowed. "I... I guess so? I mean, it worked, didn't it?"

Feichin let out a soft breath. "Oh, child." He bowed his head and studied his hands. "I have no standing to tell you what to do. But I will say this: I would rather die now in physical torment of any creative sort that Grenidor or his scientists could devise than have been fed to my body's satisfaction while I remained... what I was. Do not spurn El's grace."

"I... thank you." She sighed. "You and Bartok would get along well."

Feichin inclined his head. "Yes, I would be honored to speak with him at some point."

Aria couldn't help smiling. *I'm discussing the state of my soul with a saved vampire and pointing him to a doctor, a scientist, who talks about God. I'm not sure I'm ready to serve this God. Sometimes, I feel like I'm ready, and other times... He demands too much. I'm not ready to make that kind of commitment. Because I don't think this God would be happy with token words. It's all or nothing. Hot or cold.*

Her throat seemed tight with sudden emotion. *How long can I wait before I decide? This is important, and I don't want to be rushed, and I don't want to mess it up. I don't have forever to decide. Time is running out.*

Feichin was watching her, and she had the disconcerting feeling that he could read her thoughts on her face.

"I have other topics to discuss with you if you are willing."

She nodded.

Feichin steepled his thin fingers together and studied them for a moment before he began. "I spoke with a dark one, a being I believe is much like Conláed, but... different. Perhaps he is a fallen

43

one of Conláed's species, as I was a turned Fae. He said many things, most which were disturbing and intriguing to various degrees. Among them was a general idea that I believe was meant to steer me towards killing you." His quicksilver blue eyes flashed in the lamplight. "Do not fear me. Everything he said is now utterly horrible to me. I did not know what he meant at the time because I did not know of you. But he obviously had some knowledge of you. I suspect that, like Conláed, he operates at least somewhat outside of time. He may know, or at least have reason to believe, that you will play some important role in something that is yet to come.

"Or perhaps you already have, in the time between when I was given that impression and now. Perhaps not. There isn't much to go on. In any case, I warn you to be careful. Not of me. But if something with Conláed's power wishes you harm, it would be wise to be cautious. He will have plans within plans, and he does not think as we do."

Aria licked her dry lips. "But why? What part can I play?"

Feichin tilted his head, studying her face. "I don't know. I do know your death would grieve Lord Owen, and the dark one hates Lord Owen with an intensity that surpasses the worst moments of my hatred of Grenidor. Anything that would cause Lord Owen pain would delight the dark one. That reason alone is sufficient for me to protect you. I owe Lord Owen more than my life."

Why would hurting me hurt Owen so much? Does he care more for me?

Or is it simply that I'm more vulnerable than the Fae? Perhaps I'm just a target of opportunity.

I want him to care for me not just because I'm vulnerable but because I'm me! I want to matter!

Bartok's voice startled her. "Are you all right?"

Aria glanced up at him and then at Feichin, who had slid away from her. *Can Bartok see Feichin?* She wasn't sure. "I think so." Her voice shook, and she cleared her throat. "I'm fine. I was talking with Feichin."

The Fae must have made himself visible in response because Bartok failed to entirely hide his surprise at Feichin's proximity. But he recovered quickly, and asked, "How are you feeling, Feichin?"

Feichin's icy blue eyes widened in surprise. "For what reason do you inquire?"

Bartok smiled, the warmth in his expression warming Aria's heart. "I'm a doctor. I like to see people in recovery, even if I had nothing to do with the improvement."

Feichin tilted his head, his eyes alight with curiosity. "You are a different sort of human than I have met before." His thin lips parted in a smile, showing white teeth. "I am honored to meet you. Lord Owen has spoken highly of your wisdom and your knowledge of El, as well as your generosity and kindness. I owe you a debt of gratitude for your role in my redemption."

Bartok's cheeks flushed. "You're welcome." He cleared his throat. "Your salvation is a blessing to us all, a reminder that God has not forsaken us even when the darkness feels overwhelming."

The Fae's smiled widened. "You are a wise man, Dr. Bartok."

CHAPTER 3

GRENIDOR WOKE BEFORE the sun had fully risen, the cold light slowly brightening the cheerless box of his apartment. He lay in bed with his hands behind his head, staring across the room at the folded memorial flag on the opposite wall. A tiny plaque on the frame was engraved with his father's name.

They'd be coming for him soon. The authorities were fast, and Edwin would undoubtedly help them along, eager to facilitate Grenidor's arrest. He'd probably enjoy the execution, too.

Grenidor closed his eyes and sighed. Eyes still closed, he brushed a hand over the place on his head that had hit the wall when Cillian attacked him. *If they love like we do, and Cillian is Owen's brother... can I really blame him?*

Edwin's voice startled him out of his thoughts. "You're running late today. Aren't you planning on going in? Are you feeling unwell?"

As if he really cares. Grenidor pushed himself up against the headboard, the skin of his bare chest prickling in the chill. He shrugged. "They're going to arrest me. If they're not waiting for me now, they will figure it out in an hour or two. The transport is missing, along with a particularly dangerous vampire. Records show I took him out and that I obviously tried to hide it. If that isn't enough to arrest me, it's enough to start an investigation. They'll find other… irregularities. I might as well wait here. I'd rather not be arrested in front of my men."

Edwin leaned one elbow against the door to Grenidor's tiny living room. "The transport vehicle is back in place, or at least one just like it. I couldn't get to the real one, I admit, but no one can tell the difference. There are no records of you doing anything suspicious. True, a vampire is missing, but another one just vanished into thin air before, if you recall. You were at home during the time of this disappearance and could have had nothing to do with it. The security cameras at work and in your apartment lobby confirm this."

Grenidor stared at him.

Edwin's smile widened slightly. "I told you I could protect you."

"I had the impression the offer might have been withdrawn."

Edwin gave a thoughtful nod. "No. Not yet. It's true that I view last night as a debacle. It is also true that I blame you, for the most part." He glanced up to catch Grenidor's eye for one heart-stopping moment. Then he smiled again, as if conceding a point Grenidor had not yet argued. "Yet the Slavemaster is a genius at confusing people, deceiving them into serving his own ends. It is also true that perhaps things would have gone better if I had forged a better understanding with you. You had some facts, some half-truths, and a great many suppositions. These led to your uncharacteristic indecisiveness and failure to act. I am sure this was further complicated by confusion sown by the Slavemaster's agent. I propose to correct that now by being more open and informative. Perhaps we can still save our relationship." He paused for one heartbeat, then added, "And you."

Grenidor swallowed. *He hasn't killed me yet.* "All right. I'm listening."

"First, I know you hate me. I don't care. In fact, I expect that, and would be disappointed if you were not intelligent enough to hate me. I hate you, as well. You can take the fact that I hate you and still protect you as a compliment, if you will.

"I'll give you a bit of insight, from my… outside… perspective. All intelligent beings hate all other intelligent beings. Oh, not the simple 'I'll do anything to get you, cut off my nose to spite my face!' sort of hate. That's simple and trivial. No, I'm just being honest in that all truly intelligent beings work to maximize their power and influence over others. This naturally means that the advancement of others is, at best, inconsequential, and likely in conflict with your own.

"However, sometimes we can work with some as allies against others for mutual benefit. One can follow a leader as he rises in power, provided he trusts you or values your services. You can work with me, to your benefit, as I can work with you to mine.

"It is good to have some expendable flunkies, cannon fodder, pawns, or whatever you would like to call them. But you also need some lieutenants, those who can think for themselves, but still choose to serve out of self-interest.

"For this reason, I have tolerated your efforts to avoid my control, and even some laughable efforts to control me.

"Let me be very clear. I'm in this for my benefit, but your benefit can be incidental, just to get you to cooperate or to put you in a position to more effectively serve my ends. I *will* dominate." The word resonated with tightly restrained power.

"I have tolerated some failures and some lack of cooperation while you learn. The reason I have done so is that you have some promise; we are very much alike, you and I.

"I see some disgust and denial.

"But consider, just as I deal with you, you deal with me. You are in it for your gain with little concern about mine at all, and you didn't even stop at human sacrifice. Your words, not mine. Who are you to criticize me? At least, I live up to our agreement and I do give you what I promise while you try at every turn to obstruct me."

Grenidor sucked in a breath, trying to sort out his many arguments and objections. He latched onto Edwin's talk of hate. "That's not true. Not everyone hates each other. Surely some people love others selflessly. Maybe not adults, but children. A parent loves a child! Most people don't hate others."

Edwin snorted. "The parent is going to die. Their primary ability to continue their influence is through their bloodline. They guard their children

49

as they guard their power in life, and for the same reason. Though, to be fair, they may not be aware of this. This is the purest love that exists! All other love is even more self-deluded and self-serving. Or, sometimes, a mental illness.

"And your assertion that most people don't hate is weak. Firstly, I said all *intelligent* beings, and most people are not intelligent or, at least, do not behave as if they are. Secondarily, to the extent that they are intelligent, they do put themselves before others. This is the true definition of hate… self before others, to the detriment of others. You don't have to actively wish harm to others. You just want to advance yourself at their expense. Call it realism if you prefer. The name doesn't matter.

"You're lucky. Advancing myself, I pull you along. So long as you are useful." Edwin gave him a toothy smile. "After your death, you will be in my camp, if you want to think of it that way. There are only two camps, really. There are the Slave-master's minions, and there are those on my side. Both those who choose independence in physical life and those who choose to serve me intentionally will end up in our camp for eternity." His smile widened. "Do you understand what I mean by eternity?

"Time becomes meaningless when we talk about eternity because time is a feature of this physical world. Eternity is beyond human com-prehension, but imagine it as stretching infinitely forward and backward, forever onward without ceasing.

"It would be better—wiser—for you to enter eternity as a lieutenant with whom I am pleased than as someone against whom I hold a grudge."

Edwin's eyes flashed, and Grenidor had a momentary vision of fire consuming his body, a screaming agony that tensed all his muscles at once.

"I shouldn't have to explain that you can't be in the Slavemaster's camp. Not that you would want to be, of course." Edwin's lips lifted again in a predatory smile. "You *cannot* be in his good graces with sin on your record. And oh, do you have some impressive ones." He grinned. "But no matter. I'm sure you understand the benefits of cooperation with me anyway."

Grenidor studied Edwin as he talked. The man, or whatever he was, looked as he always did. A forgettable face, slightly paunchy, clothes just worn enough to look unthreatening. A physique that didn't justify the inhuman strength he possessed. *Not just inhuman. Supernatural.* Grenidor swung his feet to the floor and pulled on his uniform, still listening.

"Now, the meeting with the Fae." Edwin's eyes never left him as he dressed. "It was a disaster, but perhaps not entirely unmitigated. I wanted you to kill the vampire Feichin before the meeting took place because I saw two possibilities. The most likely was that he would kill you and run off. That would mean I would have to start over with another human. While I have contingency plans, none of my other prospects are quite as promising as you are. However, that would still have been preferable to the other possibility, which is—mostly—what happened. Feichin completed his transformation from Fae through vampire to full-fledged agent of the Slavemaster. He will now attempt to help other vampires make the same transition. Vampires are bad, but I can deal with a

51

vampire. I cannot directly attack one who is actively in service to the Slavemaster. To the extent he is successful, my ability to aid you is diminished.

"I did not expect that you would survive the meeting unless you killed Feichin, so things did not go as badly as I had expected. However, the Slavemaster is now out to destroy *you*, specifically. You've gotten his attention and shown that you are dangerous." He paused and then added, "Let this be a lesson to you that my advice is not to be ignored without consequences. I do tell you things to benefit me, but I also give you advice for your own benefit. I do not tell you which is which or explain. I don't *want* you to know which is which. Just do what I tell you or risk missing something intended to benefit you." He waited a second for this to sink in, then continued.

"Just as the Slavemaster's agents are protected from me, my agents are protected from him, at least from direct attack. So he will lie to you, perhaps using the Fae to deliver messages, hoping to get you to commit to being his slave. Most likely they will promise love, or something else imaginary but attractive.

"This is a trap!" Edwin's eyes blazed with fury. "The instant you choose to commit to him, I can no longer protect you as I do now. He will take that opening, and you will die." His voice resonated again on the last word, adding inhuman emphasis. *Die* seemed to reverberate within Grenidor's bones. "But death is only the end of *this* life… your current physical state of being. There is still the matter of eternity, under my dominion, after that little attempt to betray me. You have no idea how bad 'worse than death' can really be."

Edwin's voice softened. "Take the rest of the day off. Rest. Think. No one at the office will notice. But tomorrow, our work will begin. We must eliminate the Fae before they can begin to convert the rest of their kind and vampires. I can't directly attack them, but I can help you do so."

Grenidor paused, one shoe on, the other in his hand. "I think I *will* take the day off." He pulled off his shoe and straightened. "Thanks." He forced a smile, knowing it looked more like a grimace.

Edwin inclined his head. "Of course." He gave Grenidor what appeared to be a genuine, sympathetic smile. "It's a lot to take in, I realize. But I would not have chosen to work with you if you did not have the capability both to understand your position and to further my work. A willing partnership between us benefits us both. Don't throw that away." He disappeared. Present, then NotPresent.

It was a not-so-subtle reminder of his power.

Grenidor licked his lips and sat at his tiny breakfast bar, rubbing his hands over his face.

Start at the beginning.

Does Edwin lie? Or is he incorrect and just think he's right? Or… is he right? That would mean I'm insane, or maybe "unintelligent," because this disgusts me. And I do believe love exists, even if it's rare.

No. I get the sense that Edwin does *lie, on purpose and often… but sometimes he tells enough truth to make his lies plausible. Maybe he believes he's telling the truth now?*

Again, no. His story changes. It's always plausible, but it's not what it was before, and it was plausible then too. He lies.

I knew that before, and somehow he made me believe him again. The sudden realization set his heart thumping harder. He forced himself to take deep, calming breaths, pushing the fear back down to manageable tension.

He says he can't attack the agents of the Slavemaster... the other side. But he also says he can protect me from attack. But earlier, he said the other side would never attack anyway. And his reaction to Niall... that didn't look like he could protect me. He dodged Niall like he was an open flame. The way he looked at Niall... or didn't look at him... that could be an illusion since I know he isn't really a pudgy, balding man. Or could it be a bit of truth accidentally leaking into the illusion? Would he deliberately create that impression? I think not. I think his illusions have let some truth through before, too.

He just told me the progression was Fae, to vampire, to agent of the Slavemaster. But he also told me at first that Fae and vampires were only a cultural difference. And he told me that Fae are already agents of the Slavemaster while vampires are not. That is supported by the fact that he can't attack Fae and they can't see him, but he can approach vampires, and they can hear him.

I see the Fae, and they are not insane. I believe they really love and they don't hate. At least not as I think of hate. I don't know if they can. Vampires can. Maybe that's the difference between Fae and vampires. Edwin says hate is mandatory for intelligent beings. Fae are obviously intelligent, though they're different than we are.

Maybe they're better.

That alone makes it clear that Edwin is the bad side. He might be right that I'm much like him.

Look at what I've done. And I have been using him, just as he's using me. Worse, I've used him against my own kind, and at least he's used me against his declared enemies.

I'm just as much on the bad side as Edwin is. I don't want to be, but I am. Edwin says this is inevitable; all thinking beings are like him to some degree.

Fae can be vampires. Humans can be... me.

But Fae can be, well, Fae... not vampires. Can humans be anything other than little Edwins?

I wish I knew Bartok better. Then I'd be able to judge for myself. But at least a few people think he's not insane. He might even be admirable. He's what I wish I was. Maybe he's an example.

If I tried to change sides, is there any possibility I would be accepted? No, I think not. They may be glad I stopped, but they wouldn't accept me. How could they? I've killed and tortured their friends. I wouldn't accept one of them who'd done what I've done.

Wait.

If Feichin really did forgive me and really did change back into a Fae, rather than a vampire... would I accept him? And what does forgiveness really mean anyway? He didn't kill me, at least, and from his perspective, I deserved it.

He killed Davis. But as Fae, I think he is (and was) probably better than I am. Maybe, just maybe, I might accept him.

He took an uneasy breath, pausing to consider that thought and what it meant.

I've done worse than he ever did. He licked his lips, thinking on that fact and acknowledging it.

Feichin was provoked beyond measure. I tortured innocent Fae and vampires. I even sacrificed humans for my own purposes.

Maybe they would be glad I turned from Edwin, but still kill me immediately, lest I turn back and betray them.

He pondered that thought and realized it held more than a little attraction. It would, in fact, be wonderful. Compared to continuing with Edwin, a quick death he knew he deserved would be mercy.

Yes.

I will go to Owen and the rest of the Slavemaster's side, and I will ask for mercy.

If they kill me, so be it. It is the best I can hope for, and better than I deserve.

What comes after death? Well… the best I can hope is that Edwin is lying about that and that death is the end, after all.

So how can I contact Owen and the Slavemaster's allies?

He had no idea where they were, no way to contact them, and no way to avoid Edwin.

Except… maybe one.

The Bible.

CHAPTER 4

GRENIDOR SWIPED into the building to a bored nod from the guard. Only the fear of attracting attention kept him from running through the halls. *He can find me. I know he can find me.*

But Edwin didn't appear. Grenidor nodded at the lieutenant outside his office and slipped inside, trying to look as normal as possible. The Bible was still in his desk drawer. He pulled it out and dropped into his chair with unexpected relief, already opening the book.

He barely remembered his history lessons from childhood, and the Empire permitted only highly circumscribed versions of history to be taught. Unlike much of the rest of the population, he hadn't received any of the drugs or other behavior control measures. But he was still sadly ignorant of history; the leaders of the Revolution and then the Empire itself had been planning and shaping the population for years. He did have a tracker, of course. That would be a problem.

Last time, Edwin hadn't appeared as soon as Grenidor closed the book, but rather when he'd stopped thinking about the words. So something about focusing on the Bible and what it contained was important, not merely the act of holding the book in his hands.

The page was thin and slightly crinkled beneath his hand, and he smoothed it as he read. *Or do you show contempt for the riches of his kindness, forbearance, and patience, not realizing that God's kindness is intended to lead you to repentance? But because of your stubbornness and your unrepentant heart, you are storing up wrath against yourself for the day of God's wrath, when his righteous judgment will be revealed. God "will repay each person according to what they have done." To those who by persistence in doing good seek glory, honor, and immortality, he will give eternal life. But for those who are self-seeking and who reject the truth and follow evil, there will be wrath and anger.*

He rubbed his hands over his face. *Well, I can't expect mercy. But I'll ask anyway. At least they'll kill me quickly. Probably. Maybe.*

His office made him feel like a trapped animal, the familiar tingling between his shoulder blades rising as he expected Edwin to appear at any moment, Bible or no Bible. He had no way of finding Owen or even Niall. But he needed them.

He kept one finger in the book and stood. *Keep thinking about the Slavemaster. If I think about something else, Edwin might come.*

I don't want to see him angry.

He strode through the halls again. *Slavemaster, I want to be a slave. Keep me alive long enough to find out how. Or at least let me die quickly. I don't want to belong to Edwin.* He kept that thought in his mind, nodding to the guard again without meeting his eyes.

He went back to his apartment. The tracker would make it too obvious if he went anywhere else, and at least Niall knew where he lived. *If he's coming back. Why should he?*

He was closing the door behind him when Niall appeared only an arm's reach from him. Grenidor squawked in surprise, nearly dropping the Bible. "Where did you come from?"

Niall tilted his head, brows lowering in confusion. Glittering words appeared in the air in a neat script. *Is that a rhetorical question?*

Grenidor stared at him. "What happened to writing on paper?"

I wished to preserve our limited supplies of paper for Lord Owen. I have been working on this... it is not something Fae have done before, at least to my knowledge. Is it easily readable? The words hung in the air for a moment, then vanished.

"Easily enough." Grenidor swallowed. "How do you know when I'm done reading?"

Your eyes. The boy studied him for a moment, then motioned at the door with a questioning look on his face.

Grenidor felt fear fluttering inside him but pushed it down. "I want to join you and the others. I don't want to work with Edwin anymore. I don't even care if you kill me. Feichin can do it if he wants. It's still better than what Edwin will do."

Niall's eyes widened. *You wish to join us?*

C. J. BRIGHTLEY

Grenidor gave a sharp nod, not entirely trusting his voice. Niall's narrow, solemn face broke into a brilliant smile. Grenidor caught his breath at the boy's sudden, heart-wrenching beauty. How had he not seen that before?

Niall bowed his head. *Come with me.*

"Wait. I have a tracker. They'll know if I go anywhere."

Niall frowned. *I can remove it physically if you have a knife. Or I can disable it if you prefer. Disabling it will require "magic" as you humans call it. I do not know if you are comfortable letting me use it within your body.*

"You'd cut it out with a knife?"

Yes. The cut is small, and I can heal it for you easily if you allow me. Aria's healed without magic in a day or two. He held his thumb and forefinger half an inch apart.

Grenidor swallowed. "Cut it out."

He led the way into his apartment. Niall suddenly tensed and pushed him farther away from the door.

A tall, slim man appeared at the doorway. No, a Fae, judging by his pale beauty. His cheekbones were sharp, his eyes a bright, clear blue. He wore dark, fitted jeans and a soft, thin sweater that highlighted a body fit for a magazine cover. He looked familiar, and Grenidor swallowed bile when he realized that he might be one of the escaped captives. M13, perhaps.

"Hello? Colonel Grenidor?" He smiled charmingly as he knocked on the doorframe.

"Yes?" Grenidor asked.

Niall reached for the knife block on Grenidor's counter and slid the largest knife out. He held it low, near his right leg. Then another knife for his left hand. *Do not listen to him, Colonel Grenidor. Please.*

The Fae, or vampire, or whatever he was, stepped inside. *So much for the legend about needing an invitation*, Grenidor thought.

"May I speak with you a moment? I have information that may interest you." His voice was beguilingly sweet. Helpful.

Niall shook his head.

"Stay there, please. I can hear just fine." Grenidor took a step backward.

The stranger nodded, though a flash of irritation narrowed his eyes. "You haven't been listening to the boy, have you? He's a prankster, this one." He smiled again, holding Grenidor's gaze. "You've been looking for Owen and Cillian, haven't you? And the others, Aria Forsyth and the human fighters? I know where they are."

Grenidor shuddered, breaking eye contact. Vampires were rumored to have some kind of mind control abilities, but he'd never given it much credence. Now, in an instant, he'd imagined Owen's broken body with a new surge of vengeful joy, a sense of hatred not his own.

"You would betray them to me?" he asked.

"Call it what you like." Another smile, this one more gentle. "Isn't that what you want? To catch them?" He seemed a little confused that Grenidor had not already jumped at his offer.

Niall had kept himself between the other Fae and Grenidor, the knives lowered but ready. Glittering words appeared in the air between them. *Lachtnal, please leave.*

The Fae, or vampire, snarled something at him that wasn't English. Niall flinched at the hatred in his voice.

He asks for mercy, Lachtnal. You also may receive mercy if you only ask El.

In a split second Lachtnal produced a narrow blade as long as his forearm from some hidden sheath, and a shorter blade, perhaps a kitchen knife of some sort. He lunged at Niall, lightning fast and nearly silent.

Grenidor stood, his back pressed against the wall, as the fight swept across his apartment and back. Blood sprayed in a quick arc and spattered on the floor, immediately smeared by Niall's bare feet.

Preternaturally fast and strong as Niall was, the vampire was just as fast and even stronger, with the benefit of longer reach, experience, and hatred. Blades flashed faster than human eyes could follow.

Lachtnal drew back and Niall let him, still keeping his body between Lachtnal and Grenidor. Niall held his right arm pressed against his side, not quite covering a deep wound that bled freely down his ragged shirt and soaking into his pants. More stripes of blood crossed his chest and arms. Lachtnal was also marked, blood dripping from a deep gash across one bicep and another crossing his ribs. The fabric of their shirts stuck to them, plastered against skin and bone.

Please, Lachtnal. You know I do not want to fight you. Niall's eyes were filled with tears.

"You dare speak to me of mercy!" Lachtnal snarled.

El will give it to you if you only ask. Please, Lacht-nal! Please come back with us. Lord Owen—

Lachtnal's hand blurred into motion. Niall flung his arm up, trying to block Lachtnal's throw, and Lachtnal stabbed him in the chest with the longer blade. Something thudded into Grenidor with stunning force, and he stumbled backward.

Then the pain hit. Lachtnal's smaller knife was buried nearly to the hilt in his left bicep, the tip stuck in the bone. Grenidor kept his feet only because he'd fallen into the wall behind him.

Through eyes blurred with pain, he watched Lachtnal yank the blade from Niall's chest with a twist of his wrist to free it from the bone. Niall crumpled, falling to his knees, then forward to one hand.

Lachtnal, come back with us. Lord Owen can help you return to El. Please.

Lachtnal growled. If it was language, it was cursing, but Grenidor wasn't sure the sound was meant to be words at all. He raised the knife over Niall's neck.

"Shoot the tall one!" Grenidor screamed.

Lachtnal looked up, startled, and Niall's hand snaked out, catching his ankle. Niall's blade flashed as Lachtnal twisted and fell. Lachtnal made a strange noise and jerked, then grew still.

Silence.

Niall lay half-beneath Lachtnal, his head beside Lachtnal's and hidden from Grenidor's view. He slowly pushed Lachtnal's body off himself and slithered out from beneath the vampire. He lay on his back, eyes half-closed, barely breathing.

How badly are you injured? The letters wavered in the air as if they were a reflection on water.

"I'll live. I've got a knife stuck in my arm. It's bleeding a bit." He felt light-headed with the pain. He gripped the handle in his right hand and tried to pull it out, but it was stuck firmly. Breathing too fast. Dizzy.

Niall gave a faint grunt of acknowledgment. *Where are the soldiers?*

Grenidor blinked, but then he realized Niall was just as confused by his deception as Lachtnal had been. "There are no soldiers. I lied to distract him."

Niall rolled slightly to the side and placed one blood-covered hand on Lachtnal's forehead. With his eyes closed, he remained motionless for long, worrisome heartbeats.

Then he rolled to his stomach. Slowly, painfully, he pushed himself up to his hands and knees. He looked over at Grenidor and seemed to evaluate his injury.

"And you?" Nausea rose in Grenidor's stomach when he looked at the boy. He was covered in blood. The deepest wounds were bleeding profusely, leaking bright red into his clothes, and dripping onto the floor, already slick. The stab wound in his lower right side had been first, and then the last wound, right in the middle of his chest, straight through the sternum. The blood was the same color as human blood. Grenidor thought distantly that the room looked like a murder scene and then realized it nearly was.

I'll live. But we must move quickly. Niall staggered to his feet, nearly falling, catching himself on the edge of the bar. Still leaning on it, he made his way to Grenidor. *Is it stuck?*

"Yes."

May I help? Niall looked up at him. A bruise was beginning to shadow the boy's left eye.

"Yes."

Niall gripped the knife handle and pulled it out with one quick motion. He pressed his hand to the wound for a moment, and the pain lessened. Then Niall sagged against the wall, eyes closed. *I would heal it more, but I need my strength to run. When we reach the others, they will help you.*

Grenidor swallowed, his throat tight. "Of course. Can I do anything to help?"

The boy slowly slid down the wall, eyes fluttering open for a moment, then closing again. *Five minutes. Wake me in five minutes. I cannot*

The words faded, the sentence left incomplete.

Grenidor examined his arm. There was an ache, muscle fibers still torn inside, but the bleeding had stopped and the pain was manageable. He looked across the room to Lachtnal still lying motionless on the floor. The vampire's face was turned upwards, his perfect profile relaxed as if he were asleep.

Blood pulsed out of Niall's wounds, a slowly spreading stain. Even if he'd live without it, losing that much blood couldn't be good. Grenidor found a towel and pressed it to Niall's chest tentatively. At the first touch, Niall's hand shot out and grasped his wrist with crushing force. Immediately his grip loosened.

Thank you. The boy let his eyes close again, not protesting as Grenidor secured the folded towel against the wound with an old leather belt. He did the same for the stab wound in the boy's side. Despite Grenidor's familiarity with vampires and Fae, he'd had little physical contact with them, and the feel of the cool blood and flesh beneath his fingers was thoroughly disconcerting.

Grenidor took a deep breath. He wouldn't be coming back to his apartment for a long time, if ever. He washed his hands in the kitchen sink and packed a bag with a few extra shirts, socks, underwear, a pair of pants, and all four framed photos from the top of his dresser. A toothbrush and toothpaste. A razor. A bar of soap.

Nerves twisted inside his gut. Edwin might know what had happened. Perhaps Edwin had even sent Lachtnal! Edwin had said vampires were the enemy, but he talked with them, at least sometimes. Edwin apparently wanted vampires killed, but that didn't prove much. That was what Edwin was like.

Would Edwin appear in the apartment? He'd been cautious around Niall, but with the Fae child helpless, Edwin might see an opportunity to attack. Perhaps he would send others instead.

In any case, Grenidor and Niall had best move quickly. He hoped that Edwin really couldn't track the Fae, or Grenidor himself, if he stayed close enough to Niall.

He knelt in front of Niall, and the boy blinked at him.

"We need to go."

Niall blinked again, slowly, as if he wasn't quite sure of his vision.

Grenidor motioned at the longest knife. "It's dangerous to leave him alive, isn't it? I can do it if you want."

Do what?

"Kill him."

The boy's eyes hardened. *Don't. I did not leave him sleeping for you to kill him while he is defenseless. He may yet return to El. Feichin has proven it is possible.*

"You want me to leave him alive?" Grenidor's voice squeaked a little.

Yes.

Grenidor took a deep breath, his thoughts shifting wildly between disbelief and hope. If Lachtnal could be left alive, perhaps Grenidor could find mercy, too.

Lachtnal was far too dangerous; he should be killed. Eliminate the threat; that was basic imperial policy. Common sense. Leaving a monster, a dangerous, intelligent, merciless opponent behind was idiotic, at best.

Yet who was Grenidor to demand that an unconscious vampire die for his crimes, when Grenidor's own crimes were so much worse? Who was he to pass judgment on Lachtnal?

Maybe he could tie up the vampire. No, it might just wake him.

"Fine." His voice was almost steady.

Do you still prefer me to cut out the tracker, or should I use "magic"?

"Cut it out." He rolled up his sleeve and handed the boy the knife near his hand. "You know where it is? Maybe I should do it myself."

Niall looked up at him, eyebrows raised skeptically. The letters appeared, faint and wavering. *I don't want to have to heal a cut vein.*

He put his cool, white fingers against Grenidor's arm and then the knife flashed in and out. Pain followed belatedly. Grenidor grimaced. The boy pressed a finger against the wound and the little metal capsule popped out, no larger than a grain of rice. Grenidor picked it up and put it on the counter. "I'll leave it here. Maybe it will take them a while to realize I've gone."

Grenidor held out a trembling hand to the boy.

"He would have killed me, wouldn't he?"

Not if you'd accepted his offer to betray Lord Owen.

The boy's hand was cool in his, sticky with blood and stronger than any boy his size had any right to be. There was a tremor in Niall's hand, and despite the boy's strength, Grenidor couldn't help the sudden guilt that surged over him when he realized how his own hand engulfed Niall's small one.

"Will you... How much does it hurt?" He'd tortured Fae and vampires in many creative ways. But he'd never thought so much about their pain as in the last few minutes.

Niall looked up at him, letting him see the tears standing in his eyes, the way he was biting his lip to keep from crying out. *How do you quantify pain? I will live. I will also remember it. Yet the pain in my heart is greater than the pain in my body.*

He swayed for a moment and words flickered again. *Do you have a pen and paper?*

Grenidor found a notebook and a scratchy ballpoint pen. Niall leaned on the bar as he wrote, his hand leaving streaks of drying blood across the paper. His handwriting was hurried and unsteady but legible. *I will not be able to write in the air in public. Light is meant to be seen. To create something meant to be seen, and simultaneously hide it, is difficult at best, if not impossible. Also, I am not yet skilled at the technique, and it takes great concentration. I would not be able to do it and pay sufficient attention to our surroundings.*

It is possible that my ability to hide us will fail anyway; hiding myself is more or less reflexive, but hiding you requires strength and focus, and my wounds are the enemy of both of those. He stopped to press a hand against the towel strapped to his chest, his eyes closed.

If we are detected, leave me and try to get away. I will attempt to escape as I can, and I will return for you when I am able. Stay alert and watch for anyone who seems to notice us, because I will be concentrating on maintaining our concealment and will not be as alert as usual. If you see someone notice us, warn me first, and then walk away.

Grenidor swallowed. "Right. If you say so."

Niall shook his head as if clearing it, squared his shoulders, and led Grenidor out of his apartment and away.

GRENIDOR FOLLOWED NIALL through the streets, his stomach churning with the realization that no one noticed him. How many times had Fae or vampires passed him on the street without him realizing it? How many times could they have killed him? In the crisp, clear morning light, with dozens of people on the sidewalks, no one noticed the pale, dark-haired boy covered in blood and the haggard man with a military haircut who followed him.

"No one seems to see us," he whispered.

Niall did not answer. The boy was pushing ahead with grim focus. His shaggy hair fell forward, covering his face.

"Are you all right?"

Still no answer.

A gust of icy wind caught Grenidor's bag and he shifted his grip. He sidestepped to avoid a woman, not expecting her to notice him. She looked up and her gaze almost slid past him, just like those of everyone else. Then she saw the blood on his shirt. She gave a little shriek of surprise and terror.

"She saw me!" Grenidor gasped, his heart suddenly pounding.

Niall stopped and stared at the woman for a moment, his thin body trembling and silent, then turned away, pulling Grenidor after him. Grenidor watched her over his shoulder. She blinked, shook her head, and then walked onward, ignoring them.

Niall led him off the busy street into an alley and nearly to the end, where he gripped Grenidor's hand in his own small one. He looked back at Grenidor with a questioning look and then tugged him forward gently, as if to say "follow me." Grenidor swallowed and nodded.

Niall pulled him through the wall. The old marble was solid, but they passed through as if it was an illusion. It felt like walking through gelatin, except that the resistance affected his mind and his thoughts rather than his body, as if he'd been separated from himself for a moment. Grenidor stumbled, disoriented, but Niall was already leading him down a long-abandoned escalator, now frozen in place.

"Where are we?" he murmured.

Nearly there. Abandoned subway. Forgotten entrance.

In the dark, he followed Niall only by the gentle, cool grip of that small hand in his. The walk seemed interminable, but it was probably only a few minutes before they reached their destination.

Flashlights flared in his face. In the sudden, glaring brilliance, he saw Niall's slim figure collapse bonelessly. He disappeared before he hit the ground.

"Hands up behind your head. On your knees."

CHAPTER 5

ARIA LOOKED UP as Niamh darted past her.

Niall stood near the entrance to one of the tunnels, visible because flashlights lit him in an almost physical assault. A moment after the lights flared, he fell, limp as a marionette with the strings cut. Niamh was already there, her arms around him. His head flopped forward onto Niamh's chest, and she lifted him as if he weighed nothing. Perhaps, to his mother, he did.

Cillian reached Niall a moment later. Owen staggered to his feet, and Aria offered him a shoulder. He leaned on her as they hurried after Cillian.

Only then did Aria see Grenidor on his knees, hands behind his head and eyes squinting into the glaring lights.

"Is he all right?" he asked. "Neel? Nile? The Fae boy." He gestured with one elbow, careful to keep his hands behind his head. "He led me here. I don't see him."

Gabriel grunted. "They'll tell us if they want us to know. What are you doing here?"

Cillian placed the edge of his knife to Grenidor's throat. "May I kill him?"

Grenidor froze, apparently unable to see Cillian. Aria could see his eyes, wide and frightened, but far from panicked. More... resigned, and tired, and hopeless. He swallowed and closed his eyes, breathing slowly. He didn't say anything.

"No." Owen and Niamh spoke at the same time.

Cillian glanced at his sister. "I expected that from Lord Owen. But you, Niamh?"

The razor edge of the knife scraped softly against Grenidor's skin as he breathed.

Niamh's nostrils flared. "This blood is not only from Niall but also Lachtnal. I would not kill Grenidor for Lachtnal's crimes. Let us hear Niall's testimony."

Cillian sheathed the knife and moved toward Niall, still limp in his mother's arms. Other Fae had already gathered around Niamh and Niall. Owen bowed his head over Niall and for a moment there was only silence, the adult Fae breathing softly over the boy's head. Aria felt their song, though she couldn't hear it, a breath of fresh air and hope. *Love like an unending song.* Then Niall sighed and turned into Niamh's embrace, snuggling like the child he was.

Owen stepped away, only a little unsteady on his feet. Grenidor flinched backward, and Aria guessed that Owen had made himself visible. The flashlights wavered as the humans surrounding them were also surprised.

Owen extended a hand to Grenidor. "Come."

Gabriel growled, "What are you doing?"

"Niall brought him to us for a reason." Owen knelt in front of Grenidor. Grenidor licked his lips and swallowed convulsively, though he did not otherwise acknowledge his fear. "Come, Colonel Grenidor." He extended his hand again.

Grenidor took it cautiously, careful to make every movement slow and smooth. "You're not going to kill me?" His voice was a little hoarse.

Owen shook his head. "No. Dr. Bartok and I wish to speak with you." He stood, pulling Grenidor up with him. "Gabriel, I request your hospitality for our guest."

Gabriel let out a short, sharp breath. "You're making him your *guest*? You offer him that honor? That protection?"

Owen gave a faint, solemn bow. "Apparently he needs it."

Gabriel muttered something unintelligible to Aria's ears. Owen huffed softly, the sound like a laugh that didn't quite make it past his lips, and leaned forward to murmur in Gabriel's ear.

Gabriel sighed and waved a defeated hand at the others. "Fine, fine. Get him some soup or something. And check him for weapons."

Aria watched with interest. *Gabriel seems to agree that Owen has the right to welcome Grenidor and that his protection of Grenidor will be honored by the human resistance. Gabriel didn't argue with that; he was incredulous, but he wasn't actually arguing.*

Niall was surrounded by Fae: Ardghal, Sorcha, Fearghal, Lorcan, and others whose names Aria still could not remember. They sang over him as he lay against Niamh, voices rising in the still, cold darkness.

Niall sat in the middle of a mossy clearing, his eyes closed and a circlet of leaves on his head. Others danced around him, darting in and out among each other in a laughing game, jumping over each other and rolling beneath each other. At first, it appeared chaotic, but Aria felt the pattern in it after a moment, so intricate she couldn't quite predict the next movement, although she knew that Owen could have, if he were there with her. As she thought of him, she saw him watching from the side of the clearing his blue eyes bright and calm. His lips lifted in a slow, proud smile. At a motion of his hand, all movement stopped.

Aria blinked, focusing on Grenidor again. He glanced around as he followed Owen through the human encampment. Bartok had been on the night watch and was still asleep with one arm flung over his face. Grenidor stood looking down at him with an odd expression.

Owen knelt beside Bartok and touched him on the shoulder. "My apologies, Dr. Bartok, but Colonel Grenidor is here. I believe you wished to speak with him."

Bartok sat up, frowning as he scrubbed his face. "What?" he rasped. Then he looked up and blinked. "Oh. … *Oh.*" He looked around. "And Niall?"

Owen looked across the train platform. "His injuries will be healed soon. There are many here who will sing for him." He looked at Grenidor. "You also were injured."

Grenidor shrugged. "I'll survive. Niall healed it some."

"Is there still pain?"

He grunted noncommittally. "Some."

"May I?"

Grenidor nodded, watching Owen with wide, cautious eyes.

Owen put a hand on Grenidor's sleeve for a moment, then asked, "Is that better?"

Grenidor swallowed. "Yes. Thank you." He opened his mouth, then closed it again. "I was… I don't even know what to say. Everything in my life is broken, including me." He took a shuddering breath and dropped his head into his hands.

Bartok smiled. "I know someone who can help with that."

SIOFRA JOGGED TOWARD OWEN and spoke into his ear a moment. He nodded and murmured something to her, and she jogged back into the darkness.

Owen approached Gabriel. "Someone is coming. A human. He is alone and has one sidearm, some kind of pistol. Siofra did not know the type. He will be here in minutes."

"You let him come?" Gabriel looked surprised.

"Siofra said he looks cautious, not dangerous."

Gabriel shrugged. "Very well, If we have to move later, we will."

Siofra preceded the man into the station, though he didn't seem to realize she was there. He paused at the entrance until his sweeping gaze caught Gabriel waving to him.

He approached, tense but confident. "Are you Gabriel?"

"Who asks?"

The man stuck out his hand. "Beckett. It's not my real name, but it's what's on the papers at the train station."

Gabriel shook and smiled. "Right. What do you have for us?"

"A problem." He glanced around. "How much should I say now?"

Gabriel waved him toward their makeshift table made of stacked boxes of supplies. "Might as well get comfortable. Speak as freely as you like; save me some time repeating everything."

Beckett dropped onto the cardboard box seat with a sigh, stretching out his legs. "Someone found me out. Says she needs out of the Empire and doesn't have a tracker. Wants me to put her in touch with the resistance. I tell her I don't know what she's talking about. She's scared. I think she's telling the truth because the IPF isn't on my head yet."

"Are you sure?" Gabriel's voice had a dangerous edge.

"As sure as I can be. I've been sitting on it for two days and I made tracks for six hours before I found you here; didn't see anyone or anything tailing me. I might have missed a drone, but not much else."

"And your tracker?"

"That's why I have a cat." Beckett pulled one arm out of his jacket and pulled up his sleeve to reveal a tiny white scar, nearly invisible on his cold-prickled skin. "I removed it and put it in a little plastic capsule. Normally I wear it on a brace-

77

let, but I clip it on my cat's collar and lock her in my apartment when I need to get out unnoticed. She moves around enough that it doesn't get flagged for suspicious inactivity."

Gabriel raised his eyebrows. "That's inventive."

Becket shrugged. "I took it out the day I got it. I won't be tagged and tracked like some endangered animal. I saw what happened to everyone else; they forgot about it in a day or two. I didn't wait that long."

"Any idea who she is?"

"Yeah. A bookstore owner. I went there a few times because one of my associates used it as a drop. I asked her about maps last time. Since I worked for the rail system, I wanted to give a framed rail map to my dad, you know, a good story. Maybe I wasn't convincing enough. Anyway, that's how she found me at the station. Asked for me by name."

"Dandra?"

"Yes, that's the name she gave me."

"Where is she?"

"I don't know. She said she'd meet me back at the station tomorrow when my shift starts. I came to see whether I should meet her or bug out."

Owen stepped forward. "I, or one of mine, will meet her and escort her here. We have matters to discuss with her."

Becket startled so badly he fell off his box chair.

The Fae king offered him a hand. "My apologies; I did not mean to surprise you so thoroughly. Dandra is an acquaintance, and far from an agent of the Empire. We will help her. My name is Owen."

Gabriel shot him an unreadable look. "Agreed."

Beckett waved a hand to keep Owen back, rising cautiously with a hand near his gun. "You're one of those vampires, aren't you?"

Owen's lips flattened. "If you had ever met a vampire, you would not ask me that."

Beckett glanced back at Gabriel. "What is he? Is he dangerous? Appearing like that is not natural."

"Yes, he's dangerous, but not to you. You can trust him more than you can trust me. But the explanation is long. If Dandra discovered you, is your cover blown?"

Beckett sat again, keeping one eye on Owen. "Not that I'm aware of, for whatever that's worth. Dandra asked for me by name, but only in her capacity as a bookseller. She must have suspected that my office was bugged, which it is; she said she needed to catch a train, but asked me to accompany her to the platform to 'complete our business' before she had to leave. That was smart. It avoided the bugs, and if anyone was listening and decided to bring her in, she'd just told them she'd be gone by the time they arrived. They'd be figuring out what trains arrived and where she might get off, rather than looking for her to leave by the front door.

"She had a map in her hand to explain why she was there, in case I didn't bite. She casually mentioned that the resistance would love to get a map like it, and I probably flinched. I'm a suspicious type, but I hadn't suspected her. I'd asked for her to keep an eye out for maps for me, so even though

I was surprised to see her at the station, I wasn't entirely shocked until she mentioned the resistance. She said the store was closed because of excessive interest from the IPF. She also said the Christians being arrested are her friends. She wants to talk to the resistance about them.

"She said she didn't have a tracker. So… since she knows about the trackers, either she's telling the truth and she's not from inside the Empire, or she's an agent."

"She's not an agent." Gabriel sighed and sat back. "Owen, do you want to go? You're better at covert work, for obvious reasons."

"I will go."

Aria, who had been listening, stepped forward. "I'd better go too. She thinks you work for the Empire, Lord Owen."

Owen frowned. "Why?"

"You knew too much. You frightened her." Aria shrugged. "I'll go with you. She'll feel safer with me."

"Thank you."

Beckett glanced between them, his gaze settling on Owen again. "*Lord* Owen?"

Owen inclined his head. "Yes. In English."

Beckett looked back at Gabriel, apparently hoping to be informed that this was a joke. When Gabriel didn't smile, he looked confused. "So, go back and meet her tomorrow? My cover isn't blown, don't bug out, keep on keeping on?"

Gabriel nodded. "If you have no other reasons for concern, yes. Dandra isn't working for the Empire. We'll deal with her from here."

"Got it. Do I need to do anything to help tomorrow?" He glanced at Owen.

"No. I will handle it." Owen smiled. "Thank you for the information."

Beckett gave him an incredulous look.

CHAPTER 6

"HOW DID BECKETT know to come here?" Aria asked Gabriel.

He grimaced, then sighed. "He wandered around until he found us. His name's not Beckett; I don't know his real name, but he's a former spy. Intelligence officer, I should say. He's good at finding things and finding people, and good at losing a tail. I'd never met him, but Leo told me about the guys he'd worked with, the intelligence and counterintelligence experts."

"So he works for Leo too?" Aria frowned. "Then, shouldn't he know about Dandra?"

"No. He's resistance, like us. Leo got out of intel and into clandestine missions work. Well, as clandestine as evangelism can be. Beckett is semi-independent, like most of the resistance."

Aria chewed her lip. "And you're in charge? But he didn't know you."

Gabriel rubbed a hand over his face, and the light caught the weariness around his eyes. "Well, more or less. We're scattered. We operate in cells with only occasional communication. We use dead drops and disposable cell phones and all the old stuff. It's for security reasons; even if the Empire gets lucky and wipes out one group, the resistance can survive."

"It's hard to coordinate that way, isn't it?" Aria's confused look deepened. "What does the resistance actually do? Do you have any plans?"

"We survive." Gabriel gave her a bleak look. "That's basically the goal. Survival. Things have been easier since the Fae arrived; they're keeping us hidden. Before that, we were getting slowly picked off. The Empire has a few recon drones; we've hijacked a few, they hijack them back, we introduce viruses... it buys us time.

"There aren't enough of us to win. We're resisting by not giving up, but there's no way to win." His shoulders slumped. "We all know it, but no one talks about it. You can tell, though." He lifted his chin in a gesture encompassing the camp. "You don't see a lot of hope out there. Bartok's been good for us, as much as I hate to admit it." He gave her a sidelong glance. "If there's no hope here, might as well put our hope in something after death."

"You don't really believe it's just wishful thinking, do you?"

His gaze slid away from hers.

"What do you care? It's not like I'm much of a Christian anyway." His lip curled in disgust.

"Can't you be forgiven for losing hope? Does God turn away from us because we're weak?"

C. J. BRIGHTLEY

Gabriel ran his thumbnail over the seam of his trousers, studying the fabric rather than meeting her gaze. "I don't know. I'm sure there's a verse about it somewhere. Bartok would probably say no. But I've lost more than he has, and I'm more cynical. So what if I see miracles I can't explain with science? I also see the Empire's overwhelming power. If God is good, why was Owen tortured? Why is the Empire allowed to gain power while the people don't even think clearly enough to question it?

"Will they be held accountable for decisions they made while drugged and stupid and brainwashed? Where's the justice in that? Where's the mercy?" His voice cracked. "Owen can forgive them, but how can I?"

He pulled at a fraying thread then smoothed it down again, as if the motion kept his emotions in check. "I've asked for help from outside the Empire, but there's not much hope of that. The Empire is too strong, and the other nations have their own concerns. Vampires, and famine, and other monsters..." He gave her another sidelong look. "Vampires are the smartest and most dangerous, but there are other things outside the Empire. Vertril weren't designed in a vacuum, you know; they're derived from real creatures. Other things too, if you believe the whispers and rumors and legends."

"Do you?" Aria breathed.

Gabriel smiled mirthlessly. "Vampires are only legends, don't you know?" He shrugged one shoulder. "I'm sure some of the myths are only myths. But I imagine there's a grain of truth in many of them. Parsing that truth out of the myths and legends and lies and stories and fables... I have more urgent concerns." He waved a hand. "These people trust me because we're at war and I was a colonel and they were school teachers and IT technicians and lawyers. But this? This is beyond me. It would take a miracle to bring down the Empire."

"But I've seen miracles." Aria hated that her voice shook. "Isn't Owen being alive a miracle? Isn't it a miracle that I'm alive? That Grenidor's here? That the Fae are helping us?"

His voice hardened. "I mean a real miracle, one that changes the things that matter. One that breaks the Empire wide open so people can make their decisions in the full light of day."

"You mean a political miracle. Isn't it harder to change a heart than to change a government? I'm not sure." The edge of thought beckoned, revelation and realization taunting just out of reach. "Does it matter what the government is if we're all so blinded we don't choose right anyway? Does God care about the government? Or does he care about our hearts?"

Gabriel's grumble was so quiet she barely made out his words. "I don't care what God cares about. I just want to be free."

"ARIA, COME WITH ME." Owen held out a hand to her in invitation, and she let him help her up.

She followed him out into the brilliant sunlight, bare tree branches tracing fine shadows across their faces. He turned to face her in the small clearing, standing beside a concrete fountain

85

no longer flowing with water. Other Fae were already gathered, and they nodded to her, each in turn.

"Kneel."

Aria knelt in front of him, feeling her cheeks flush. It was an archaic, extravagant gesture, out of place in modernity. "What are you going to do?"

He dropped to one knee, his blue eyes clear and bright. There was a joyful solemnity in his face. "You were born Fae. That makes you my subject, and me your king. I have not formalized that relationship. I will do so now."

She swallowed, her throat suddenly feeling tight. "What exactly does that mean?" Her voice quavered a little. "Does that mean I have to do everything you say? Always?"

He cocked his head to one side, eyes searching her face. "Are you afraid? Of me?" He let out a breath, the joy in his face gone. "Have I given you reason to fear me?"

"No! I just don't understand what this means." She couldn't look away. Time might have stood still around them; this moment was private and immeasurably important.

He closed his eyes for one heartbeat, the air between them silent and utterly still. Then he looked at her again, eyes glittering in the sunlight. "The relationship between a king and his subject is one of obedience, trust, and gratitude. As king, I bear great responsibility for your physical and spiritual well-being. I think those are the words in English; I have not spoken of these things before using human languages. If you are injured, the pain of it is in my heart, though my body remains whole. If you choose rebellion, my part in your choices is scrutinized by El, and if I have failed in my leadership of you, I bear some responsibility for your sin.

"I do not make your choices for you. But I command obedience with authority given to me by El. To defy me is to defy El, and bears the same consequences. In the same way, I answer to El for the commands I give you. No one is held to a higher standard than I am or bears a heavier responsibility than I do. I am to be your example, your protector, your solace, your rescuer." His face had taken on a sharper, brighter look, the light catching his cheekbones if he were carved of living pearl.

"A Fae subject is responsible for obeying his king in all circumstances that do not directly oppose El's will as made clear to the subject in his own communion with El. Yet a king does not make frivolous demands; authority is not given by El to the king for the king's comfort." He smiled a little, his expression softening. "The bows you see and the deference given to me by my friends is not required of them; it is a natural response to the authority and affection that bind us."

Aria's heart thudded. "What will you ask of me?"

Owen sighed softly, the disappointment in his eyes hidden, but not so quickly she didn't see it. "I do not ask you to swear your allegiance. The idea is new to you, and humans are not accustomed to this type of relationship. You also are young, almost painfully so, and I forget how little you know of obedience, trust, and protection.

"What I offer is a gift. I wish to affirm my part of the relationship. I affirm my acceptance of the weight of kingship over you. You may swear your allegiance when you wish, either now or later. Or never. It is your choice.

"You were not raised under our covenant, and I do not know what El will ask or require of you. I know only what he requires of me. This is not required, but I believe it pleases him. I know it pleases me."

Aria felt her eyes filling with tears. "But why would you do that? It can't bring you anything but pain. I'll disappoint you." *I already have.*

Owen's smile was so gentle that Aria felt it like an embrace, though he didn't touch her. "How could I not? You are mine. You were meant to be mine. I am your king. It is what I am, and what I want to be, and what I was made to be. It doesn't matter what it costs."

Aria's throat felt so tight with emotion that she couldn't speak. She nodded, tears slipping down her cheeks.

Still kneeling, Owen placed a hand on her head, his fingers cool and strong. He sang, but she did not hear the music with her ears. His song wove through her heart, notes weaving together in an impossibly intricate harmony and melody, rippling like water in a brook over tiny stones, eddying around her in reflected light. He asked for her trust, for her obedience, for her cooperation, for her heart, but he demanded nothing. He gave, and he gave, and he gave.

She found herself weeping in earnest, the ugly kind of crying that made her nose congested and her eyes swell. "I'm sorry," she choked out, not able to look up at him.

He pressed a kiss to her forehead, his lips cool against her burning skin.

SEVERAL HOURS LATER, Aria sat with Bartok while he spoke with Grenidor, but she didn't say anything. She just listened.

Grenidor didn't seem to want to talk, but the words kept coming, as if his guilt and grief overflowed without his consent. "I started pursuing the vampires for a good reason. They killed my sister, I think, and others. Senators and homeless people, even before the revolution. They are… were… *are* a threat. They prey on humans as food! I felt myself changing… I did things I wouldn't have considered at first. I would have thought the methods too cruel when I was younger and more innocent. But we had good reasons.

"I was put in charge of the program years ago, when it was still fairly new, because of my work on the few pieces of biological evidence we had back then. I devised a series of medical experiments. We wanted to see if the vampire capabilities could be used to address human ailments: to treat infectious diseases, treat or cure cancer, even treat traumatic injuries. We had no success. The vampires could heal themselves, but their blood offered no benefit to humans. Still, we were determined. We got more desperate and more creative. Crueler. There were behavioral differences between the Fae and the vampires, but biologically they appeared the same. I was determined to prove that they were the same, partly to justify the cruelties that already made me uncomfortable, partly to justify myself to General Harrison, and partly because we wanted to understand that the behavioral differences weren't an indicator of a species difference, but rather, something as trivial as a cultural difference.

C. J. Brightley

"What I proved was that it was a decision. Feichin proved it. He claimed to be Fae, and I think he actually was—until we broke him. He murdered one of my researchers." Grenidor's voice tightened until Aria thought he meant to weep, but then he merely cleared his throat and continued. "It gave me a sick sense of satisfaction—not the death, of course, because Brent Davis was a friend—but the scientific proof of what I'd known for years.

"By the time I started talking to Edwin, the whole program was already evil. Not everyone in it, but I was, and some of the others. I thought I was doing the right thing, most of the time, but I knew I cut corners, I knew I justified the cruel things by hoping that good would come of it.

"I felt noble, sacrificing my peace of mind for the good of the Empire. Then Edwin somehow led me further into evil. He made me—no, he didn't *make* me do anything—he prodded me into becoming much worse. I would never have thought of human sacrifice if not for him. I certainly wouldn't have…" His voice caught. "Wouldn't have shot an unarmed prisoner in the knee. Earlier, I would have drawn a line somewhere before I got to that. With Edwin's influence, I justified it as legitimate, or at least necessary, scientific inquiry.

"And the Christians…" He stopped for a moment, staring at his hands.

Bartok tensed but said nothing.

"Edwin wanted that. I bought his help with their lives. It was easy. Just a few phone calls and a little paperwork. I didn't realize it was so easy to cross those lines. The crimes are mine. But I want to be free of him. I don't want to be any worse than

I am, even if I can't ever be better than this... and I can't even do that without help." His voice cracked.

Bartok bowed his head, his eyes closed in grief. Then he began to speak. He told the story again, the words different but the meaning the same: undeserved mercy was available for the asking. How God created the world, and man, in his foolishness and disobedience, broke the perfection of creation. How sin separated man from God, bringing death and pain and sorrow into the world. How for long years, God spoke to and through the Jews, telling of the Messiah who would come, and how when He came, those in power did not accept Him, feeling threatened by His message. How Jesus died for humanity's sins, though He was sinless, and how He defeated death and rose again, triumphant. How salvation was through God's grace alone, free to everyone who asked in humility and hope.

For ten minutes, Grenidor had not looked up, his face hidden behind one hand. His voice rasped with emotion when he finally asked, "But is there mercy for me? After what I have done?"

"Yes! Even you." Bartok sighed. "I know you've sinned. But God offers grace even to the worst of sinners. His grace is greater than our sin."

Grenidor made a choked sound. "I can't. How can I ask for grace when I've never given it? It's too much."

"Nothing is too much for God. But you have to ask."

Aria thought Grenidor might be weeping, but he made no sound.

Feichin's sudden presence next to her made her twitch, but Grenidor didn't notice him until he spoke.

"Colonel Grenidor?"

Grenidor looked up, his eyes red. "Come to kill me? Go on." He let out a ragged breath. "It's what I deserve."

"No." Feichin looked away, as if steeling himself, then met Grenidor's gaze, silvery-blue eyes glinting. "I am not practiced at forgiveness, so I do not know its depth. But I know that El's grace extended to me, and I have no standing to call your sin greater than mine. If your question is whether you *can* be forgiven, as far as I can tell, the answer hinges on whether you ask, not the depth of your sin."

Grenidor stared at him. "You, of all people, want me to be saved? You think I should be?"

Feichin inclined his head. "My anger has not entirely faded, but I cannot hate you, not when I deserved hatred and received love. Neither of us *should* be saved, but that does not mean we should not accept mercy when it is offered."

Grenidor shuddered and looked down. "Thank you."

He said nothing else, and after a moment, Feichin nodded to Bartok and turned away.

CHAPTER 7

NIAMH TILTED HER HEAD, appearing to listen.

"What is it?" Aria whispered.

Niamh frowned slightly, then cupped a hand around Aria's ear.

"—botched it up." Gabriel's voice was low and intense, with an undercurrent of emotion that Aria couldn't interpret. "I'm done, Bartok. I fold."

"What are you saying?" Bartok's voice was clearer.

"I'm done! We haven't made any progress on any front. We're fighting a losing battle. " Gabriel's voice rose. "God hasn't listened to my prayers in years. What have I got to lose? Nothing, Bartok. I've got nothing left. Owen's dying, or haven't you noticed? I haven't told anyone about Jesus because I'm sick and tired of calling myself a Christian when I see no evidence that it really matters. This is a godless revolution and a godforsaken resistance and I'm done!"

"God never forsakes us, Gabriel. You know that." Bartok's voice was barely audible.

"I *don't* know it." Gabriel's voice cracked. "My son bled out on the oil-slick pavement and God wasn't there! He's still not here, no matter how much I pray. Or how much you pray... I bet he'd listen to you more than me anyway." Bitterness made his words sharp. "I'm stepping down, Bartok. You're in charge. I'm done."

There was silence. Niamh and Aria stared at each other; Niamh's eyes were wide, the whites perfectly white and the blue shot through with silver. *I wonder what she's thinking*, Aria thought. Niamh's slim fingers were icy against Aria's ear.

Bartok's voice came at last, low and a little rough. "I'll pray about it, Gabriel."

"You do that." Gabriel's voice was flat.

ARIA ATE BESIDE BARTOK in silence.

"Have the Fae been out to get food again?" he asked abruptly.

"Yes, earlier today, just bread and meat. They went to several different shops." She frowned as she thought about it. "I'm not sure it was enough, actually. They're trying to avoid suspicion." She glanced over at the distant encampment, absently noticing that her eyesight seemed to have improved a little. Even at this distance, and in the dark, she could clearly see the subtle expressions on the Fae faces. She watched them for a moment before looking back at Bartok. "Why?"

"Their attempt at eating human food wasn't especially successful, was it?"

She snorted. "No. The best reaction so far was to the apple. That was 'acceptable.' Everything else was 'vile.'"

"That's what I thought. Do you think they'd be willing to experiment with new foods?"

She glanced at him curiously.

"Well, I'm a pediatrician. I've dealt with picky eaters before." He smiled a little. "I think their palates are just inexperienced. If they *can* eat human food, which it appears they can, it should be possible to find some foods they like. From what I've seen so far, it seems they disliked strong tasting foods, like the cheese they bought that time. Maybe a fresh mozzarella or a cream cheese might work better. The zucchini was fairly mild and they didn't like that, but I could imagine they might be super tasters... their other senses are heightened, so it makes sense that taste would be as well. So they might be very sensitive to the bitter tastes in some vegetables. Kale would be out. Bell peppers might be palatable. Texture might also be an issue, but I don't know yet. Did they give you any other clues to work with?"

"Owen said they didn't chew much because they didn't like swallowing mush. I've seen them eat pig hearts and liver, but nothing else. Cillian said they prefer organs but can eat most meats."

Bartok nodded, frowning thoughtfully. "I think they're a lot like children learning to eat solid food. We eat the same meats and think of them as not especially bland. But we cook and season our meat. They eat it raw, and it's much more bland that way. Organ meats typically don't have much connective tissue either, and meat isn't crunchy. They might be sensitive to texture; it sounds like they're accustomed to bland foods in a narrow texture range. They might be able to supplement the raw meat they eat with human foods, but they probably don't know what to buy that would be tolerable for them. If they're willing to try some new things, I can work with them on a diet."

"I'll ask them. Now?"

"Whenever." He shrugged.

Aria stuffed the last bite of bread in her mouth and stood. "Well, if they're going hungry because they don't want to attract attention by buying what they want, it wouldn't be kind to make them wait."

A few hours later, she and Bartok went out with Niamh to keep them hidden except when necessary to purchase supplies.

They could steal whatever they wanted. But they don't. I bet it never even occurred to them. Aria smiled at the belated realization.

"I hoped they'd have samples out, but I don't see any." Bartok frowned as they navigated the entrance displays. He spoke to Niamh over his shoulder, holding a melon. "Would you smell this and tell me what you think?"

Her nose wrinkled while she stood three feet away. "Not good."

"What about this?" He held up a bunch of celery.

"Not good."

"This?" He held up a plastic package of fresh mozzarella cheese.

Niamh sniffed it carefully. "It is not bad. Strange, but not unpleasant."

Bartok nodded. "Good. What about this?" He held up a fat green pepper.

She grimaced and shook her head. "No. Even from here, it is vile."

"Banana?"

Niamh shook her head hurriedly. "No."

He held up a box of prepackaged granola bars.

Niamh held it up to her nose. "I smell more of the plastic than the food inside. I cannot tell."

Bartok shrugged and put it in the basket. "I thought that might be the case, but I thought I'd check." He picked up a few more things.

"What about applesauce?" Aria held up a jar.

Bartok shrugged. "It's worth a try. It's more expensive than apples, but if they'll eat it…"

"Ooooh," Aria smiled. "We're getting this." She put a carton of caramel ice cream in the basket. "If they won't eat it, I will." She grinned at Bartok. "I might even share. A little."

He smiled back at her, and she felt her cheeks flushing. He put a few more things in the basket without checking with Niamh. A few minutes later, they were on their way back to their hiding place.

BARTOK SAT in the middle of a group of Fae with foods spread out before him. Aria smiled as she watched him, not yet approaching. He was a thoughtful man, not dramatic but quiet and steady.

As she drew closer, she noticed that there were five Fae sitting in front of him visible, and three more just outside their circle, hidden. Just days ago she hadn't been able to tell whether a Fae was visible to humans or not, since they were always visible to her. She'd guessed, based on the reactions of the humans around her, but she hadn't been sure. Now something about them made it clear.

She stopped, studying them for a moment, trying to decide *how* it was clear. The difference wasn't identifiable, but somehow she knew. *Either I'm getting stronger in megdhonia, or I'm learning finer discernment.*

Aria felt rather pleased with herself when she reached the circle and sat down next to Bartok. "How is it going?"

"About as I expected." He motioned to Cillian, who was sitting in front of him, to ask if he wanted to elaborate.

"Mashed potatoes are acceptable. The granola bar is like eating fine gravel." He grimaced. "Uncooked pasta is not good. Plain cooked pasta is acceptable, as is pasta with cheese."

"Is that macaroni and cheese?" she asked.

Bartok nodded. "It's pretty mild, a blend of cheddar and cream cheese."

"The cereal is bad, but..." Cillian frowned. "I kept wanting to eat another few pieces, just to be sure. That was strange. Milk and various forms of bread are fine - muffins and plain wheat bread." He smiled. "Butter is good. I like butter."

Aria raised her eyebrows. "Sounds reasonable."

"Applesauce is too runny and sweet. Plain apples are tolerable, though a bit crunchy. Only sweet ones, not tart. Peanut butter tastes acceptable but is too sticky. Cream cheese is acceptable but a little sticky. Tolerable, but not a favorite."

Lorcan spoke for the first time. "Chocolate chips are good, too."

Cillian nodded. "Also strange. Delicious at first, but they lose their attraction after a few bites. Yet we wanted to keep eating them."

Bartok caught Aria's eye and shrugged, smiling. "They aren't very good chocolate, but they were the only ones I could find."

Owen approached from the side. "What are you doing?"

Cillian glanced up. "Furthering our experiment on alternate nutrition sources."

Owen sat beside him. "Any success?" He looked to Bartok.

"Yes. You should have enough other foods to supplement the meat you prefer to help avoid attracting attention by your food purchases. I'm not sure about the nutritional value of these foods in comparison to the meat you've been eating. I know what it provides, but I don't know what you require. A human would suffer from severe vitamin and mineral deficiencies on what you eat, but you seem to be fine. Maybe your bodies are just more flexible at utilizing the fuel."

Aria spotted the pecan ice cream, defrosting slowly on the cold concrete floor. She looked around for bowls but saw none, so she jogged back to the human encampment. She found a few bowls and a handful of spoons and returned just as Owen was chewing thoughtfully on a handful of chocolate chips.

"I agree. Very odd. Enticing, but… not entirely good. Yet I want more." Owen eyed the bag cautiously. "What are they made of?"

"Cocoa solids and oil. They're not exactly real chocolate; they're like imitation chocolate made from some of the same ingredients."

Owen looked at him blankly. "What is chocolate? Is it a plant?"

"Cocoa comes from a plant, yes."

Owen studied the bag again. "It doesn't smell like a plant. Strange."

Aria scooped small servings of ice cream into the bowls, stuck a spoon in each one, and passed them around. "Try this." She served Owen first, then Cillian, then the others. She caught the eye of one of the Fae who were hidden and offered him a bowl. His eyes widened in surprise, but he gave her an appreciative look and reached out to take it. Bartok didn't blink; perhaps he had assumed other Fae were watching.

Owen licked his lips with a thoughtful expression.

"This is good, too," Cillian announced with pleasure filling his voice. "What is it?"

"Caramel ice cream." Aria grinned at him and then at Bartok and Owen.

For a few minutes, they simply enjoyed their ice cream, the air cold but the feeling warm between them.

CHAPTER 8

ARIA LEANED AGAINST the cardboard box wall containing their rations. Bartok had been on watch earlier, and when his shift ended he made his way to her, stopping to pick up a little camp stove and a few packages. He sat beside her wordlessly and swished milk and powder together in a thermos. He melted butter in a little skillet.

He turned away and crunched something out of her view, then asked, "You're not allergic to anything, are you?"

"No. Why?"

He didn't answer, but he dropped the whatever-it-was into the batter and swirled it around before making the first of a series of small pancakes, which he stacked on a camp plate. He handed the plate to her.

"You made me breakfast?" She raised her eyebrows.

C. J. BRIGHTLEY

"It's hardly gourmet, but I figured I might get points for effort." He nodded at it. "Chocolate chip and walnut pancakes. From powder, but pancakes."

She swallowed. *He likes me. And I like him, but I'm not sure if I like him like that. Actually… I think I do. How am I supposed to deal with this?* "Is this a date?"

He raised his eyebrows back at her. "I figured I needed to be a bit more obvious. But I'm not…" He frowned, then looked down. "I'm not proposing. And I'm not trying to compete with Lord Owen. He's remarkable, and I can't blame anyone for choosing to follow him, no matter where it leads or how much it costs. If I were you, I'd be in love with him, too. I'm just trying to be honest about the fact that I'm interested." He looked up, and she could see the weariness around his eyes. "I'm not going to be weird about it or anything. And I don't expect anything from you. I'm just… here, if you need me."

She hesitated and looked down at her plate. "No syrup?"

"I'm not a magician!"

The tension broke between them. Bartok made another plate of pancakes for himself and then leaned back against the boxes next to her. He sighed and gave a jaw-cracking yawn, covering his mouth belatedly. "Sorry. Long night."

"Anything happen?"

"No. I got a lot of thinking done… hence, the pancakes." He took another bite and chewed thoughtfully. "I think Feichin is important. I don't think Petro was necessarily the main target of…

whatever was talking to Col. Grenidor. I think it was Owen. Perhaps Feichin too."

"Why do you say that?"

"There are a lot of ways to tempt an angel, if that's what Petro is. Something like an angel, anyway. But there are not a lot of ways to strike directly at the Fae. I think they're protected from direct demonic influence. They can be hurt by people and indirectly tempted. But I don't think a demon, or whatever it was, can directly strike at them, or even directly tempt them. If it could be done easily, I bet it would occur more often."

Aria snorted. "You think their lives are easy?"

"Not at all. But I think they are protected from direct interference. Feichin said he spoke to a dark one. I imagine that dark one would try to tempt Lord Owen if it could. I think it can't. Maybe that's part of their covenant."

"Maybe..." Aria blew out her breath as she thought. "Lord Owen and Cillian have both mentioned that Fae withdrew from human interaction because of how humans took advantage of them. And they don't lie, so they probably aren't good at telling when people are lying to them. Maybe God protects them from the dark ones because they're vulnerable; they're so honest, they don't even know how to look for deception."

Bartok nodded. "That makes sense. Not that people aren't vulnerable to deception, too; we've been falling for Satan's lies since the first sin. But we're like turned Fae; we abrogated God's protection by our own sin."

Niamh stepped out of the darkness, and Bartok twitched in surprise.

"May I join you?" she asked.

103

"Of course." Bartok gestured at the stove. "Would you like some pancakes?"

"No, thank you."

"You might like them."

A smile flashed across her face. "I thank you, but no. I wished to speak with you about Petro and the dark one."

They nodded, and she sat beside Aria. "I thank you, Dr. Bartok, for what you have already taught us." Her smile faded, and for a moment, she was absolutely, inhumanly, still. Then she said, "My brother, Lord Owen, is resting now, but he can hear us. Lord Owen, Cillian, Feichin, and I have been considering the implications of Feichin's redemption. First, of course, we rejoice in El's grace to Feichin and in his return to fellowship with us and with El. We rejoice in the revelation of El's love for us, which we had not fully appreciated in our attention to obedience. But also..." She stopped, looking down at her white fingers clasped in her lap. "We are... concerned."

"About what?"

Niamh swallowed. "Upon reflection, we have realized that Petro has followed three beings who have rebelled to various degrees that are in some way different than others of their type. He has examined the consequences of those sins. Lord Owen lied, albeit under duress and for love of others, not for himself. He asked for forgiveness and received it. Feichin sinned in judgment and hatred. He asked for forgiveness and received it. Aria," Niamh turned her gaze upon Aria, "was born under our covenant but raised under the human one, unaware of the importance of obedience. Perhaps she also will be saved in the way of humans." She stopped and inclined her head. "It is to be hoped."

"I…" Aria didn't know what to say to that. *I'm still thinking about it.*

Niamh nodded, as if accepting that Aria wasn't ready yet. She hesitated and took a deep breath. "Petro appears to be investigating sin and its consequences in anomalous cases. In particular, it seems he is looking at those who are not human, but who may claim forgiveness under the covenant offered to humans. We fear he is looking for some loophole. So… what sin is Petro considering?"

Bartok sucked in his breath and let it out slowly. "I hesitate to even imagine. Let's not borrow trouble. Our responsibility is to obey God to the best of our ability, and to trust in his grace and forgiveness when we fail."

Niamh blinked, then tilted her head. "You are not concerned?"

"There is no purpose in fear." Bartok gave her a lopsided smile. "The only thing we can do is pray that Petro will choose wisely. It is in God's hands."

Niamh's gaze held Bartok's for a moment, then she inclined her head. "You are a wise man, Dr. Bartok, especially for one so young."

Bartok snorted. "I'm not that young."

"To us you are." She smiled, perfect white teeth gleaming in the light. "That is a compliment, Dr. Bartok. Few humans have ever been called wise by Fae. It is a rare honor, and you should not forget it."

CHAPTER 9

FEICHIN STOOD a little way from where Grenidor sat alone, hunched over a large piece of bread, some cheese, and a bowl of now cool soup. Grenidor hadn't eaten yet; he'd merely sat there, staring at his food, apparently lost in thought. Feichin watched in uncanny silence, his expression hard and unreadable.

Aria wondered whether Feichin had really forgiven Grenidor. Whether he was planning to kill him. How much he would enjoy it.

Grenidor rested his elbows on his knees and sighed, rubbed his hands over his face. He ripped a piece of bread off the larger chunk and toyed with it.

Aria looked again at Feichin. *Should I warn Grenidor? Should I call for Owen?* She looked around helplessly.

Feichin turned away, his face hidden from Aria. He disappeared into the darkness.

Aria found her heart pounding with belated terror. She made her way to Bartok, who was reading the Bible again, lying prone on his bedroll.

"Can I sit with you a while?"

"Of course." He sat up and stretched. "I was reading the part called Ephesians, and there's an analogy about spiritual fighting as if we're wearing spiritual armor. It talks about how our struggle isn't against flesh and blood and men, but against the powers and principalities of darkness."

She frowned at him. "I don't know what that means."

"Well, our lives here are real. They're important. But they're also just a prelude. My father said life on earth was the physical shadow of a spiritual reality. We're making choices, and our choices are part of a great spiritual battle. Our choices don't only affect us now; they affect eternity."

The darkness pressed down, the little pool of light from the lantern suddenly small and pathetic. "Feichin told me that the dark one wanted him to kill me."

Bartok stiffened a little beside her. "Did he say anything else?

"He was warning me. It wasn't meant to frighten me." The image of Feichin's silver-bright eyes and thin lips lifted in a faint smile came to mind. She glanced toward Grenidor, who was eating alone. Feichin was nowhere to be seen. "He thought maybe the dark one wanted to strike at me to hurt Owen. Or maybe the dark one had other reasons. Maybe I play some part in something important that he wants to see happen or prevent."

Bartok stretched again and rubbed a hand over his jaw. "You must have been one of the targets of the demon's attempt at goading Petro into fury with the idol and the blood-covered bullets."

Aria blinked. "Why would you think that?"

"Owen was there as a target. So targeting you separately, through Feichin, must mean there is something about you specifically, beyond simply hurting Owen."

"Oh."

The silence seemed heavier. Aria's heartbeat pulsed in her ears. "But why?" she breathed.

Bartok sighed. "I don't know." He turned to meet her eyes. "But you're not alone."

ARIA NEARLY GROANED at the exquisite agony of stretching her aching muscles. Without a watch, she found it difficult to estimate how long she had slept, but it must have been hours. She sat up and looked around at the camp, the neatly folded bed-rolls and cold camp stoves. She must have slept long past dawn. *I wonder if I should be embarrassed by that. But I think I needed the sleep.*

Owen caught Aria's eye from some distance away. "Come. It is time to meet Dandra."

She hurriedly grabbed a nutrition bar from an open box and followed him into the darkness of a tunnel. Just when she could no longer follow him by sight, he slipped his hand into hers and led her onward silently.

They stepped into a larger tunnel and followed a narrow walkway along the wall. Once she must have stepped too close to the edge, because Owen grabbed her arm and guided her back to the left, his grip firm but courteous.

"Sorry," she murmured.

A moment later, he wrapped his arm around her more strongly and flattened her against the wall. His body pressed against her, and he covered her ears with his hands. A second later, she heard the oncoming rush of a train, a blast of air, and a roar so loud it hurt even through his palms muffling the sound. He shuddered against her.

The train passed, the roar receding in the distance. Owen stumbled away.

"Where are you?" She didn't entirely succeed in keeping the fear from her voice.

"I'm here. Don't fall," he croaked.

She waved her arms carefully in the inky blackness until she found his shoulder. He was leaning against the wall only a step away, nearly doubled over.

"What's wrong?"

He flinched at her voice, another shudder running through him.

She ran a hand over his shoulders and the back of his head, trying to determine if he was injured. She frowned, unable at first to figure out what she was feeling, then realized his hands were clamped over his ears.

He straightened, breathing heavily, a catch in his voice when he answered. "Our hearing is much more sensitive than yours."

She whispered, "Are you all right?"

Even that soft sound made him wince. "Well enough." He leaned against the wall for a moment, his breath steadying.

"It's that bad?" She kept her voice low. "Grenidor tortured you with sound, didn't he?"

"Yes." He let out a long breath, as if putting the pain behind him. "Let us go. We are close."

"You don't have to cover my ears for me. I can do it myself. Just cover your own ears," she whispered. He squeezed her hand but said nothing.

A few minutes later they rounded a long curve to face the rear of the stopped train. Passengers were boarding, and Owen led her up the tiny hidden ladder and around a corner onto the platform proper. No one saw them, and Aria smiled to think how easily Owen kept them unseen.

He led her through the station to the main entrance, stopping in a corner from which both the entrance and the doorway to the manager's office were visible. The spacious tiled entrance was lit by halogen lights competing with the winter sunlight reflected off the floor. An icy breeze ruffled Aria's hair, and she shivered.

They waited without speaking, though the sounds of the crowds shuffling through the station and the beep of the ticket machines echoed around them. Aria glanced at Owen's face at intervals, wondering what he was thinking. If she hadn't studied him so closely in these past few weeks, she wouldn't have known that he was still healing. One fading bruise barely peeked out of the collar of his plain black shirt. He walked with an almost unnoticeable limp; if she hadn't been holding his hand earlier, she wouldn't have known it at all. Studying him surreptitiously, she could see that he looked a little tense, a little worn by pain. Somehow it didn't diminish his inhuman beauty.

"What are you looking at?" he murmured, finally looking down at her.

"Just… you. It's been a rough few weeks for you."

His eyes swept over the crowds again. "I appreciate your concern."

If he had been anyone else, the words might have sounded cold and dismissive. But in his voice, they merely sounded sincere. Slightly distant, but sincere.

Then he looked down and smiled at her, a warm smile that made her feel disconcertingly weak in the knees. It wasn't intentional; she was sure of that. But now that she realized how cool the Fae expressions generally were, she appreciated that warmth all the more.

"There she is." Owen caught Aria's hand and drew her forward.

She didn't see Dandra immediately, but then the familiar figure emerged from the crowd and headed for the manager's office door, looking like any other comfortable, middle-aged woman wearing a thick coat against the fading winter chill.

"Speak to her first, please."

Aria nodded. "Dandra, it's me."

Dandra jumped, her eyes darting around to settle on Aria. She gave a startled smile.

Aria drew her off to the side. "Owen is with me. Lord Owen, actually. Don't be frightened."

Owen stepped forward, and Dandra gave a little shriek of terror. "You!"

Owen inclined his head. "Yes. Do not be afraid."

Dandra swallowed and she raised her chin a little. "How could I not be?"

111

Owen's nostrils flared. "I mean you no harm. Come, I will take you to the resistance."

Dandra glanced at Aria. "Talk to me. Who is he, and who does he work for?"

Owen frowned. "At least come to the side a little more."

Aria glanced at him. "I thought you were good at hiding."

He drew them both a few steps farther out of the crowd. "It's more effort when I'm tired."

The light and shadow played across his face for a moment, and for a split second, she could see the weariness around his eyes, the way he held his lips tight as if to keep himself from betraying any pain.

"I'm sorry," she murmured.

He nodded. "No matter. Dandra, don't be afraid. We are here to help you."

Dandra edged closer to Aria. "Are you all right?"

Aria impulsively gave her a hug. "Yes. I'm so glad you're safe. I was worried about you."

The older woman looked startled, then smiled, wrapping her arms around Aria in return. "I was worried about you, too. Did you get my message, then? The books?"

"Yes. That was clever. Although I don't think I understand everything. You'll have to explain. I didn't know you were on some secret mission."

Dandra huffed. "It's not like that. I'm not part of the resistance. But now, I think my mission and that of the resistance align more closely than before. Are you part of the resistance?" She studied Owen warily.

"Not exactly. I lead *a* resistance."

Dandra hesitated, looking back at the manager's office with a bit of longing. "You're not safe, are you? You're dangerous."

Owen inclined his head. "Not to you. I think we misunderstood each other before. Come."

He led them back to the tiny service ladder. They clambered down to the hidden walkway. Owen offered Dandra a hand, and she ignored it. Aria wasn't sure if it was because she didn't yet trust Owen, or if she simply didn't see him in the shadows.

At the bottom, the darkness was deeper, and Dandra gripped Aria's hand gratefully. Owen took Aria's other hand and began to lead them through the blackness.

They were nearly at the first turn when Owen's grip tightened. A moment later, a distant rumble had become a deafening roar.

"Cover your ears!" Aria shouted. She pressed her hands against her own ears.

Owen's strong body pressed hers against the wall again, even as he reached out to crush Dandra against the wall, too.

The roar receded, and Dandra gasped, "That was incredibly loud. Let's get out of here."

Owen's voice rasped with pain. "A moment, please."

"Are you all right?"

Owen made some inarticulate, agonized sound.

"Shhh!" Aria hushed her. She felt for Owen but didn't find him until she stumbled into his back. He had fallen to his knees and was clutching his head, palms pressed against his ears. He shuddered, and she patted his shoulder in silent sympathy.

A heartbeat later he staggered to his feet, his breath ragged in the echoing darkness. He took Aria's hand again, and Aria groped for Dandra's hand. He led them onward in silence.

OWEN LET OUT a short, sharp breath. "El, give me strength," he murmured. Then, only a little louder, "Get down."

Aria dropped to the floor, wrapping one arm around Dandra.

A moment later, she heard the terrifying growl of a vertril in the tunnel in front of them.

"What is that?" Dandra sounded less panicky than Aria would have expected.

"A nightmare."

Eyes straining, Aria managed to make out the beast as it leaped at them, an ink-black blur hurtling through the shadows.

Owen dodged forward, evading its teeth, to catch one ear and a handful of the vertril's pelt. With terrifying strength, he jerked it out of midair, down and around, twisting it so that its feet scrabbled vainly for purchase on the smooth concrete. Faster than thought, he drew his sword. The vertril's nails caught a seam in the concrete, and it twisted against him, savage teeth grazing his arm as it snapped, pushing the Fae king over the edge of the narrow platform and onto the tracks. Owen landed on his feet, let it go, and danced backward, sword ready.

He's drawing it away from us.

114

It leaped again.

He twisted, one foot narrowly missing the electrified third rail, slipped under the beast, and slid his sword across its throat. Blood spurted, mostly missing him, the dark droplets disappearing against the black of his shirt and in the shadows.

The vertril wasn't dead, and it snarled, blood and saliva dripping from its maw, snapping helplessly as Owen evaded it yet again to cut its throat more deeply. Blood spilled over the rail, and Owen stood over the beast for a moment as its feet twitched.

Life slipped away, and the creature stilled.

Owen put his left hand flat against his chest, as if something pained him, though he was facing away and Aria couldn't see his face. Then he grabbed the vertril's leg and pulled it off the tracks. He shoved it under the overhang where no train would run over it, then he wiped the sword against the dead vertril's fur, removing most of the blood.

The Fae king vaulted easily back onto the narrow walkway, sheathing his sword in the same motion. He took Aria's hand.

"I thought you killed them all." Aria's voice shook.

"Not all. They grow quickly."

"Do your ears still hurt?"

"I'm fine." He squeezed her hand as if to thank her for asking.

The tunnel seemed darker, though the light hadn't changed. *How did I see that? My eyes aren't that strong.*

Aria gripped Owen's hand, grateful for his strength. Dandra clung to Aria's other hand,

115

though she said nothing. *I bet she didn't see the vertril at all.*

Ten silent minutes later, they rounded the last turn and approached the sentry. Owen spoke to him, then led them across the open platform.

"Let me speak with you first. We have matters to clarify between us," Owen said, turning to Dandra at last. "Sit." He gestured to the concrete floor near a lantern.

Dandra looked like she wanted to refuse, but Aria smiled reassuringly at her and sat down. Dandra followed, her eyes darting around and settling on Owen again.

"You're resistance?" she asked finally. "I thought you were IPF, maybe, or one of their spies."

"No. I am not part of the human resistance to the Empire. I am not human. But I do object to much of what the Empire is doing, and I have lent my support to the resistance for a time."

"You're not human?" Dandra gave him a skeptical look before looking to Aria for confirmation.

"He's telling the truth." Aria had her own questions. "Why did you close the store? I was worried about you. But when I asked Lord Owen about it, he said he hadn't told Petro about you."

Dandra's gaze shot back to Owen. "*Lord* Owen? And who is Petro anyway? Why did you threaten me with him?"

Owen tilted his head, his gaze sharpening. "You don't know?"

Dandra sighed. "You came into my shop asking for maps that were forbidden. I told you I couldn't get them. Then you came back again, saying someone named Petro told you I could get them. I don't know who or what Petro is, but it was enough to worry me. Then, as I was leaving the shop that same night, I found a paper in my hand." She shivered. "On the back, it said I had to flee, that I had only a few days. Signed Petro."

Owen blinked, his gaze distant for a moment. "He was avoiding undesirable consequences, I imagine." He focused on her again.

"What?" Dandra gave him a confused look.

Aria frowned. "So you threatened her with Petro because you thought she would understand who he was? Why would you think that?"

Owen sighed softly. "I was desperate. It was a question, not a direct threat or a lie, and I meant her no harm. But I *knew* she lied to me, and my people were dying, or worse, while they waited for me to extract them."

"But I couldn't get the maps!" Dandra's voice rose. "Not without endangering others. It would mean near certain discovery, and probably execution, for whoever got the maps for me."

Owen inclined his head. "I understand now. I had reason to believe you might be a Christian, and I did not know how much Christians know about other created beings. When Petro spoke of you, he said you would know him by the name Petro; that is why I used that name with you. I have known him by other names at other times. Rather than a threat, it could also have been reason for you to trust me; if you knew Petro, you would understand that I was not working for the IPF." He looked down and added softly, "Also, I did not fully comprehend the cost of what I was asking. Petro does not give complete explanations; he merely gives facts. Sometimes."

Dandra frowned. "I suppose if you're being excruciatingly technical, I probably *could* have gotten the maps, but people would have died for it."

Owen gave her a faint, wry smile. "That would not enter into Petro's calculations."

"How did you know I was a Christian?" Dandra brushed at her hair with a trembling hand.

"I guessed. Many Christians came to your bookstore and held meetings, and you received shipments with Bibles and other Christian books, which you distributed to them free of charge. Your shop also hosted several resistance discussions and clandestine drops, so you might have been a member of the resistance, but I doubted it. I didn't think you were aware of the resistance operations in your shop, and you didn't have the look of a political subversive."

Dandra's eyes had grown wider and wider as he spoke. "You knew about the meetings? Did you tell anyone?"

Owen looked confused. "Who would I tell? And for what purpose?"

"You didn't betray them to anyone? Then why did the IPF come knocking on my door a few days later?"

Owen blinked. "I don't know."

Aria sucked in her breath. "That might have been my fault." She grimaced and glanced at Owen, then back down. "After I followed you and you killed the vertril, the IPF questioned me. I mentioned that I'd first seen you at Dandra's. I don't even know when they went back. It might not have been immediately."

"They came by a few days after he did. I was already closed up. Petro's warning was enough for me, but I watched the place to see what happened, and the IPF came by." She turned a slightly accusatory look on Owen. "You can see why I might have suspected you."

His face remained entirely neutral. Aria wondered whether he was offended by the accusations and hiding it, or whether he thought they were simply irrelevant.

"They weren't especially suspicious. They took a quick look and then left. I went back later and left the clues for you, Aria."

"What would they do if they found you?"

Dandra licked her lips, choosing her words carefully. "Six months ago, I would have said they would deport me, or at least allow me to leave the Empire. But now? Do you know what we do?"

"Not really."

Dandra grimaced as she thought, then glanced across the platform. "Who's in charge? It's a long story and I don't want to repeat it."

"I'll go get Gabriel and Bartok," Aria said. She stood, noticing Dandra tense at the prospect of being left alone with Owen. Perhaps it would be good for her to see that Owen could be trusted.

A few minutes later, she returned with Gabriel and Bartok in tow. It appeared that Owen and Dandra had been utterly silent in her absence. Owen glanced up at her, then back down, and she noted that his hands were shaking a little as he motioned Gabriel to sit beside him. He hid the tremor by resting his hands on his knees and nodding politely to Bartok, who sat across from him. *He's tired and probably hurting more than he's showing. What would it be like to be brave?* The thought caught her for a moment, because she'd never felt particularly brave. She'd done things recently that she could never have imagined, but she'd never felt brave. *Maybe Owen doesn't feel brave either. Maybe no one ever feels brave. It's something you do, not something you feel.*

Owen introduced them quietly. "Dandra, this is Colonel Gabriel Peterson, leader of the human resistance, and Dr. Tobias Bartok. This is Dandra."

Gabriel nodded. "Dr. Bartok is actually my second-in-command if we're going to be specific."

Aria blinked. "I thought Eli was."

"Eli is a friend and a good assistant. But Bartok is a leader. I'd trust him best if something happened to me. I think everyone else would, too, despite our disagreements."

Bartok gave a quick, almost embarrassed smile. "You had news for us?"

Dandra glanced between them. "Right. So, you know Leo, don't you?"

Only Gabriel nodded.

"We're a missionary organization, though we're not like those in the past. Leo's intelligence background has shaped how we operate. I was a missionary years ago, back when such things were permitted. I worked with college kids." The ghost of a fond smile flickered across her face.

"What's a missionary?" Aria asked.

Dandra blinked. "You really don't know much, do you?"

Aria frowned. "Sorry! It's not like I got much explanation of anything."

"A missionary is a Christian who works in evangelism, or sharing the gospel. Well, I suppose other religions have missionaries, too, but I was a Christian missionary. A missionary works to bring the gospel to people who haven't heard it before, or who haven't accepted it yet.

"What's the gospel?" Aria's frown deepened. All the Christian words felt like a secret code meant to exclude her, or perhaps to make her feel unworthy. Unworthy of *what*, she wasn't entirely sure, but she didn't like the feeling.

Dandra's voice softened. "Gospel just means the good news of Jesus Christ; it's the story of the grace God offers through the life, death, and resurrection of Jesus. Every Christian is supposed to be a missionary to their own community, but when we say 'missionary', we mean someone who works in evangelism full-time. Missionaries are often supported by donations from the church or other Christians, so they don't have to hold another job to pay the bills. They can focus on outreach."

Aria nodded, still feeling a little confused but not wanting to admit it.

"I was a missionary when I was young, and when Leo told me what was going on here, I volunteered. I'm not a missionary now, though; I'm field support. Our missionaries are organized into small, independent groups that have very little knowledge of other groups. If a missionary or group is discovered, they can't be forced to betray others. We'd hoped that the government wouldn't interrogate them so harshly since they don't have any information, but that's not always the case." She looked down at her hands twisted in her lap. "Several cells are supported by one field support person, like me."

"That sounds like the cells the resistance uses," Aria said.

Dandra looked up, surprised. "I suppose it is. I serve as an information and supplies conduit. Bibles, money, and other materials are shipped to me so the missionaries don't have much on them. If a Christian, missionary or not, is discovered with only a few Bibles and a little money, generally they're ignored. But if for some reason they're arrested, often they're merely deported. Sometimes, if the authorities are feeling irritable, they're imprisoned. Sometimes they're tortured. But if they have a lot of materials on them, say ten Bibles, more money, whatever, they're likely to be executed as a subversive. Technically evangelism has been against imperial law for several years. They just haven't enforced the laws much; other threats have taken precedence."

Gabriel nodded. "Vampires, for one."

Owen gave him a cold glance.

"I didn't say Fae! I said vampires. I didn't even say the Empire was right. But that's what the government's been focused on, and you know it."

The air around them seemed brittle with tension.

"Vampires?" Dandra whispered. "What vampires?"

"That is a discussion for another time. Continue your explanations." Owen's voice was low and clear, and the authority in it made Dandra blink and sit up straighter.

Aria asked, "Why do the missionaries need money? What's wrong with holding a job?"

"The government pay scale is carefully planned. If you make more money, you can live better, but you can't accumulate any savings. Lack of savings means you're dependent on your job, and that means you're beholden to the government. You can't take time off and you can't really sit around and think about things; everything is watched and everything is controlled. If you get a better job, you are assigned better housing that costs more. It's not optional. You also need better clothing. You have to keep up appearances; if you don't, your superiors will notice and there will be disciplinary action."

Gabriel blinked. "Really? I didn't know that much was controlled."

Aria nodded. "That's true. Even at school, it was true. If you had a better scholarship, you had better housing that cost more. And the professors would comment if you didn't dress well enough. It was a lot of pressure, but no one really questioned it. It was just a fact."

Dandra continued, "The point is that if you have a job, your movements and associates are controlled. Your freedom to talk is limited. So the missionaries need outside support, and they have to remain more or less unnoticed, at least as missionaries. I support five cell leaders, each of whom has three other missionaries in their cell. I know the leaders by sight and by their code names, but not by their real names. I know how to contact them by drop and I could signal them if I needed to.

"The bookstore was a perfect cover. I could get shipments of books and paper goods, including cash, from outside the Empire without it being unusual. I could only order from the approved suppliers, of course, but my contacts on the outside could add what I needed to the expected deliveries. The drop-in customers provided some cover, and book discussion groups provided adequate reason for small groups to meet and talk for an hour or so. Because of this, I could probably identify by sight at least a few of the other missionaries, although I wouldn't know how to contact them and I don't know their names. I didn't want to. They would know that they meet at my shop, but they wouldn't know I'm part of their organization.

"In order to avoid suspicion, I didn't engage in missionary activity myself. Of course, I wouldn't have anything to do with the political resistance either; that would endanger the missionaries, as well as cast doubt on our mission. We're after souls, not political power. Even if the Empire is horrible, which it is, opposing it isn't our purpose. It might be yours, but it's not ours.

"When Owen came to the shop asking about maps, I assumed I had drawn the attention of the IPF somehow. I thought they were suspicious of me and were trying to trap me into revealing support for the resistance. 'Petro' might have been some resistance leader, or perhaps a code name for some committee that the IPF thought I supported.

"Petro's note in my hand was even more frightening. It might have been him," she nodded toward Owen, "trying to frighten me, but that didn't seem right. I was already scared, and that seemed like an unnecessary complication. And mostly... I didn't know how the note got in my hand. That shook me, but I thought at first maybe I'd picked it up without noticing while I was distracted. Later, when I got home and looked at it again, I realized it was written on Aria's bookmark, which I had watched her put away. I knew, without a doubt, I would not have picked it up without noticing, even if she'd left it on the table. That scared me--badly.

"Maybe Petro was something unnatural, spiritual, maybe. Or maybe I was imagining things.

"However it got in my hand, the note was alarming enough that I knew I needed to leave. I'd like to think I'm brave, but the IPF could break me with torture and drugs. I knew too much about the missionaries and the cell leaders, and I didn't want to get them killed.

"But I didn't want to go without leaving clues for Aria. I couldn't do so before, because of the rules, and I had to be careful because I didn't want to implicate her. I hoped the investigation would blow over completely and I'd be able to return since I didn't really do anything suspicious, but I couldn't be sure I'd be back at all. She was searching for the truth, but she hadn't made contact with any of the missionaries, and I didn't want to identify them to her, in case she was an imperial agent. If I left her clues, she'd find the truth if she was looking for it, and I wouldn't endanger anyone if she was merely fishing for information."

She sighed and looked down, twisting her hands together. "Then the crackdown started. The arrests proved my fears weren't groundless. If you didn't set them off," she glanced at Owen, "something else did. From what I know, which isn't much, the pattern of arrests indicates that there was no compromise at my level, or even of the cell leaders. It's only been individual missionaries." Her voice had tightened as she spoke, but only now did Aria realize she was barely restraining tears.

"Some of them have been executed already. I know we've avoided the political resistance until now. I hope you understand why."

Gabriel nodded.

"But now I'm asking for help. Not because we're afraid to die; we all knew that was a risk before we came. But as we've worked, we've realized that everyone is just too...." She stopped, clenching her hands into fists. "It's like everyone is drugged or something! We've had a few converts, mostly among the forgotten people, the manual laborers, taxi drivers, and dockworkers. But when the missionaries have talked to others, they get... I don't want to say stonewalled, because that's too deliberate. It's more like people just can't quite follow the conversation or the logic evades them. They're perfectly capable of holding a job, even a challenging job sometimes, but they can't fathom questioning the all-sufficiency of the government. The very concept of sin and redemption evades them because they don't seem to fully understand the choices they're making. Maybe they're not really making choices. They're just on auto-pilot."

She glanced at Aria. "That's actually why I noticed Aria. I thought she might have been part of the resistance because she wasn't drugged and—"

"But I was. I got a wire in my brain and everything." Aria scowled.

Owen murmured, "You were less affected by it. Your heritage, though forgotten, still protected you."

"—and she was asking... what?" Dandra stopped and looked at him. "What about Aria's heritage?"

Aria licked her lips. "It's a long story. I'll tell you later."

Dandra hesitated, then nodded. "All right. I thought you might be part of the resistance because you were more alert than the others. You questioned things no one else questioned. But I asked about you and found that you were indeed a full-time student, just as you said, and in a politically sensitive field. No resistance agent would be in your position. You'd have a tracker, and none of the resistance fighters did, so far as we knew.

"Besides, you disappeared right as the purge started, and I had no way to contact you. I hoped you hadn't been arrested because of your association with the bookstore, either as a suspected Christian or part of the resistance. Perhaps you actually *had* become part of the resistance and had gone underground. I hoped you had, although I thought it more likely that he..." she motioned at Owen, "was an imperial agent, had gotten irritated at your interest, and had arrested you."

Owen raised his eyebrows but said nothing.

"If so, perhaps you would be released after an investigation. I prayed for your safety. If you *were* released, I thought you might come to the bookstore looking for me, or more likely for the book that proved the records had been changed. I left the clues for you hoping you would find the Bible. God's Word is powerful. Even if I was not there to explain it to you, if you sincerely sought God's wisdom and guidance, you would not be disappointed."

Aria studied her hands in her lap. *I should have decided by now. I should trust God. But I don't. There's too much darkness. Too much evil.*

The silence drew out uncomfortably long, until finally Gabriel asked, "What exactly do you want?"

Dandra opened her mouth to speak, but then she stopped, looking over Aria's shoulder with wide, horrified eyes. Aria turned around.

Niall stood a few feet away from Owen, the blood on his clothes dried dark and crusted on the cut edges of the fabric, the original color of his shirt lost among the stains. He knelt deliberately and pressed his forehead to the ground, dark hair falling over his face.

"Niall, I am glad to see you well." Owen's voice was soft.

Niall rose and scooted closer, letting his uncle wrap one strong arm around his shoulders.

Glittering letters appeared in the air in front of Owen. *Lachtnal offered your location to Colonel Grenidor. When Colonel Grenidor did not take the bait, Lachtnal attacked. I tried, my lord Owen, to bring him back. He refused. I left him sleeping in Colonel Grenidor's apartment, but we do not have long.*

"Your pain is gone?"

Yes. Colonel Grenidor was injured, as well. Has he been healed?

"Yes." Owen looked at Gabriel. "We need to move. It will not be long before Lachtnal finds someone to pursue us."

Niall's glittering words appeared again, but this time, it was a flowing Fae script, infinitely more elegant than the precise Roman characters. Owen answered him in the same language, and Niall bowed his head in acknowledgment.

Dandra's eyes had gotten wider as she watched. "What is he doing?" she murmured to Aria.

Niall turned his steady, cool gaze on her. *My apologies. My name is Niall.*

Dandra swallowed. "I'm Dandra. You write in the air?"

I cannot speak. He motioned toward his mouth, glancing away as if embarrassed by the inability.

"I didn't see what happened earlier. You're healed?" asked Bartok.

Yes. Thank you for asking.

Bartok frowned and glanced at Dandra, then back to Niall. "Would you like a clean shirt?"

Niall blinked, as if startled by the thought. He looked down at himself, then back at Bartok. *It matters not to me, but if you find it disconcerting, I will remove it.* He stripped off his shirt and wadded it into a ball, which he held in one hand. *We should go soon. They have not had a turned Fae to lead them before. Lachtnal will track us.*

Owen sighed. "Yes." He rubbed his hands over his face as if he was trying to stay awake.

"Do you still have getlaril in your body?" asked Bartok.

"Yes." Owen frowned at the floor and pushed himself to his feet. Niall kept a steadying hand behind Owen's back, but his uncle didn't need it.

"Aren't you cold?" Dandra asked in disbelief.

Niall shook his head. *The cold does not bother us.* In the darkness, his pale skin was nearly luminous. Still quite thin, he was a study in youthful beauty, lithe and graceful. No trace of his injuries was visible.

129

"I didn't know you could write in the air. Why didn't you do that earlier?" Aria asked.

It takes great concentration, and I was not practiced at it. It is a variation of the techniques we use to condense light, but greatly refined. I may be the first to use it in this way.

Also, light is meant to be seen. When we were fleeing before, I was using megdhonia to keep us hidden. To create something meant to be seen, and then hide it, is difficult, if not impossible. Even now, the technique is challenging, and I would not want to communicate in this way while pursuers are close.

Niall gave his uncle a sharp, questioning look. Glittering words appeared in the air in one of the Fae languages, and Owen answered him in a low voice. Niall flinched, his expression sympathetic, and he glanced toward Aria as if seeking her support.

"What can I do?" Aria and Bartok asked together.

"Is the library still abandoned?" Owen asked, looking around to meet everyone's eyes.

Aria had the distinct sense that his question was a deliberate attempt to change the subject. "I think so," she said.

"Which one?" Bartok asked. "The big one, the Library of Congress, is still empty. But it's guarded, I think; there used to be motion detectors and other sensors around it."

Owen licked his lips thoughtfully. "What about the island?"

Bartok blinked. "What island?"

"In the river. Roosevelt Island? I think that's the name."

Gabriel sucked his breath in through his teeth. "I've heard rumors of vampires there, but nothing confirmed. I don't want to be trapped on an island, though."

Owen seemed to be listening for a moment, and then glanced down at Niall. He murmured, "We have a little time yet. Lachtnal will not act until he is strong again, and without anyone to sing for him, he will take time to recover." His voice lowered further. "I grieve for him."

CHAPTER 10

OWEN ROSE WITH FLUID GRACE. "Come," he murmured, one hand brushing Aria's shoulder. She stood and looked across the platform to where Lorcan and a young Fae boy stood just inside the room.

The boy was younger than Niall; if he'd been human, she would have guessed he was about five years old. Since he was Fae, that meant he was perhaps thirty, give or take a few years. He was slim, though not as gaunt as any of the Fae she'd already met. His skin was much darker than Owen's was, or indeed any of the Fae she had seen before. Near her own color, actually. His hair was a medium brown, much like her own, though curlier; defiant ringlets stood out from his head as if unaffected by gravity. His eyes shone a clear hazel tinged with gold. *How can I see that from this far away? My sight is improving!*

She followed Owen to the younger Fae. Owen bowed, a slight, solemn movement filled with regal courtesy. Lorcan dropped to a knee for a moment, bowing to Owen, and the unknown Fae boy beside him followed a heartbeat later.

The boy rose and spoke, the language different than the ones Aria had heard before but with something of the same flavor. Age, and freshness, and power. *I should understand, but I don't.*

The boy's eyes turned toward her. He said something else, and Owen answered him. The boy paled and bowed toward Owen again.

Lorcan said, "Shall I translate, Lord Owen?"

Owen glanced at Aria, then shook his head. "I will." He motioned toward the boy. "This is Aodhagan, your brother."

"What?" Then, as the weight of what he'd said percolated through, "*What?*"

"Aodhagan is your elder brother. He was there when the rest of your family was killed. I sent Lorcan to find him, if he was still alive. He has been in hiding since the death of your family. He remained alone in the forest for about nine years. Then he found another clan to join; they knew he was Fae, but did not know his family. They have cared for him as their own. He speaks no English."

Aria could not seem to find her voice. The boy stepped forward, bare feet soft and silent on the floor. He studied her as if he was not yet sure whether she was dangerous, eyes shifting between brown and green like leaves in shadow. He said something else that sounded like a question, and Owen answered him again in a low voice. The boy flinched, as if Owen had described something graphic and cruel beyond words.

"What did you say? Is he... is it offensive that I'm human?" Aria's voice shook. "It's not my fault. I'm sorry."

"No. He grieves for what has been taken from you." Owen's voice shook also, and she glanced at him. He was looking at her with an expression of sorrow and compassion, unshed tears glistening in his eyes.

The boy said something else, and she looked back at him.

"He says you look like his—your—mother, but a little younger."

"How old is he?"

"Thirty-two. He was eight years old, an infant, when your family was killed. Human infants and Fae infants are similar, but different. Our appearance matures more or less linearly until adolescence; he would have looked like a human infant a few months old. But our physical capabilities surpass those of humans quickly; at that age, he would have been able to walk and run, to feed himself, to speak his own language, and to have some understanding of what was happening. Enough to understand that there was danger, and to conceal himself, though not enough to fight back with any hope of success. He was able to survive on his own in the forest."

She swallowed a lump in her throat. "How?" She and the boy watched each other as Owen spoke softly into the space between them.

"Fae can command some level of obedience from wild creatures. We do not often require animals to come to us as food; we prefer to hunt, as we believe it is respectful to give the animal a chance to flee. But when wounded or otherwise unable to hunt, we have the right and authority to compel animals to come to us to provide their bodies as food. It is one of the first things Fae parents teach their children. For safety, you understand."

Aria's throat felt tight with emotion she could not name. "He's still a child." Her words came out like a sob. "I'm old."

Owen snorted softly. "He's older than you are. We mature differently; he is a child by our standards, but his mind is not that of a human with a face like his. Nor is it the mind of a human of his age. He remembers you as an infant, not yet able to walk."

The boy asked something, his eyes flicking to Owen and back to her.

"He asks if he may come closer."

"Of course." *Does he think I am afraid of him? Or is he afraid of me?*

The boy took a step closer, then another, his eyes wide and every movement cautious. She knelt in front of him. Eye-level, they studied each other for silent minutes. He stepped even closer, tense as a rabbit approaching a fox. Then he leaned in, his head to one side, and put his nose into her hair. She felt the soft brush of his inhalation. He drew back, his eyes filled with tears. He stood, trembling and silent, with tears rolling down his face. He muttered something and brushed at his cheeks.

"He apologizes for his tears. Despite your similarity to his mother and his trust in my honesty, he did not truly believe you were his sister until now."

The boy said something else, with a deeper bow to Owen. Owen replied without translating.

Aria felt the tears on her own cheeks with surprise; she hadn't been thinking about her own emotion, only that of the beautiful boy in front of her. She leaned forward and put her arms around his shoulders.

He shuddered at her touch, but he didn't pull away. He merely stood, wordless and shaking, while she pressed her cheek to the top of his head. Despite his age, he felt like a child in her arms, and her heart ached for him as if he was a child. "It's all right. I'm all right. I'm sorry. You'll be fine," she murmured, as if he could understand her words. Then the tension in him broke, and he fell against her, his face hidden in the curve of her neck and his arms around her as he sobbed.

"GABRIEL, I PRAYED about accepting the leadership position," Bartok said. "I don't think that's what God has for me."

"What?" Gabriel breathed

"I prayed about it." Bartok sighed. "I… you know I've never wanted that position. But I asked God with an open heart."

"And?"

"No. It's not for me."

"Oh, God." Gabriel closed his eyes. "I can't do this, Bartok."

"You're not alone." Bartok wrapped an arm around Gabriel's shoulder. "Let's pray about it. Right now."

Gabriel fell to his knees, heedless of everyone watching. He bent forward to bury his face in his hands, forehead to the ground, weeping.

AODHAGAN SAT with his head in his hands, elbows on his knees. His hair stood out from his head, nearly hiding his fingers against his scalp.

Aria sat down beside him. "I know you don't understand me. But I wanted to say thank you for coming."

The Fae child looked up and studied her face. His eyes were ringed with red, as if he'd been crying, although they were dry now. He reached out one tentative hand and brushed the tips of his fingers across her cheek, his touch cool and light as a feather against her skin. He said something, the words so soft and sorrowful that she didn't need anyone to translate his grief.

"I'm sorry I'm human. At least mostly. But I've had a good life, I think. My parents loved me. They're gone now, though." Her voice caught on an unexpected sob, and she bit her lip. "I miss them. I don't remember your... our... parents. I wish I did."

With one cool finger, he traced the damp line of a tear down her cheek.

A moment later, Cillian sat down beside her. "Lord Owen has asked me to translate for you, if you wish." He said something in the other language, presumably the same offer.

The boy bowed his head in an expression of respectful gratitude and murmured something.

Then he spoke to her, his eyes meeting hers.

"Were you mistreated?" Cillian asked her. "Were you hurt? Were you told of us and how you were stolen?"

"No! No, not at all. My parents were very good to me. I wasn't even... I didn't even know I was adopted, much less that I was Fae." She stopped. It

137

was the first time she'd said the words aloud. *I am Fae.* Or at least *I was Fae. I could have been Fae.* She wasn't yet entirely clear on how it worked. "I don't think my parents knew. The government thought that I was a stolen human child, and when they found me—took me —they found people to adopt me. I would never have known they weren't my biological parents if not for..." She waved her hand vaguely, encompassing everyone on the train platform. "I guess if not for Lord Owen."

Cillian spoke softly, the sound of his words like water in the air. The boy's eyes never left her face.

"Does he have many memories of our parents?"

Cillian relayed her question, and the boy responded.

"He asks if he may show you his favorites."

"What?"

"Show you his favorite memories. It is simple and painless, but he will not do it without your permission."

She swallowed. "Show me his memories? How do you do that? Why didn't anyone tell me about that?"

Cillian blinked at her as if he found the questions puzzling. "I don't understand. Are you afraid? He will not hurt you."

"No, of course not." Her eyebrows drew down in gentle confusion. "Please tell him I'd like that."

After a few quiet words, Aodhagan reached forward as if he meant to brush her hair back behind her ear. For a moment, she felt the cool touch of his fingertips on her temple.

Then she saw out of his eyes. His body was like that of a child perhaps five months old, slightly chubby legs, delicately rounded knees with adorable dimples. He was sitting cross-legged, and, astonishingly, a smaller baby was in his lap. Despite his tiny size, he was strong enough and coordinated enough to hold her up, the baby's head supported in the crook of his elbow. *That's me*, she realized with a start.

His thoughts, like his words, were not in a language she understood, but she could feel the emotion behind them. There was a feeling of love and protective wonder when he looked at the baby's face; the feeling was similar to what she'd felt for Johan, her human brother, but orders of magnitude stronger. *I feel like I've never really loved before. I thought I did, but everything I felt was like a pale reflection of what it was meant to be.*

His gaze shifted upward, and he listened to a Fae woman speak. Aria's breath caught when she saw the woman's face. Her mother! Seeing her was like looking in a mirror and seeing herself a few years older. The rush of warmth and comfort that flooded her memory confirmed the Fae woman's identity. Her mother was wearing a short dress of pale brown cloth that might have been the finest silk, which draped to show a perfectly curved body while somehow seeming more modest than revealing. Inhabiting Aodhagan's body, Aria felt his smile and heard his soft voice say something in response. Their mother smiled and looked over her shoulder.

Another memory, the shift between them smooth and almost unnoticed. Her mother and father sang over Aodhagan and infant Aria. Her

139

father was darker than any Fae she'd seen before, his skin a creamy coffee-brown, his hair like a tuft of dark thistledown above an angular face with wild, joyful eyes. The curls had come from her mother, whose hair fell in tight ringlets down her back. As they sang, the infant Aria waved her arms and Aodhagan sang wordlessly, attempting to follow the intricate harmony.

Aria blinked and found herself staring at her brother's face. He smiled at her, tentative and gentle. He said something softly, and Cillian translated. "It was good to share a little with you. Thank you."

In sharing his memories, she had also seen that he still loved her as he had when she was an infant. "Thank you," she said, and meant it.

Aodhagan's expression sobered, and he asked another question.

"He wishes to know what happened to the other child who was stolen. He is a cousin born two months after you were. His name is Dagda," said Cillian.

Aria felt her throat tighten with emotion. "He was adopted too. He died a few years ago. It was a car accident. His father--his adoptive father--died with him."

Aodhagan stared at her while Cillian relayed this, his lower lip trembling a little.

"Was he loved?"

Aria nodded. "He was. I didn't know him, but I saw pictures. He was loved and had a good life."

Aodhagan shuddered at Cillian's soft words. He whispered another question, and Cillian answered without asking Aria.

The Fae child buried his face in his hands, and his shoulders shook as he wept.

A MOMENT LATER, Owen lowered himself to sit beside Cillian and said, "Dr. Bartok and I would like to join you. Please make yourselves visible to him."

Cillian translated for Aodhagan, whose eyes widened. He looked at Owen, who nodded that he should obey as well.

A moment later, Bartok sat cross-legged beside Aria. Aodhagan studied him with cautious eyes. Bartok smiled at him, and he blinked, glancing at Owen again before giving Bartok the barest hint of a smile.

"Dr. Bartok and I were discussing the implications of your apparent humanity, despite your Fae genetic makeup. For generations, we Fae have believed our Fae-ness, if you will, is primarily inborn. We knew Fae newborns were similar to human newborns, but we did not fully comprehend how very similar they are. We did not realize they could be mistaken for each other at a genetic level. We assumed most of our megdhonia, or magic, if you want to call it that, is the result of inborn talent, refined by what our parents taught us, both intentionally and merely by example. We underestimated the importance of this training." He nodded to Bartok.

Bartok said, "Humans, and presumably Fae as well, see by using light sensitive structures called rods and cones in our eyes. The rods are sensitive to brightness, and cones are sensitive to color.

141

Most people have three types of cones, each sensitive to one color: red, green, or blue. By seeing mixtures of these three colors we can perceive about a million or so colors. Some people are missing one type of cone. These people are called colorblind and see a narrower range of color. For instance, if you're missing the red cone, you can see only the colors formed by mixtures of green and blue.

"But a few people, maybe one in ten thousand or so, have four kinds of cones. In theory, these people can see around a hundred million shades of color. But in testing, it has been determined that the great majority of these people can't judge color any better than someone with only three cones. They have the equipment, but evidently judging color is not only a physical ability but also a learned ability.

"If a human child was raised by Fae, she might learn a little of how to touch magic, even though she lacks the basic capacity to do so to any great degree. Colorblind, if you will. Conversely, if a Fae child is raised by humans, she has the native capacity, but wouldn't learn how."

His gaze rested on her face. "It's only a theory, of course. We don't actually know anything about Fae children raised by humans. But it makes sense."

Aria felt her heart thudding with sudden desire. "Teach me! Teach me to be Fae."

Cillian frowned. "I don't know that it would be possible. You are not an infant. Your mind is not as... well, as *flexible* as it was."

Owen glanced at Bartok, as if he hadn't expected Bartok to take the conversation as far as he had. Bartok gave a rueful smile and a slight shrug.

Cillian spoke carefully, watching Owen's reaction. "Also, I am not sure we even understand *how* we teach Fae children megdhonia. We thought it was less teaching and more innate than it might be, in reality. We may be teaching without understanding what we are doing."

Owen nodded thoughtfully. "This is true. We apparently understand ourselves as little as we understand humans."

Aria leaned forward. "I know! I know I will never be Fae, not as I would have been. But if I have any raw ability, I should at least try to use it! I must have a little, because I can always see you, even when you're hidden. Maybe that's why the brainwashing didn't affect me as much as it affected other people. I probably can't learn in twenty years what I would have learned in five if I'd been taught from the beginning. But surely I can learn something! Besides, we can't be sure unless we try. Even if I can only learn enough to better appreciate your singing... it's worth trying." Her voice broke. "Please."

Owen looked down for a moment, then murmured, "Yes. It is." He looked up to meet her eyes. "You wish for a good thing, Aria. We will try."

She smiled, the first genuine, joyful smile she'd felt in days, perhaps weeks.

Bartok smiled too, and she caught the sadness in it more strongly this time.

"I DON'T UNDERSTAND how magic can be real. I understand that it works... I just don't understand *how* it works." Aria frowned up at the darkness.

"Neither do I." Bartok's voice carried a smile. "I think it's a bit like how people always wonder about science and religion. Secular scientists say they understand how the world works, or at least how their field works. They say that science is true. Devout people of many different religions some-times set themselves against science, as if the study of the world is inherently anti-religion. But I don't believe that."

"What do you believe? You're a doctor; you can't be anti-science." Aria glanced at him out of the corner of her eye.

"Of course not. Science is the study of God's creation." He clasped his hands behind his head, the shadows moving across Aria's face as he shifted. "Science is always advancing, and we're always discovering something new or reevaluating something we thought we understood. Take light, for example. For many years, light was thought to be made of particles called photons. Light behaved as if it were made of particles... except for when it didn't. Sometimes light behaved as if it were made of waves. Light could be demonstrated to be both particle and wave. But those can't both be true. What this really meant was that both concepts rep-resented an imperfect understanding of light. Modern physicists have newer concepts to explain this apparent contradiction. Nothing that is true contradicts anything else that is true. If it seems to do so, that means that either one of the postulates is false, or the logic is bad, or you have insufficient understanding. Our understanding of what is true can be incomplete.

"Science admits this. The scientific method is one of hypothesis and testing and reevaluation. Scientific 'truths' are only 'true' so long as we haven't found anything that contradicts them yet. When we do, we reevaluate. By iterating, we hope to draw closer to the truth. Our testing capabilities change as technology changes, and as we reevaluate our assumptions.

"God's truth doesn't change, and the Bible says we've received sufficient revelation to make our decisions. We learn more through study of the Bible, and through prayer and worship and sanctification.

"It's a false dichotomy. We see contradictions, and people think they have to choose science or religion, as if they can only believe in one or the other. But the contradiction just means that we don't really understand as much as we think we do."

GABRIEL, BARTOK, AND THE SQUAD LEADERS were huddled around the documents Owen had extracted from the H Street facility, the simpler mission conducted before the rescue during which he had been captured. That night was a blur of emotion. Aria glanced at the group, then back at the Bible beside Bartok's bedroll.

Would he mind if she picked it up and read a little? Probably not. She thumbed through, not sure exactly what she was looking for, stopping in the middle of a book called Luke. She glanced up toward the people still discussing the papers, then began to read.

"What are you reading?" Bartok's voice startled her.

"I've read this section three times and I don't understand." Aria's voice cracked.

Bartok looked where she was pointing. "Luke 15. The lost sheep, the lost coin, and the prodigal son. What don't you understand?"

"I... I think I just need to think about it." Aria pushed the book toward him.

Grenidor's voice caught her attention and she looked past Bartok to where the group still gathered around the papers.

"How did you know that?" The colonel sounded confused rather than irritated.

"Why do you ask?" Gabriel replied tersely.

"No one should know that about the vertril program."

"Why do you need to know how we know anything?"

Grenidor scowled at him. "If you have a spy, you'd best call him back. Because the... thing... that manipulated and threatened me, whatever it is, will be angry that I'm here. He probably knows about any spies you have. Your spies are in danger."

Gabriel's rancor faded. "No, no spies. We have a few low-level people who might help with low-risk activities, like the kid who helped Aria escape, but we don't want to use them often. It's too risky. We got the data from the hard drives Lord Owen got from the facility on H Street."

Grenidor blinked. "I... we hadn't noticed any were missing."

"Exactly." Gabriel smiled.

Owen had been nearby, and he made himself visible. "I took only a few hard drives from computers I suspected might have the most interesting information, and one from each department." At Grenidor's baffled look, he added, "Then I dismantled the computers, smashed the pieces, and burned the pile of pieces. I contained the blaze so as not to destroy the building or risk the lives of the guards. I hoped that the absence of a few pieces that might have been melted into slag would be overlooked in the mess."

Grenidor's frown deepened in confusion. "I'd assumed you wanted to destroy the data."

Owen tilted his head. "Surely, you keep offsite backups. Computers are not expensive or difficult to replace. Why would destroying a computer eliminate the data?"

"How would you know that?" Grenidor breathed.

Owen chuckled softly. "Do you think we are so naive? I go barefoot by choice. I can and do read. I'm curious about many subjects and have spent more time among humans than you have been alive. I am hardly a computer expert, but I learned how to use them back when they were programmed by punching holes in paper cards."

Grenidor swallowed hard. "Oh."

CHAPTER 11

LACHTNAL STEPPED out of the darkness into the light surrounding the guard post. The two guards were inside the compact guard post building, and the gate was closed. He approached slowly, careful to keep his hands visible and his face composed in a friendly but serious expression.

"Halt. State your business." A voice came over the speaker. "The microphone is to your left."

A gray square on a post a few feet in front of the glass window had a little sign on it. *Speak into the microphone. Look at the square on the window to be identified.*

He stood in the painted square on the concrete in front of the microphone and nodded at the two guards visible through the glass as he spoke. "I need to speak with whomever is in charge when Colonel Paul Grenidor is not available."

"Why?"

"I have information that might be of interest to him."

The guards studied him, then one of them spoke into a phone on the desk. The glass was nearly soundproof, and despite his excellent hearing, Lachtnal could catch only a few words of the conversation. *Vampire wants to... Colonel... wait...sir.*

"Lieutenant Colonel Blakeley will be here in a minute. Wait please."

Lachtnal nodded. "Thank you." He stepped back out of the square. His gaze roamed around as he observed the guard shack and the surrounding gate and walls.

The wind gusted, reminding the guards that winter wasn't quite over yet. Lachtnal didn't seem to notice the cold, wearing only a thin, fashionable sweater, dark slacks, and soft black shoes.

The younger guard, whose nametag read Rink, murmured to the other, "He's wearing shoes. Are you sure he's a vampire?"

"He's not wearing a coat, and he's not shivering. It's 38 degrees out there," Jackson replied.

A few minutes passed in silence. Through the glass, two more men appeared. Lieutenant Colonel Michael Blakeley had the tall, sinewy build of a runner. Beside him, Dr. Walter Burke was shorter and stockier, still wearing the white coat of the research lab from which he'd come. Blakeley flipped a switch on the control board behind the desk, cutting off all recording and transmission to the main guard desk inside.

"Blakeley here. Who are you and what do you want?" The voice was neutral.

Lachtnal stepped in front of the microphone and said, "Colonel Grenidor has become a traitor to the Empire. He has allied himself with the Fae. I know where they are, and will be happy to lead you to them."

Blakeley frowned at him through the thick glass. "Where are they?"

"An abandoned train station just north of the old courthouse. I can lead you to it. There are approximately forty-five humans and twenty-four Fae there."

"Why are you supplying this information?" Blakeley's suspicion came through the speaker clearly.

"I want to ally myself with humans."

"Ah." Blakeley gave him a cool look through the glass. "You want to do to your people what you say Grenidor is doing to us?"

Lachtnal's face contorted in rage for a split second, then just as quickly smoothed into a tight smile. "You have no understanding of the internal issues of my people. I offer this information in good faith because I object to what some of my people are doing. The ones dealing with Colonel Grenidor want to dominate everyone, and I will not be told what to do."

Blakeley licked his lips and considered Lachtnal. Lachtnal held his gaze through the glass, his expression earnest, though he was still tense with anger.

"I will investigate what you say and act appropriately. If you truly want to be our ally, this can be mutually beneficial. However, you must understand that we do not fully trust you. At least, not yet. If you will voluntarily enter and submit to being confined to a holding cell—a comfortable one—you will be well treated. Just while we verify your information, you understand."

Lachtnal snorted. "You think I'd trust you when you want to put me in a cage? I think not. I will come back to speak with you again. If you want to speak to me, turn out that light," he pointed behind himself to a streetlight, "during the hours it should be on. I will check it periodically, but it may be hours or even days before I respond."

"You want to be difficult to find?"

Lachtnal smiled again. "I think it safest if you don't know exactly where I am. Nor am I one to be called like a dog. I would like to partner with you, but it will be a partnership of equals."

"Understood."

Lachtnal vanished. The guards watched the console for a minute as, the tension eased a little. Jackson, the elder guard, a man nearing forty with close-cropped, salt-and-pepper hair, said, "I read that he really left. No weight on the pressure sensors, no heartbeat or sound of respiration in the coverage area. No motion detected. Concur?"

Everyone nodded.

"I saw a trace of him as he left, just a flicker. He was heading north, and fast," said the younger guard.

Blakeley turned to the others. "Talk to me. Tell me your impressions of him and of his information."

Jackson sighed, as if he didn't want to talk at first. Then he said, "I don't know that one. But I've been in on the capture of several other vampires. Or Fae. Whatever you want to call them. My theory is that some of them are only trouble if you mess with them. They're very dangerous, but far from aggressive. They'll only strike if provoked, and sometimes not even then. Others are just bad. All the time. Dangerous until they're dead. This is one of the bad ones. You can see it in his eyes." His lip wrinkled in distaste.

"And you? What do you think?" Blakeley turned to the younger guard, a fresh-faced young man in a crisp new uniform.

"I got just out of training, sir. I don't know if you want my opinion."

"What do you think?"

The guard fidgeted, then said, "I only know vampires from training videos and reports of encounters. The videos are interesting, because they don't always show up. We don't know why. Maybe when they want to be seen. Maybe it's a technical glitch.

"So I don't really know much about them. But I do know evil when I see it. That guy was evil. Not just dangerous. *Evil*. I wouldn't trust him under any circumstances."

Blakeley licked his lips thoughtfully and turned to Burke. "Doctor? What do you think?"

Burke frowned and rubbed his hands down his white coat. "Well, he referred to the others as 'Fae' rather than vampires. That's informative."

Blakeley nodded and motioned for Burke to continue when the guards looked confused. Burke's voice took on the air of a lecturing academic.

"I've been studying these creatures for nearly a decade, and they divide themselves into two groups. The ones that call themselves Fae are safe to be around unless they are defending themselves or another Fae whom they judge to be defenseless. They can change sides, but while they call themselves Fae, they are basically safe. Certainly they're not aggressive.

"Others call themselves turned Fae, or refer to themselves as formerly Fae... they have no real name for what they are, but they do not claim to be Fae any longer. Those are the ones we now call vampires. We've incorrectly attributed the name vampire to all of them for years, and only recently begun to understand that Fae are distinctly different from vampires. Biologically they are the same, but behaviorally, they are different enough that having different names for them is useful.

"'Vampires', for lack of a better word, are always dangerous. The characterization of them as 'evil' is unscientific, but I can't argue with the accuracy. However, the Fae might actually be admirable. Despite their capabilities, they do not appear to be wantonly destructive or violent. Only when provoked do they—sometimes—become vampires. As yet, we're unsure exactly what produces the change. Our uncertainty about the cause of this change is what concerns me.

"I haven't written this in my reports thus far because I can't prove it. But since you asked, there it is. I could be wrong, though, so don't take it as scientific, proven fact.

"That one was held captive before. He was designated M13. I would have called him Fae. He never tried to hurt anyone while in captivity. But now... I think he might have turned. I don't know why. I don't know how. But he's not like he was."

Blakeley nodded, eyeing the space where Lachtnal had stood, then he looked at the faces of the men around him. "I agree. I brought you," he nodded at Burke, "because I trust your opinion more than most. Even your unproven opinion is worth something." He glanced out the window again, then at the control board behind the guard desk. "We're all agreed that Colonel Grenidor is trustworthy, right? He's a good guy?" Nods answered him. "So here's what I think. He knows more about vampires and Fae than anyone else alive. Maybe not in quite as much detail as some of the research scientists, but he has a better understanding of them than the rest of us. If he thinks an alliance with a group of them is possible—and is a good idea—then he's probably right.

"However, his actions are risky. Maybe he doesn't know that at least one of the vampires is out to get him and the others. So Grenidor is in trouble. I support him, even though if I asked General Harrison, I'd probably be told to organize a raid to arrest Grenidor and capture or destroy the Fae, or vampires, or whatever they are." He looked at the others. "Are you with me so far? If not, say so."

The guards glanced at each other and nodded. The older guard said, "I don't know the colonel well, but he always seemed to have a good head on his shoulders. He could be right."

Burke frowned. "True, but even evil people can tell the truth sometimes, and we have to keep in mind that if Colonel Grenidor has been bent to the wrong side, he must be stopped. The consequences otherwise would be terrible. But..." he hesitated. "I also should tell you something." He glanced at the desk, confirming that the switch transmitting their conversation to the main desk was still off. "I could get shot for telling you this. But… I'm already close to treason for agreeing with you, and I can only be killed once." He cleared his throat nervously, looking around their faces again. "Before I was transferred to the HHIREP program to work on the vampires and Fae, I worked on the drugs used for population control. You know about those, right?"

The elder guard nodded, but the younger one looked confused.

"The general population received drugs to help with establishing the Empire's authority. Nothing too strong, you understand, just enough to help people trust the government. Scientists are exempted, of course, as are certain branches of the military. Guards are exempted. The drugs dull the intellect and certain jobs require full intellectual capability and alertness."

The younger guard frowned. "Oh. That explains a lot."

"Right. Well, there are clinical cues you can use to determine how strongly an individual is influenced by the drugs. The signs are obvious enough that a trained observer, such as myself, can make a reasonable evaluation after a few minutes of watching someone. Even watching the subject on television provides enough information to make a reasonable guess as to whether they're influenced or not.

"I've never paid much attention to politics, but I was watching an official announcement a few days ago. You know, the one about the increasing threat of vampire attacks and how to stay safe indoors after nightfall. The High Council was in the background, a clip of them talking from a few weeks before, just as an official backdrop for the public affairs official, with no sound except the announcer. Do you remember? I... I think probably eighty or ninety percent of them were drugged. That scares me."

Blakeley's gaze grew distant as he thought. "I think you're right. I hadn't noticed at the time, but I think you're right. Grant is one of the alert ones, isn't he? And Seymour?"

Burke nodded. "That's what I think."

Blakeley rubbed his jaw. "Right. So... we agree that Fae are good. Vampires are bad. I'm not sure what the difference is, but we can all agree that there *is* a difference, and it's important. M13 is bad now, even if he wasn't before. He wants Grenidor and the Fae with him dead. That implies that Grenidor is on the good side and probably the Fae with him are as well. That is... if we can believe anything M13 says at all."

The guards nodded again. Burke hesitated, then nodded as well. "So far as we know now, I'd agree with that assessment."

"Right then. Keep it quiet, but see if you can feel out who else might be reliable. Who might be trusted to aid Grenidor with us? Don't raise suspicions. Be careful." Then he looked at the younger guard. "Actually, you just keep your mouth shut. You don't know people yet. We'll need you later."

BURKE WALKED BACK through the empty hallways toward the lab. He'd intended to leave for the night, but the conversation with the vampire had unnerved him. He'd wait a while before leaving.

He shuffled lab reports for a while, feeling restless; then he crossed the hall to speak to Dr. Federico Pyorski. Pyorski's scientific contributions were unquestionable, and he had every reason to be personally loyal to Grenidor. Grenidor had given Pyorski every piece of lab equipment and every assistant he'd requested, and Pyorski had returned the favors by consistently producing groundbreaking work. Among other innovations, he had identified the radiation that bore his name; Pyorski radiation was used in the magic detectors as well as the Pyorski test which differentiated vampire blood from human blood.

Burke knocked on the doorframe. "Rick? You have a minute?"

"Of course." The older scientist smiled amiably. "You're here late. I was just waiting for those samples to finish before I called it a night."

Burke nodded. "Right. I had a report I was writing up." He slid into the chair across from Pyorski's desk. "I was thinking. What do you think of the Fae?"

Pyorski frowned. "In what regard?"

"Well, I've wondered whether there are actually two classes of them, and perhaps only one class is actually hostile. You have a lot of experience with them. What if someone were to approach wild Fae with an eye to ending the hostilities? Is there any possibility of success?"

Pyorski sat back and crossed his hands behind his head. He stared at the ceiling thoughtfully. "My research is only on the physical aspects of the vampires. Or Fae. Whatever. I don't have much insight into their behavior. I have noticed that some are much more dangerous than others. I don't have enough information to judge why. It's not a physical difference, though."

"But it's possible that there are two camps, if you will? Cultural differences can be significant among humans. Maybe they are among vampires as well."

"I suppose it's possible. Why?" Pyorski raised his eyebrows.

"I was just curious. It seemed like something we should know, after all our research." Burke frowned, then stood. "Thanks."

"Of course. Glad to help." Pyorski smiled benignly as Burke stepped back into the hallway.

Pyorski waited several minutes, his head cocked as he listened to the sound of Burke shuffling papers across the hall, then his footsteps fading.

Then he rose and locked the door. He went to a cabinet behind his desk and unlocked the top drawer. He removed a plain wooden box, which he unlocked with the same key.

Pyorski carefully lifted out the a glittering golden bull statue and placed it on the table in front of the box. He pushed his chair aside and knelt stiffly on the cheap burgundy carpet. He pulled a tiny penknife from a pocket and slid it across his finger with a wince, then smeared the welling blood over the idol's head and back.

"I call on your aid. I think there may be a problem that requires your attention."

LIEUTENANT COLONEL BLAKELEY went back inside. Before he reached his office, he turned toward the cafe. He put a couple of dollars in the machine and waited while it made his coffee. He sat by a window and looked out to the darkened courtyard. It was only about seven o'clock, but darkness came early in winter.

He tapped his fingers on the plastic tabletop thoughtfully, sipping the steaming liquid. When it was no longer scalding, he drained the cup and stood briskly. He tossed the cup in a trashcan and strode back to his office.

He lifted the phone and dialed, but Burke didn't answer. He flipped through his personal phone to find Burke's cell number as he stood. He glanced over his desk, picked up a few critical pieces of paper, and stepped back out into the hallway. He dialed as he walked, knowing the concrete would make the signal spotty but unwilling to wait.

"Burke, meet me at the front gate." He waited for Burke's terse "Right, sir," then hung up.

A few minutes later, he was back in the guard post with Dr. Burke, and the two guards Rink and Jackson. He flipped the switch to the main desk again, keeping their conversation private.

"Forget feeling out Grenidor's supporters. He probably doesn't know his group is betrayed. If he's right about the Fae, it justifies almost any risk. If he's caught with the resistance, he'll be executed before he can explain anything. I think we should warn him. Who's with me?" Burke's voice rang with tension.

"Don't you think that's risky? What if he's wrong?" Rink said.

"Well... then whoever goes with me will probably die at the hands of vampires or be exe-

159

cuted as traitors. It's a real possibility. But I'm going tonight."

Burke spoke first. "I'm with you. Grenidor's changed recently, and not for the better. I still think he could be right. This might be the best thing he's done in years, and it's consistent with my own observations."

Jackson nodded. "I agree. I'm in."

Rink's eyebrows rose. "All right. You all know more than I do. If you go, I'll go."

Blakeley looked around. "Right, then." He took a deep breath and let it out slowly as he thought.

Jackson spoke first. "One of us should stay, don't you think? To send messages? Warnings. To help from the inside, if we can."

Blakeley sighed. "Well, yes. But that's at least as dangerous as going."

"I'll do it." Jackson nodded. "You're right, it is. But you're both known to Grenidor, and he'd barely recognize me. If security suspects anything, Rink would be tarred with suspicion immediately because he's so new. I'm older. I have a good record. I'll send you intel if I can."

Blakeley's frown deepened. "Wait. We'll leave Rink instead. Rink, wait an hour, then call the desk and ask to speak to Lieutenant Colonel Curtis. He's next in command after me. Tell him—"

Rink frowned. "He's not a major?"

"Well, he is, but he's promotable; it's already been approved. Address him as Lieutenant Colonel. Ask him to physically come to the gate because you need to show him something here and can't be more specific. Direct orders from me." He explained the rest of the plan and looked around.

The others nodded, albeit reluctantly. "Agreed?" asked Blakeley.

Jackson sighed. "I don't like leaving him here. He'll be suspected."

Rink shook his head. "Sir, I can do this. It makes sense for you to go."

They left as quietly as they could and jogged west, then north toward the location Lachtnal had given them.

When they felt they had their bearings and would be able to navigate underground, they found a Metro train entrance and followed the stairway down. Then they followed the maintenance ledge along the tracks for long, silent minutes.

"How much farther, do you think?"

"I don't know. We have to be getting close."

Jackson's flashlight, their only source of light, bobbed in the inky blackness.

Suddenly Jackson squawked in surprise. He dropped the flashlight, and it fell to the tracks some six feet below them. It illuminated nothing, but ambient light made the shapes of the three men barely discernible to each other.

"What are you looking for?" came a voice out of the darkness.

Jackson faced the other two stiffly, both arms pulled up behind his body as if someone invisible immobilized him.

Blakeley took the lead. "We're looking for Colonel Paul Grenidor. We have reason to believe he might be nearby and he might need help." He stood tensely, as if he wanted to draw his pistol but was resisting the urge.

"What reason is that?" The cool, masculine voice sharpened a little.

"A vampire came to the guard post at Eastborn looking for me, trying to tell me where he was. I'm Lieutenant Colonel Michael Blakeley. Colonel Grenidor is my commanding officer. I wanted to let him, and the others with him, know that his position is compromised. Maybe he already knows that, but I couldn't be sure. I'm on his side, whatever side that is."

Jackson flinched at something the others didn't see, then stumbled toward them. He whirled to face the place where he had been standing, his shoulders tense and one hand on his gun, though he didn't draw.

The voice came again. "You all have trackers. You seem to be attempting to lead the Empire to your commanding officer."

"Uh..." Blakeley blinked. "We'd forgotten. I'd forgotten, anyway. I don't think about them often."

"Trackers?" muttered Jackson. "What trackers?"

"I will not take you to the location of Colonel Grenidor and the others. But I will request that they meet you at a new location. It would help me—us—trust you if you consent to let me remove or disable your trackers."

"What exactly does that entail?" Blakeley asked cautiously.

"I can disable them using megdhonia. You would call it magic. Or I can cut them out. It is a small wound, quickly healed even without the assistance of megdhonia. Perhaps half an inch long at most." The voice carried a hint of subdued amusement.

Blakeley glanced at the others. "It's probably safest to cut them out. What do you think?"

Burke hesitated. "Our decision is final, either way."

"We already made our decision when we left the base."

Blakeley stepped forward. "All right. Fine. Cut it out. Make it quick."

A figure stepped out of the darkness. A moment later, the flashlight flipped into the air toward Blakeley, who caught it reflexively and flashed it into the stranger's face.

The Fae winced, half-closing his eyes and turning away from the glare. "Put it aside. Our eyes are more sensitive than yours." He was the one who had spoken to them; his cool voice was smooth and cultured, at odds with the ragged clothes he wore. He was barefoot, but the cold didn't seem to trouble him. "Thank you, Tadg," he murmured to an unseen companion. "Please convey their request to Lord Owen and Grenidor, and return to tell me their chosen location, if they agree to meet with him." He appeared to listen for a moment. "Yes, thank you."

His gaze had never left the humans before him. Jackson pointed the flashlight at the ceiling, letting the reflected light illuminate the stranger. All three men were tense, careful not to move too quickly. The Fae was unnervingly handsome, with intense blue-green eyes flashing in a pale, fine-boned face. He stood without moving for a moment, a faint smile on his lips.

"Remove your coats and shirts. The trackers are just beneath the skin of your right arm."

Blakeley went first, removing first his coat, then his fitted dress shirt, pulling his arm out and letting the shirt hang from his other shoulder. Stripped down to his undershirt, he tensed against the chill, and the skin of his arm and right shoulder prickled in the icy air.

The Fae stepped forward, a knife appearing in his hand from some unseen sheath.

Jackson drew his pistol and pointed it at the Fae's chest. "Don't hurt him."

The Fae turned his cold blue-green gaze on the guard. "I have already told you I intend to cut out the tracker. Pain is inevitable. If you are afraid I will kill him, I could have killed you all before you knew I was here. I would think your lives are enough evidence of my good intentions."

Jackson swallowed. "All right." He lowered the gun again.

The Fae looked back at Blakeley's arm, prodding the wiry muscle with a cold, white finger. The knife flashed. Blakeley hissed in surprise.

The Fae held up a tiny metal capsule. "Here it is. Shall I heal the wound, or let it heal without assistance?"

Blakeley swallowed. "Um... whatever you prefer. It's not too bad."

The Fae smoothed his thumb over the wound, and it disappeared. Blakeley stared at him. "That was strange," he murmured.

"In sensation or in concept?" The Fae blinked at him.

"Both." Blakeley smiled, looking a little surprised. "That was... unexpected. You didn't have to do that. Thank you."

"A gesture of goodwill, and one of which Lord Owen would approve. I desire to emulate my king." The Fae inclined his head. He turned toward Burke.

Burke unbuttoned his shirt without protest. "You were captive, weren't you? M20, perhaps?"

"That is the designation that was given to me." The Fae's voice tightened with restrained anger. "It is not my name."

Jackson's hand brushed against his pistol again, and Burke gave him a hard glance.

"I'm Burke. Dr. Walter Burke. What *is* your name?" Burke smiled nervously.

"Fearghal." The knife slipped into the skin and back out before Burke could wince. Fearghal pressed the skin beside the wound, and the tiny metal capsule popped out. "Hold it." He healed the tiny wound and turned to Jackson.

The guard sighed, then slipped off his jacket and unbuttoned his outer shirt.

Fearghal looked to the side, as if speaking to someone the humans could not see. "Yes," he said. "I will take them. Thank you."

"Who are you talking to?" Jackson asked.

"Tadg. He told me that Lord Owen and Colonel Grenidor will meet you. I will take you to them." He nodded toward Jackson's arm. "Are you ready?"

Jackson nodded.

Fearghal removed the tracker and healed the tiny wound. Jackson remained tense, and Fearghal met his gaze. "Are you afraid of me?"

165

The guard swallowed, then nodded. "Everything I've learned says I should be."

Fearghal's lips curved in a faint smile. "And much of what you've learned is wrong. Leave the trackers here, along with your cell phones and any weapons you carry." He glanced at Blakeley's expensive watch and narrowed his eyes. "Also, your watches and any other electronics." He waited while all three men complied. "Follow me."

DR. FEDERICO PYORSKI picked up the phone and dialed a number from memory.

"Dave. Yeah, it's Rick Pyorski. I want all the vertril activated immediately."

A startled exclamation made him grimace in annoyance.

"Colonel Grenidor's orders." Another frown. "Yeah. Vampires are causing problems. How many are there?"

"One hundred sixteen.

"When will the others be ready?"

"Fifty next week, and another fifty the following week. The others are puppies."

"Release them as soon as possible. Make sure they're hungry." Pyorski hung up the phone with a smile.

CHAPTER 12

"WHAT DO YOU normally wear?" Aria asked.

"Pardon?"

"These aren't your normal clothes, are they? They're all made by humans. What would you wear, if you hadn't been captive?"

Niamh looked down at her worn jeans with pink rhinestones and the clashing brown shirt. Even in clothes that didn't fit and didn't match, she was stunning. "You are correct. Our clothes were taken from us when we were captured. I assume they were studied."

"Why?"

Niamh tilted her head a little. "I am not sure I have the words in English to describe our clothes. They are of different cloths than humans use, though they are made of the same materials. We sometimes use human weaving methods, though nothing like what you do with machines. We use old techniques, simple weaves. But we also use megdhonia. We do not mind the physical effort of making clothes with our hands, but we use the practice of making attire to train children in fine megdhonia techniques. Detailed work requires focus. It is a precursor to healing techniques."

"I wish I could see them," Aria murmured.

Niamh smiled. "Truly? It is interesting to you? Our lives have been hidden from human notice for so long; I could not have imagined that clothes would intrigue you."

Aria let out a breath. "Of course."

Niamh's smile softened. "I will show you, if you wish, through a shared memory."

"Please do!"

Niamh brushed Aria's temple with her slender, cool fingers, as if brushing Aria's hair behind her ear.

Between one heartbeat and the next, Aria looked through Niamh's eyes. The Fae woman was sitting cross-legged on the forest floor. Her legs were covered by a soft brown fabric and her feet were bare. A much younger Niall sat in front of her, looking like a human two-year-old, all big eyes and floppy dark hair. He frowned at a bit of fluff cupped in his hands.

Niamh spoke, and the words were layered in Aria's mind, English over Fae. "Feel it, Niall? Feel how they move together. Gentle, now."

The fluff moved slightly in Niall's hand, twisted a little, then began to fold back on itself as if the fluff were turning itself inside out one strand at a time. The process was rhythmic and calming, yet she could feel the methodical precision in the pull of megdhonia. She felt Niamh's talent reach

out and correct an infinitesimal mistake in the
cloth, and she felt Niall's soft gratitude, even as he
continued staring at the fluff, his concentration
unbroken.

Minutes passed, perhaps an hour, the child
and his mother unmoving. The fibers slowly
morphed from a handful of fluff into a filmy piece
of off-white cloth.

The memory shifted, and she saw Owen standing before a gathering of Fae. The Fae king wore a
shirt and trousers of similar material of a darker
brown. The shirt had no collar and a simple neck
opening, a triangle open halfway down his breast-
bone. The lower edge, unhemmed, hung loose
over the top of his trousers. The cloth was so fine
and light that it might have been made of shadow,
outlining every graceful line and curve of his body
as the wind gusted. The fabric settled again as the
air stilled, the shirt falling softly from his shoulders, scarcely showing the muscles across his
chest, hiding everything else.

A young Fae woman in the front row caught
Aria's attention; she wore a short dress of only
slightly thicker green cloth, caught at one shoulder
and belted with what appeared to be water droplets. Long, pale legs caught the light, smooth as
cream. Yet another Fae youth wore a patchwork of
cloth in the shapes of leaves, fluttering in the wind.
Tiny water drops along the edges, or perhaps they
were diamonds, glittered in the sunlight.

Aria blinked, disoriented, as she saw Niamh's
face across from her.

"I know the megdhonia techniques were unfamiliar to you, but perhaps you understood a lit-

tle of how it was done." Niamh's voice held a gentle question.

Aria's face heated. "Yes. Thank you." She cleared her throat. "All the clothes were different. Does the king... Lord Owen... wear anything special? Is there a crown?"

Niamh chuckled softly. "No. Those are human conceits. We have no need to signify who holds authority. Sometimes, because of the effort required, clothes of fine cloth are a gift from one to another to indicate esteem. My husband made me a beautiful dress, woven with his power and purity of heart." Niamh's voice caught for a moment, and she pressed her lips together. "I danced in it for him, a gift of my grace to him in the sight of El. But we have no expectation of any particular ornament, nor strong preferences about style. Placing great focus on ornamentation is not beneficial for our communion with El."

"Still..." Aria's blush deepened. "Some of those clothes were practically indecent."

Niamh tilted her head. "I do not understand what you mean."

Aria studied Niamh's expression. "Truly, you don't understand why that cloth might make a girl blush? I know he's your brother, but..."

Niamh's eyes showed only confusion. "But what?"

"I'm sorry. I'm thinking like a human." Aria forced an embarrassed smile. "It must be nice to be so innocent."

Niamh drew back, the movement almost imperceptible. "Your words are kind, I think, yet they sound like an insult that I don't understand."

"No. I didn't mean to insult you. I wish I were more like you." Aria felt tears threatening again, sudden longing welling up in her heart. *What would it be like to be so pure?*

Niamh's expression softened. She hesitated, then leaned forward to press a cool kiss to Aria's forehead. "Rest now, young one."

CHAPTER 13

As INSTRUCTED, Rink waited an hour before calling the main desk. "I need to speak to Lieutenant Colonel Curtis as soon as possible."

"What's wrong?" The guard barked.

"I just need to speak with him. It's important."

"He's at home. Is it important enough to wake him up?" Concern faded to boredom.

"It is."

Rink heard buttons clicking and then the guard gave him the officer's phone number. "Thanks." He dialed again. "Sir, this is Lieutenant Jake Rink at the Eastborn front gate."

"What? Who are you?"

"I'm a guard, sir, at the front gate of Eastborn Imperial Security Facility. I need to speak with you directly, sir, here at the gate. Lieutenant Colonel Blakeley's direct order, sir."

Curtis growled something not entirely under-standable, his hand muffling the phone. "Blakeley's orders? He wants me to come in now?"

"Yes, sir. Sorry, sir."

"Be there in fifteen." Curtis hung up.

Rink paced nervously while he waited, study-ing the darkness outside the guard post. Tension made him feel vaguely ill, and he hoped the vam-pire would not return.

Thirteen minutes later, Lieutenant Colonel Curtis jogged out of the darkness, his breath puff-ing in white clouds before him. He stomped into the guard post.

"You're Rink? What is it?" He stuck out a hand and the young guard shook it fiercely.

Rink checked the switch again, ensuring their privacy. "Sir, a vampire came to the gate several hours ago and asked for Lieutenant Colonel Blakeley. Blakeley brought Dr. Burke with him, if you know him."

Curtis nodded.

"The vampire claimed that Colonel Grenidor was with a rival group of vampires and was a trai-tor to the Empire. He offered their location to us. Lieutenant Colonel Blakeley told Jackson and me to stay quiet while he and Burke figured out what to do.

"They told the vampire they'd think about it. It went away. Blakeley and Burke went back inside for a while and then came back with a message for me to give to you, but told me to wait an hour be-fore I called you."

Curtis waited, his eyes sharp. "And the mes-sage is…"

Rink straightened even more. "Lieutenant Colonel Blakeley knew Colonel Grenidor had left, but didn't know why. He also knew that the colonel suspected that there were two types of vampires, one that's bad, and one that's only dangerous when attacked. He said the Colonel had speculated privately that it might be possible to negotiate with the not-so-dangerous ones. Blakeley thought the Colonel might be trying to contact that group. I can't imagine how that bad vampire would know about it, but it might mean that the Colonel is in danger. Even more danger, I mean.

"Lieutenant Colonel Blakeley and Dr. Burke went to warn the Colonel and possibly help him. They said to tell you that they think his mission has some chance of success and that the danger to the four of them is justified by the huge potential gain."

"*Four* of them?"

"Yes sir, Jackson volunteered to go with Colonel Blakely and Dr. Burke to find Colonel Grenidor. He was on guard with me tonight."

Curtis frowned. "Why did they tell you to wait an hour before calling me?"

"Lieutenant Colonel Blakeley didn't say. If you asked me, though, I'd guess it was because they didn't want you involved in the decision if General Harrison disapproves. It's a risky move. They're probably covering your tail." Rink shrugged slightly.

Curtis grumbled, "Or maybe they didn't entirely trust me." He scowled at the darkness out the window. "You haven't seen anything of the vampire since then, have you?"

"No, sir."

Curtis absently smoothed the tucks of his shirt into his crisp trousers while he thought. "You get any of it on video?"

Rink hesitated. "Yes, sir. It hasn't been transmitted to the main desk. Blakeley's orders."

"Let me see it."

Rink pulled up the surveillance videos and they watched them in a tense silence.

"That's it?"

"Yes, sir."

Curtis's frown had never wavered. "Hm. What do you think?"

"I don't know much about vampires, sir. But as I told Lieutenant Colonel Blakeley, I know evil when I see it, and he was as bad as they come. I think Jackson agreed with Blakeley and Burke about the two kinds of vampires. Blakeley respected Burke's opinion, and they both thought Colonel Grenidor was onto something important."

Curtis turned to lean against the desk and folded his arms across his chest, thick muscles flexing beneath his shirtsleeves. He frowned at the darkness outside. "Well, if you'd told me a missing colonel was turning traitor and his second in command had decided to follow him, the obvious thing to do would be to report it up the chain and wait for instructions. But the 'testimony' comes from a vampire. I don't trust any of them, and I sure don't trust that one."

He sighed heavily. "Whatever he wants, I can't believe he means us good. Neither Colonel Grenidor nor Colonel Blakeley thought reporting it up the chain was the right decision. At least, not yet." He eyed Rink cautiously. "Do I understand correctly that no one knows about this except you and me?"

Rink nodded. "Right, sir."

Curtis hesitated, then shook his head and sighed. "How is the video recorded?"

"It's on the hard drive here, sir. We transmit it to the main desk periodically."

"Cut out the section with the vampire on it and put it on a memory stick for me. Make sure there's no sign of it in what gets transmitted. You saw nothing. You know nothing. The vampire was never here. Colonel Grenidor and Colonel Blakeley are working with Burke on something off-base, escorted by Jackson. The only reason you know that much is that you work with Jackson and were told he was on a special assignment, but you don't know what it is. Got it?"

"Yes, sir." Rink worked quickly. The alteration to the video was surprisingly easy to make.

Curtis shoved the memory stick in his pocket. "Right then. Next time they'll know who they can trust." He pulled his jacket back on. "You have my number?"

"I do now, sir."

"Good. Call me if you hear from them."

"Yes, sir."

FEARGHAL LED Blakeley, Burke, and Jackson farther down the disused tunnel, then into a side tunnel, then another tunnel. The darkness danced with the light of Jackson's lone flashlight, and the concrete walls loomed damp and cold.

"How far are we going?" Blakeley asked at last.

"Not much farther."

Fearghal led them up a long metal ladder and opened the hatch at the top, peering out cautiously before emerging into an alley that smelled of grease and old rainwater. They walked halfway down the block and entered a nondescript metal door.

The flashlight revealed a darkened hallway with cream paint and old-fashioned white wainscoting at shoulder-height. Fearghal led them down the hall and into a cavernous room, echoing and nearly empty. The edges were lined with tables and folding chairs.

Fearghal gestured. "Lord Owen and the others are not here yet. You may rest if you wish." Then he disappeared from their view.

Jackson twitched in surprise. "Where'd he go?"

Blakeley turned in a circle, his hand dropping to where his holster would have been if he'd been wearing his sidearm. He clenched his hand, then relaxed it again. "I don't know. But we're here now, and we can't go back."

Burke sat in one of the chairs and leaned back. "Relax. If he wanted to kill us, he's had plenty of opportunities."

After a moment's hesitation, the other two joined him at the table.

Hidden from their view only fifteen feet away, Fearghal smiled.

CHAPTER 14

OWEN STOOD. He was steady on his feet, but by now Aria knew him well enough to see the subtle signs that he was hiding lingering pain. There was an almost imperceptible tightness around his lips and eyes.

"You're nearly better, aren't you?" she asked, wanting the reassurance of his voice.

He opened his mouth as if he meant to reply, but then he pressed his lips together. At her inquiring look, he murmured, "El is good."

Impulsively she reached out and held his hand, just for a moment. He blinked and squeezed her hand in return, meeting her gaze with affection in his eyes.

He looked over her shoulder. One of the young Fae boys, not much older than Niall, was approaching. He knelt before Owen, then stood.

"Fearghal was keeping watch in the tunnels and intercepted three humans. They request a meeting with Colonel Grenidor. They are led by Lieutenant Colonel Michael Blakeley. Blakeley says that a vampire tried to betray Grenidor's location, and ours, to him and those with him. He comes to warn Grenidor. Fearghal has removed their trackers; they agreed to it, as if they knew they could not return. Fearghal requests that you set a meeting location if you will meet with them. Otherwise…"

Owen raised his eyebrows. "Interesting. He has earned loyalty from his subordinates if they are risking the Empire's wrath to join his side. I will meet with them." He started toward Grenidor, who had finally collapsed into an exhausted slumber on a borrowed bedroll. "Wait a moment, Tadg, and I will tell you whether Grenidor will join us."

"What did he mean by 'otherwise…'? What would he do with them, if you didn't want to meet?" Aria whispered as she hurried after him.

"Fearghal would leave them in the tunnel. They would eventually either escape the Empire or be arrested."

"He wouldn't help them escape?"

Owen raised his eyebrows at her. "Why should he? They left their posts of their own volition. He has aided them by removing their trackers. He has cast no undue burden upon them if they wish to escape."

Aria frowned. "But they can't hide! They're probably lost in the dark and he'd just leave them there."

Owen tilted his head, studying her face. "You are displeased by that. Why?"

179

"It doesn't seem fair! They're trying to help Grenidor and Fearghal would just abandon them. They'll probably be arrested and executed."

Tadg glanced at Owen as if baffled by Aria's objection. Owen licked his lips as he thought. "You think Fearghal should assist them in their escape?"

"Well, it's easy for Fae to move around without being noticed. It seems like helping them would be simple. It would cost him practically nothing, and help them so much." She frowned at him. "Besides, you went to more trouble for Joshua Whitemarsh for less cause than this."

Owen blinked. "The man who had lost his arm?"

She nodded.

Owen tilted his head back, his expression thoughtful. He winced at he did it, although he didn't seem to realize it himself. "Perhaps you are right. It would be wise to assist them if they wished to flee. Humans have long feared us, and offering unsolicited assistance might help change that."

"I didn't mean because you wanted something! I just meant because it was generous. And..." She sighed. "You *are* generous. Why not in this?"

He looked startled, then his expression closed in a way she had never seen before. "You don't understand." He strode toward Grenidor with purpose in his steps.

"No! I don't! But I want to." She grabbed at his arm, and he stumbled as he turned back toward her.

"Do you?" He stared down at her, eyes colder than she had seen since that first night in Dandra's shop. Then he blinked, and his gaze softened. "I have gone against millennia of tradition and authority and right. I have chosen mercy and endured much for the sake of giving mercy to humans when they requested and deserved nothing but wrath. I did it for love and for the sake of greater understanding of El and our covenant with Him. I have received great mercy, and I will give such mercy as I am able. More than I am able on my own strength. But not all Fae under my command accept or fully understand what this means yet. *I* don't, and I think I understand more than the others. I must protect them; it is my responsibility before El, and it is my joy, and it is the weight I bear. It is even more critical now, while our relationship to El is not understood. I have the right to command them to do anything that does not explicitly defy El. Yet what kind of king would I be if I risked their lives, perhaps their souls, for the sake of men who do not need or want their assistance?

"There are choices I make for myself, and choices I make for those I rule. Not all those choices can be, or should be, the same. I *cannot* be as generous with the blood of my people as I am with my own. No matter how much you may wish it." His voice shook, and in his emotion his voice took on the faintest accent of one of the Fae languages, giving his words the feeling of water falling on leaves. "It grieves me that you misunderstand me so greatly."

Then he turned on his heel and did not look at her again as he approached Grenidor.

Owen knelt beside Grenidor for a moment, one hand covering his eyes as if he wanted to conceal tears, but Aria didn't think he was crying. At least not externally. Tears stung her own eyes, though.

Owen took a deep, steadying breath and touched Grenidor on the shoulder. "I apologize for waking you."

Grenidor sat up with a startled curse. Aria wasn't sure whether it was the volume or the profanity that made Owen wince.

"What? What is it?" Grenidor's voice was rough, and he rubbed a hand over his face. "Sorry, I… sorry. What?"

"Lieutenant Colonel Blakeley and two others have left the Empire and wish to meet with you. I believe they meant to warn us of a traitor, although we were already aware of him. They wish to speak with you and perhaps join… us. Join you, at least, perhaps also the resistance. I will meet with them. Do you wish to accompany me?"

Grenidor frowned. "Blakeley's here?"

"Not here. We will meet him elsewhere."

Grenidor shook his head, as if dislodging the last drowsiness from his mind. "Yes. I should go. Blakeley's in a world of trouble if he's coming to see me. He'll need… I don't know what to do for him." He clambered stiffly to his feet. He'd taken off his camouflage shirt and was clad only in his BDU pants and a worn white undershirt, revealing impressive arms and shoulders for a man of his age, pale skin prickling in the frigid air. He pulled on his outer shirt, buttoning it hurriedly. "Have you told Peterson yet?"

"I have not." Owen waited while Grenidor approached Gabriel and explained in a low voice. Gabriel had been lying on his back in his own bedroll some distance away, staring at the ceiling and frowning. He sat up and listened while Grenidor talked, but his eyes found Owen. Owen nodded, and Gabriel nodded back, as if they had communicated something without words.

Owen sent Tadg back to Fearghal with a few words in Fae.

Gabriel waved Bartok over as he joined Owen and Grenidor. Gabriel explained the situation to Bartok as they walked, the conversation fading as they entered the tunnel.

A COLD SHIVER skittered down Aria's spine, and she shivered. The air was dank and still, the far-off scent of oil from the trains barely registering in her awareness. She had accompanied Owen, Grenidor, and the others out of habit; her presence wasn't necessary for the meeting. Despite her weariness, she didn't want to be left back at the camp among the other resistance fighters whom she still barely knew.

Flashlight bobbing, Aria trailed a little behind the group as they made their way through the tunnels. *I'm not really part of the group, am I? What do I have to offer?*

She swallowed a lump in her throat. *I shouldn't have picked at Owen. God knows he's done enough for humans. God! As if God cares about what's happening. If God cared, would Owen be in such pain? And what do I do? Throw more concerns and more responsibility in his face.*

But he's a king, and I don't even always feel like an adult. I feel like a child wandering through a nightmare, saved by luck and the kindness of strangers.

When will Owen's patience run out?

I shouldn't love him. I mean... I shouldn't love him that *way.*

I don't even know what I feel anymore. Is it love? Or is it something more shameful? Lust and hero worship and the desperate longing of a lonely child's heart for a friend, a protector, a father, a lover, a brother, a savior... how can he possibly be all those things?

Of course I'm disappointed in him.

But he has much more reason to be disappointed in me. What kind of friend am I?

Tears pricked at her eyes, and she wiped at them surreptitiously, the tender skin around her eyes stinging in the cold.

If I were Fae this wouldn't even be a problem! I don't see Owen and Cillian and Niamh being selfish and grumpy at each other. If I were better, kinder, wiser... if I were Fae, maybe I would... I would... She clenched her gloved hands in her coat pockets. *I would be worthy of love.*

I'm not.

I'm a liability. The thought coalesced, suddenly clear in her mind. Leaden hurt and anger solidified into despair.

I'm not even bitter. She knew it was a lie.

All right, I am bitter. Who am I to think that anyone would want me to help? All I did was get Owen captured and tortured. I brought up the disagreement between Owen and Cillian when they most needed each other. I'm no help at all.

I should leave.

The quiet figure pacing at her side said softly, "Aria? Let me give you a piece of unsolicited advice."

Aria caught her breath.

Feichin strode beside her, bone-white and horribly gaunt, eyes glinting silvery blue in the darkness. "More than most, I know what it is to feel condemned by your own actions. I was lost, buried beneath oceans of guilt and despair. I rebelled against El, and I deserved condemnation."

Her heart skittered with fear, and Aria barely suppressed the desire to run away screaming. Feichin glanced at her sideways, and his thin lips lifted in a faint smile, as if he could read her thoughts.

"Some of the guilt and despair I felt were appropriate. It was right for me to feel the weight of my guilt, and right for me to have no hope of redemption on my own merit. But I believe also that some of the guilt and despair were manipulated by the dark one. I believe he played upon my thoughts and emotions for his own purposes. I was already lost, but perhaps he meant to prevent me from believing Lord Owen's testimony when I heard it. To prevent me from grasping the hope of redemption. Perhaps even to goad me into fleeing from the grace of El." His eyes swept over her face, and he hesitated, then added softly, "I cannot see the dark one here. But I feel the weight of him around you. Your face has the look of one who is tormented by dark thoughts. I do not know you well, but I have not seen you look so hopeless before."

Aria focused on the faint silhouettes of Bartok and Gabriel in front of her. "Why do you care?" she muttered.

Feichin's soft, surprised inhalation took her by surprise, then the guilt hit her. *Wow, Aria, way to be nice. Feichin, of all people, is trying to help.*

You're so worthless that even a vampire thinks you're pathetic.

She risked a glance at him, half-expecting him to glare back at her. Or to feel his hands around her throat, his teeth ripping, tearing. *He wouldn't even have to use his teeth. He could squeeze and squeeze until I died. He could probably rip my head completely off without even trying.* A tiny whimper of fear escaped her lips.

Feichin murmured, "I speak not for my own pleasure but for the glorification of El. If the dark one toys with your thoughts, only El can bring you peace. Guilt is a weight we were not meant to bear."

"Why are you talking to me?" Aria whispered.

The Fae tilted his head, looking at her with those odd silver-blue eyes. "I imagine that you fear me because you do not fully comprehend how I am different than I was. Neither do I, but I know that I *am* different. Not because I wished to be, although I did. Not because I was determined to be, although I was. I am different because El made me different. He did what I could not do alone. He can do the same for you."

Her hands were clenched so tightly they were shaking. She shook her head. "No, why are you talking to me now? What do you want?" The words came out with an accusatory tone, and she winced but didn't apologize. *I don't care if he kills me. At least I won't be anyone's problem anymore.*

That was definitely a lie. She *did* care; she cared very much. She imagined the anger and guilt and terror, wrapped them up, tighter and tighter, into a flaming orb, fear and fury and cruelty and the crushing weight of regret.

Regret. What I should have done differently. What I should have said that I didn't, or didn't say that I should have said. It's eating me alive.

Lost in her thoughts, she was startled by Feichin's soft, clear voice. "I meant to offer you the comfort of knowing that not all the condemnation and despair you heap on your own head is yours. You can dwell in it, or you can ask El, in his grace, to drive out the dark one and fill the space left with his presence." Feichin let out a soft breath. "I meant to offer you hope." His eyes glinted in the darkness, and he seemed to wait for some word from her.

"I…" Aria stopped. *He's more like Owen than I'd imagined.* "Thank you."

He inclined his head in acknowledgment.

Then she hurried forward to catch up with Owen.

"OWEN?" ARIA'S VOICE SHOOK, and she didn't mind that he must have noticed.

He turned his blue eyes on her, as clear and beautiful and unreadable as ever. No, not unreadable… just distant. Sorrow that he didn't want to show her. Weariness that he wouldn't indulge.

"I'm sorry," she said simply. "I've never had the responsibilities you do, and I forgot how heavy they must be. Will you forgive me?"

Surprise flashed across his face, then warmth. "Of course. You know I do."

"Thank you." She wanted to wrap her arms around him. She took a shaky breath and pushed down the urge, chewing her lip.

Simply walking beside him was comfort enough.

CHAPTER 15

GABRIEL PETERSON had let Grenidor borrow a flashlight, and he kept it pointed at the ground, following Owen's bare feet as he led them through the darkness. Behind him, Gabriel's flashlight bobbed, casting shadows of his own legs.

With every step, the guilt rose to choke him until he could barely breathe. The weight of it, the tightness in his chest, the twist in his gut... the shame never ended. Never lessened. The guilt only increased, tighter and more painful, the more he understood and the more he thought about his crimes.

Edwin's voice murmured in his ear, and Grenidor tensed. *No one is there!* "Fall back, and let the Slavemaster's minions pass by you. We have a disagreement to settle."

Grenidor's steps faltered. "But…" His thoughts careened wildly from terror to despair and back again.

Edwin's voice deepened, reverberating around Grenidor's skull. "Do you think they can stand against me? Let them pass, or they will be collateral damage as I annihilate you." The sibilant *ss* made Grenidor's hair stand on end, and he shuddered.

A few humans and Fae… they stand no chance. I should let them escape. I'm doomed anyway.

He let his steps slow, Owen and the others drawing several steps ahead. For an instant, he marveled at his own calm demeanor; his hand on the flashlight was steady, his shoulders square and straight even as his heart fluttered with terror, guilt choking him, fear crawling up his throat.

Owen stopped, turning to face Grenidor. "Is something wrong?"

"No." Grenidor's voice cracked, and he cleared his throat. "No. I… you should go ahead."

Grenidor's thoughts raced.

"You are lost!" Edwin crowed into his ear, drawing the *ss* out until it slithered through Grenidor's veins, pulsing around his heart, the sound of pure malice. "Lost! Even the Slavemaster can't save you."

Even the Slavemaster can't save me. Then I really am lost. Edwin can't take the Slavemaster's underlings. So the inverse is true…the Slavemaster can't take Edwin's underlings.

Edwin won't release me. Grenidor closed his eyes, but it couldn't shut out the sound of Edwin's quiet laughter echoing off the concrete. *His laughter sounds like the screaming of tortured souls.*

"Wait..." Grenidor breathed. *Would Edwin take someone else in my place?* The thought caught him. "Would you..." *But who?* Grenidor glanced around.

Edwin paused, and though he was still invisible, Grenidor imagined him licking his lips, the sheen of spittle obscene on the pink flesh. *He's not real. He's not really a person.*

Bartok belongs to the Slavemaster! What if... could I trade him to Edwin in my place? He's human like I am.

Would that buy me back into Edwin's favor? I'd still belong to him, but I'd be a deputy, not a defeated enemy.

"No," Grenidor breathed. *The Slavemaster can kill me, but I'm not going to sacrifice Bartok for Edwin's favor. Why did I even think of that?*

Nausea rose when he understood. *Edwin is part of me. Or he's in me. Or I'm too much like him to even tell where he ends and my own thoughts begin.*

I'm so lost.

Then Edwin appeared.

Grenidor stumbled backward with an inarticulate sound of horror. He shined the flashlight up and up, the light not reaching the top of Edwin's form.

He was a man, and a beast, and a statue, all at once. Edwin's form was there. The winged serpent was in the same space, the beautiful deadly head filled with fangs, eyes glowing with hatred. Black flames flickered from his maw, consuming the light. Another form was also there, something like an impossibly beautiful man, with a metallic sheen to his skin and the hint of feathered wings outstretched behind him, like the white pinions of a

191

swan. Other impossible forms, shapes he couldn't even identify, were in the same space, the same being taking all forms at once, as if none of them truly represented him or contained him. His forms were beautiful abominations.

Edwin's voice was a shriek and a thunder, an incoherent scream of rage.

Grenidor fell to his knees, arms over his head in terror. His cries had no words.

Edwin hissed, "You've failed me for the last time, Grenidor. I will destroy you in this life, and then I will rejoice in torturing you for all eternity." His voice was many voices together, shrieking and screaming in discordant harmony. "The only memory of you will be your torture and murder of your own people and your betrayal of your whole race! I will enjoy your screaming."

Grenidor wrapped his arms around his head more tightly. His heart was thundering, his breath too fast. He choked out the words, "He's here! Run!"

"Who?"

Grenidor couldn't identify the voice, but he answered anyway. "He's angry!"

The voices rose around him, deafening and terrifying. "I WILL SMITE YOU INTO HELL! YOU WILL BURN YOU WILL DIE YOU WILL BE FORGOTTEN YOU WILL SUFFER FOR ALL ETERNITY!"

"He's going to kill me. Just run!" he screamed.

Hands touched his shoulders. Through the terror and the rage, the legion of screaming nightmares, he heard Bartok say, "God please protect this man. Whatever demons threaten him, you are greater. Please show him your mercy now."

Grenidor looked up. Edwin, or whatever masqueraded as Edwin, was writhing. The earsplitting cacophony of his screaming beat against Grenidor's ears and mind and bones.

Yet it was distant. Edwin's writhing was like that of an ant caught in the light of a magnifying glass on a brilliant day, agonized and furious. His screaming never decreased in volume yet the pain in Grenidor's ears and bones and heart instantly lessened. The serpent hissed, eyes glittering with hatred. Wings beat at him, and he flinched.

Owen had his sword out and was looking through the darkness, blue eyes preternaturally bright in the shadowed tunnel. He began to sing, eyes still searching the darkness.

Edwin's furious thundering increased, but Grenidor realized that somehow, miraculously, Edwin had not yet killed him. The pain in his ears was gone, the twisting terror in his heart subsiding. Owen's song rose around him, his voice like spun gold in the air, so pure and righteous that Grenidor felt himself aching for the joy it carried. Power ran through the song, vast and inexorable as the ocean. Bartok continued praying, his hands on Grenidor's shoulders. Grenidor trembled, and for once he didn't care that he looked helpless.

He bent forward, covered his face with his hands, and wept.

NO ONE SEEMED IMPATIENT, though Grenidor knew they should be. They waited in the tunnel while he composed himself.

Regaining some sense of dignity took longer than he'd expected. Longer than he wished. Even when the unwelcome tears had faded, he remained on his knees, trembling and weak.

"How did you do that?" he asked finally.

Bartok dropped to one knee beside him. "Did he leave?"

"Yes. How did you do that?"

Bartok's smile was caught in the glare of a flashlight. "I didn't do it. But God answered my prayer. What exactly did you experience?"

"He said I had disappointed him for the last time. He was furious, and he said he'd smite me into hell, that I'd suffer forever. I'd die and be forgotten." The words stuck in his throat.

Owen remained standing, his sword still drawn and eyes alert, though he glanced down at Grenidor's flushed face for a moment with a sympathetic expression. Grenidor looked away. *How can he care about me, after what I did to him? It's not natural.*

"When you are able, and when you choose, a more full account of what he said to you might be useful," Owen said, sheathing his sword.

Bartok nodded. "I think it's a demon. God is greater than a demon. I didn't do anything but ask for God's protection for you. Do you really need any more proof that God loves you? He died for you. Rose from the grave, defeating death and sin. No demon is stronger than that! He loves you. God wants you to be saved. He wants to forgive you. But you have to ask for grace. You have to admit your sin and ask to be forgiven under Christ's blood. That's all!"

Grenidor was shaking his head. "I can't. I can't ask it. Not now, after everything I've done. He should…" *He should hate me.*

Bartok snorted. "You think God hates you? You think your sin is so great? You realize that's insulting, don't you? As if, in our humanity, we could out-sin God's grace. Jesus Christ prayed for the forgiveness of the Romans who nailed him to the cross!"

Grenidor's breath was ragged. In. Out. In. *Can God forgive even me? Is it possible? Would He kill me for asking? …It can't be worse than what Edwin would do.* "Will you help me?" he whispered.

Bartok bowed his head again. "Lord God, you know this man's sins. He knows them. Please give him grace, Lord. In your kindness, in your mercy, please help him trust you. Help him turn from sin and live according to your will. Wash him in your son Jesus' blood and make him new."

Grenidor heard the sincerity in Bartok's words. He felt the power of Bartok's faith like a shield around him, giving him space to breathe in the middle of terror and shame.

"I can pray for you, Colonel, but you must also pray yourself. This is between you and God. Acknowledge your sins. Ask for forgiveness. Thank God for his grace and mercy. The power isn't in the words you say. God listens to your heart. Cry out to Him with your heart."

Grenidor nodded, not trusting his voice. He cleared his throat, but still the words would not come. *So you listen to my heart, do you? Are you the Slavemaster? Even if you are, I'd rather be your slave. My own decisions have been wrong from the very beginning. Bartok says you will give me grace if I ask for it. Please let that be true. Please, God, let that be true. I don't want to be what I was. I want to be new. I want to be yours.*

Grenidor caught his breath, the feeling of peace on him so sudden and startling that it was almost physical. But it wasn't physical; it was in his mind and his heart, like a song he'd forgotten but loved as a child, and a warm blanket wrapped around him as he came in from the cold, and a meal after he'd been hungry so long he'd forgotten what it felt like to be satisfied.

Is that you, God? Is that feeling you?

He bent forward, weeping in earnest now. *If that's you, I don't know why I resisted so long. I can die now, and I wouldn't even mind. Just to know I'm yours and not Edwin's anymore.*

The voice inside him was clear, the words made of pure thought. *You have always been mine. I let you choose your master because I want to be chosen. You are mine because I made you. Edwin is also mine, and he has chosen to be his own master.*

Grenidor swallowed. "Do you always speak into people's heads?"

The warmth and comfort increased. *I am the Lord your God. There is no one before me. I have brought you out of slavery, and you are mine.*

The words reverberated in his mind, deafening and yet not painful. The voice had not answered his question. Grenidor found that he didn't need the answer anymore.

He wiped the tears from his face with shaking hands, feeling as if he were coming back to himself for the first time in a very long time. He looked up at the others in the shadowed tunnel, lit unevenly by the flashlight beams.

Owen had sheathed his sword, though his hand still rested on its hilt. His blue eyes glinted in the shadows as he smiled. *How have I never noticed the kindness in his eyes before?* Grenidor smiled back weakly.

Bartok's smile was wider, his warmth more obvious. "Welcome home, Colonel."

He swallowed the lump in his throat. "You don't have to call me that. I've probably lost my rank now, anyway. My name's Paul."

Bartok blinked and smiled again, as if the name had been important somehow. "It's a good name."

CHAPTER 16

OWEN LED THEM through the darkened tunnels again, the walk interminable and silent but for the sound of their footsteps. Finally the little group emerged from a small hatchway into a tiny alley, broken glass glittering in the beams of their flashlights.

"Where are we?" Grenidor whispered.

"Nearly there."

Aria frowned as they walked. "There are a lot of abandoned buildings, aren't there? I never really noticed before."

Grenidor grunted. "I'm not surprised."

She glanced at him. "Why?"

"We didn't want anyone questioning. I think that was put in the training videos."

She blinked. "You mean the brainwashing videos. You brainwashed us not to question it."

He shrugged.

"Why are they empty, then? Did that many people die in the Revolution?"

Grenidor frowned. "Not all of them, no. Many fled outside the reach of the Empire. The borders are not as solid as we would like to think, even now. Back then, they were even more porous." He licked his lips, then added, "When I said *we*, I meant the Empire."

The moonlight suddenly burst from behind the clouds, silvering the edges of the buildings around them. Owen led them through an old wrought-iron gate and an overgrown garden filled with misshapen topiaries toward the smaller end of a stone building, its mass disappearing into the darkness.

"What is this place?" Aria asked.

"I've never been here before. But it's old." Owen brushed his fingers against a crumbling wall. "Older than it looks."

Bartok's voice came from behind them. "It's the basilica. I've never been here either, but I've read about it. It was part of the Catholic church here. I think it's modeled after the old ones in Europe."

Aria frowned at the unfamiliar word *Catholic*, but she didn't ask about it.

"There's a monastery a few miles north of here, too, I think. At least there used to be. It's a little older. I think it was Franciscan."

"What's a monastery?"

"Monasteries are where monks lived. Monks were men who swore off things of the world and took vows of poverty or silence or something, and devoted themselves to God. There were problems, of course; the church is made of sinners. But it's an interesting idea." Bartok's voice changed, as if he were smiling ruefully. "Retreating from the world does have a certain appeal."

"Indeed," murmured Owen. He pushed open a door of heavy wood and they emerged into a larger open space, the vaulted ceiling echoing above them. He stopped and looked upward, the moonlight so bright that for a moment it fought through the stained glass, shining orange and blue across Owen's face. "The building is quite beautiful. I believe it's a blend of Romanesque and Byzantine styles, though not like the older ones in Europe." He motioned, and light coalesced in the space above them, illuminating the room in a soft glow. The ceiling was extravagantly decorated, though Aria couldn't make out many details. Rows of heavy wooden pews marched toward the front of the sanctuary; green marble inlay set off the aisles from the smooth white marble floors.

Bartok glanced at Owen. "How do you know so much about architecture?"

"I don't." Owen's lips rose in an amused smile. "I read tourist pamphlets half a century ago when this place was still in use. They gave tours, though I never took one. One of the characteristics emphasized was the universality of the Christian faith, extended to all peoples. At the time, I thought it referred only to human faith."

Grenidor seemed to hunch into himself. The movement was so subtle Aria might not have noticed if she wasn't standing next to him, uncomfortably aware of his proximity. She didn't hate him, exactly, but his presence in their midst made her wary. Pity tugged at her heart. He looked haggard in the dim light, the shadows catching at the lines of tension in his face.

"What's wrong?" she whispered to him.

He glanced sideways at her, then consciously squared his shoulders and lifted his chin.

She thought the movement only made him look more tired. Perhaps Bartok saw it, too, because he reached out and gave Grenidor a reassuring thump on the shoulder. Grenidor relaxed a little.

Bartok is good. She glanced at him with renewed respect. Bartok knew exactly how to comfort a man without making him feel weak, or at least without making it obvious that he felt weak.

Bartok said, "Lord Owen, I'm a little confused by what happened in the tunnel. I thought Fae were protected from direct attack by demons and couldn't even see them. If that's right, you couldn't see the demon, and your sword would be of no use against it. But I know you sense them, at least a little. I had the impression your magic was useless against them, and you fear them for good reason. Yet your singing seemed to have an effect."

Owen nodded. "You are correct. We are powerless against dark ones, which I believe are what you call demons. Humans are as well, I think." He raised his eyebrows, and Bartok nodded. "I saw and heard nothing I could identify, but I felt an oppressive, malevolent presence. I could feel you calling upon El, and the power, purity, and strength of your communion with him. I did the same, but in my language. My song was not megdhonia; it had little power in itself. I sang praise and a request for El to cast his gaze upon us.

I thought this was an appropriate response to a dark one's presence."

Grenidor made a tiny sound, and Owen looked at him sharply. "Is something wrong?" Owen asked.

"You'd face *that* for me, with nothing but a song? After what I did to you?"

Owen let out a little huff. "It was not me alone. I begged El to look upon us. I did nothing on my own strength."

Grenidor took a shuddering breath. "But you asked. You didn't leave me."

Owen smiled. "No."

OWEN STOOD STILL a moment as if listening, then said, "Come. They are close." He led them through a passage into a smaller sanctuary, folding tables pushed against the walls.

Fearghal, whose name Aria remembered only because Owen had mentioned it, stepped forward as well. "My lord Owen." He bowed gracefully, and Owen smiled.

"Who's there?" A flashlight glared at them.

"My name is Owen. Colonel Grenidor is with me, as are some friends: Colonel Gabriel Peterson, Dr. Tobias Bartok, and Aria Forsyth." Owen motioned to Grenidor, who stepped forward.

"You're alive." The man sounded relieved and a little surprised. "I was afraid we wouldn't have such luck."

"It's not luck." Grenidor shook the man's hand. "I've been... protected. What brings you here, Blakeley? Dr. Burke?" He shook hands with Burke and the guard.

"This is Dave Jackson." Blakeley nodded to the guard, then studied the faces surrounding him. "We came to let you know that a vampire tried to tell us where you were hiding. We thought... well, we thought that if he wanted to betray his leader by telling us where you were, then maybe you were on the right side, after all. We thought you should know."

Grenidor looked down and sighed. "I think I met him already."

Owen nodded once. Aria wondered whether everyone could see the aching sorrow in his eyes, or whether it was only obvious to her.

Gabriel said, "Well, you can't go back, I imagine. Do you have anything else you can tell us?"

Blakeley's gaze swept around the group again before settling on Grenidor. "I need to talk to you, sir."

Grenidor nodded. "Would you excuse us, please?"

Everyone but Grenidor and the newcomers retreated to a far corner. Aria imagined Grenidor explaining that the Fae weren't as evil as he'd thought, and wondered how he'd explain his own actions to them. A few words caught her ear, but she couldn't quite follow the conversation. She glanced at Owen, knowing he could hear everything they said, but he merely returned her questioning look with a faint smile, his expression barely visible in the moonlight filtering through the windows.

Bartok stood next to her. "Aria, have you considered asking God for grace as well?"

She swallowed. "I've considered it. I'm... afraid."

"Afraid of what?" His voice was filled with innocent confusion.

She was silent for long minutes, trying to put into words what made her hesitate. "Afraid of what God will ask of me," she said at last. "I don't think God wants some half-hearted words. I think he wants all of me. That's terrifying! I've never been that committed to anything before. It's not just life and death. It's my thoughts and everything, isn't it?"

"Yes, it is. But it's good, Aria. *He* is good. He knows we aren't perfect, that we can't be. He meets us where we are."

She made a frustrated sound. "But *I* don't know where I am!" Belatedly she heard the whine in her voice. "I don't know *who* I am. Not really. I feel like I should know that before I make any big decisions."

He chuckled softly. "But as soon as you commit yourself to God, you will change. Besides, he knows you far better than you will ever know yourself." He sighed. "I don't want to pressure you. It has to be your decision, when you're ready. But it's important, Aria." His voice dropped. "It scares me, knowing that you..." he hesitated, as if considering his words, "...haven't yet accepted God's grace."

"Scares you?" She turned to face him, the faint light barely illuminating his face. She could see his cheekbone and the faint line of his jaw, but his eyes were only shadows, his expression lost in darkness. "Why?"

He reached out to touch her hand for a moment and then pulled away. "The decision has eternal consequences. If you die before you accept the grace God offers through Jesus..." He stopped, his voice tight. "Please consider it. Not for me, but because it matters."

Something in his voice caught at her heart, bringing a rush of unexpected emotion and tenderness. If they had been alone, she might have asked him more. She could imagine the consequences; Cillian's bubble analogy came to mind, and she imagined being forever separated from God on the outside of the bubble while Bartok and Owen and even Grenidor basked in God's presence on the inside. But perhaps it was the other way around; perhaps God was on the outside, in freedom, and those who opposed him, the dark ones, were imprisoned on the inside of the bubble.

It didn't matter. Either way, she imagined herself forever cut off from Bartok and Owen and Cillian and Gabriel and everyone else. The idea pained her in a way she hadn't expected.

No. This is not a decision to be made because I can't bear to be away from these people I've grown to love. If God is real, and if I'm to commit myself to him, I need to do it because he deserves it.

Her thoughts were interrupted by Grenidor's voice. "Peterson? Owen? Would you come here?"

Bartok and Aria followed.

Blakeley, Burke, and Jackson eyed Owen with ill-concealed nerves. Grenidor said, "They want to join us. Is that all right?"

Gabriel and Owen nodded.

Burke frowned, studying Owen with sharp eyes. He glanced at Grenidor and asked, "Is he the one you used the getlaril solution on? The one that escaped a few weeks ago?"

Grenidor swallowed and nodded.

"And you don't..." Burke glanced between Owen and Grenidor again. "I watched those videos, Colonel." His voice tightened and he stopped to take a slow breath.

The silence grew uncomfortable, and Owen asked, "Did you wish to ask me a question?"

Burke shook his head as if not trusting his voice. "No. No. I need to think."

Owen inclined his head in a vaguely regal gesture. "Come. You will be protected."

Gabriel turned to mutter into Owen's ear. Aria heard him, though she thought suddenly that the other humans probably couldn't. *My hearing is getting better. Like a Fae!* The thought gave her a warm, satisfied feeling, as if God had smiled on her for a moment.

Gabriel murmured, "Are you sure about this? They could be traitors. I don't even like Grenidor being in our camp, much less these guys. Just because they took out their trackers doesn't mean we can trust them."

Owen whispered into Gabriel's ear, "We can never be sure, Gabriel. But generosity befits us. We are El's, you and I, and we should act as El would. I think Christ would not turn away a man who came with mixed motives, so long as he came."

Gabriel grumbled something that Aria couldn't quite make out. Owen only smiled.

GRENIDOR STOOD a little to the side, his arms crossed, his face in shadow.

"Paul Grenidor, are you willing to speak to us about what you saw in the tunnel?" Owen asked.

Grenidor startled at his voice, his right hand moving reflexively to his empty holster before he caught himself. "Yes."

At Owen's wave, Bartok joined them, then Gabriel, Aria, and Niall. Blakeley, Burke, and the guard settled in a corner, obviously ill at ease surrounded by rebels and Fae whom they could not see.

Grenidor took a deep breath, steadying his voice, and clasped his hands behind his back in a parade rest position. He told them of Edwin's thousand forms, the thunderous voice that shook his bones, shook concrete dust from the tunnel walls.

"I can't trust anything," he muttered. "I saw him as a man most of the time, but his words were twisted into knots. I believed him when he said one thing, then later I would question it and he would explain it away with completely different logic, and I would believe that. Sometimes I think I saw glimpses of truth that he didn't want me to see, but I'm not even confident of that."

The others nodded silently. Bartok murmured, "Demon is as good a description as we need."

"He was so angry," Grenidor's voice cracked. "I felt the world was ending. The ground shook. My bones felt like dust inside me. My thoughts were not my own... they were mine, but not entirely independent." He swallowed and cleared his throat, steadying his voice. "He hates me. He hates everyone and everything. He told me that, and I think it might have been the one true thing he ever said."

"Is Petro like that?" Gabriel turned toward Owen, his voice tight.

"I think not." Owen's expression was thoughtful. "Perhaps they are of the same species, but Petro does not lie, so far as I know. Nor do I believe he hates." He shifted, and Aria thought she saw him wince, although the expression was so subtle perhaps she imagined it. "We believe he has killed before, perhaps in anger. He is dangerous, but we have no reason to believe he is evil."

Gabriel frowned. "Do they even have emotions? Or was it all faked? Was it an act?"

Grenidor shuddered. "When he was masquerading as human, he often pretended to be more or less friendly. That was an act. I don't think the anger was an act." He cleared his throat again. "At various times, his plans seemed to change; whether I lived or died didn't matter to him. Actually, he would have been happy when I died, but he wanted to use me first." He frowned and glanced at Owen. "He hates everyone, especially you." Then he looked down. "Because he hates the Slavemaster."

The others blinked. *The Slavemaster*. Aria mouthed the unfamiliar name. Owen frowned, his clear blue eyes kind and confused. "Do you mean El?"

"The demon is a liar," Bartok said. "His words are twisted; his ideas are twisted. We humans can be slaves to sin or slaves to righteousness. The demon wants you to choose the freedom of rebellion and the slavery of sin rather than slavery to righteousness and freedom in Christ. The demon knows the freedom of sin, and he is enslaved by it. Of course he calls God the Slavemaster." Bartok's voice softened. "Maybe it sounds confusing, but all you need to know right now is that God loves you.

FEARGHAL DEPARTED for the train station to tell the others that Owen and Gabriel wished to move their camps to the basilica. He returned some hours later with Niall; the others would follow behind with the supplies.

Gabriel, Bartok, Aria, Grenidor, Blakeley, Burke, and Jackson sat at the old tables in an uncomfortable silence. They were all tired; it was past midnight, and the long, cold walk from the train station had left Aria feeling drained. She leaned forward to rest her head on her arms. Bartok, sitting next to her, leaned down to whisper in her ear, "Do you want my jacket for a pillow?"

"No thanks," she murmured. *That was nice. He has to be as cold as I am.* She drifted into an uneasy doze.

Aria's dreams were filled with snatches of conversation from around her, disconnected thoughts of trackers and brainwashing, guilt and despair, free will and choices and consequences. She dreamed of Petro, only he no longer looked like any of the forms she'd seen. He was smoke and light, he was a reflection, he was a dragon and a flame and a man wrapped in his own brilliant wings. He spoke in a voice like thunder, and his words slipped just out of understanding, leaving her grasping for shreds of meaning that refused to coalesce.

209

Aria blinked at the light filtering through her eyelids. It took her a moment to wake enough to realize why her neck hurt and why there was cloth gathered around her shoulders. She sat up with a groan. Bartok's jacket slid off her shoulders and down to the floor. She snatched at it, startled, and accidentally elbowed Bartok as she caught it. He was deeply asleep, head resting on his arms, and only let out a soft huff in response. Bright morning light through the old stained glass lit his face in shades of gold. She couldn't help smiling at him.

Eli and the others were just arriving, the muffled sounds of their movements coming from the hallway and nearby rooms. Grenidor sat at the end of the table by himself, leaning back in the chair with his arms crossed over his chest and his head bowed forward as he dozed. Owen leaned against a wall, his arms folded over his chest. His expression was closed and remote. Fearghal, Niall, and Feichin slept a short distance away, untroubled by the hard marble floor.

She carefully draped Bartok's jacket over his shoulders and stood, wincing at the cramps that tightened her back and legs. Her steps felt stiff and awkward as she approached Owen.

"Is everything all right?" she asked.

He looked down and gave her a faint smile. "So far as I know." Despite the smile, his eyes were solemn. "You are in pain?"

"A bit sore. The table wasn't exactly comfortable."

He held her gaze for a moment, and the cramps and stiffness vanished. "Is that better?"

"Thank you." She frowned in confusion. "I thought you needed to touch me to heal me."

210

"It is easier that way, but not necessary. Your aches were so slight it made little difference."

She studied him in the warm light streaming through the stained glass. "You look tired."

He glanced down at her again, one eyebrow raised slightly. "Perhaps because I am."

"Well, normally you don't look it."

His eyes flicked across the room and back to her. His lips parted, then closed again. Then, as if he were revealing something very personal, he said softly, "I am discouraged."

"About what?" She tried to keep her voice as soft as possible.

"I had hoped, and have beseeched El, that Lachtnal would soon see the consequences of his rebellion and turn back to El. Knowing that such return is possible, I hope for it desperately. I hoped for his redemption in a matter of days, perhaps even hours." He looked away, then back down at her, a faint, sorrowful smile touching his lips. "Thus am I discouraged as I am forced to realize how impatient and immature I am. I should not weary of beseeching El on Lachtnal's behalf." He looked back across the room, as if to ensure that no one was awake to see him. Then he slid down the wall to sit on the floor, his head dropped forward to rest on his knees.

Impulsively Aria wrapped one arm around his shoulders. He flinched, the movement almost imperceptible, and she drew back. "Did I hurt you?"

"It matters not." His answer scarcely reached her ears. A moment later, he looked up and sighed softly. "And you? How is your heart?"

Aria swallowed. *Does he know how intimate that question sounds?*

211

His gaze on her face was tired and gentle. "Is it a difficult question? It was not intended to be."

"No." She took a deep breath and let it out slowly. "It is difficult only because I don't know my own heart." *I have loved you in a way that is fading, yet I love you no less. Perhaps I love you more. And Bartok has captured my heart in a way that I cannot yet describe or quantify. He is kind and good, as you are. He is not Fae and he does not have megdhonia. But while I love those things, they are not necessary.* She licked her lips, wondering which of her thoughts were visible on her face.

Owen studied her expression for so long that she felt her face heat. Then he put his head back against the wall and closed his eyes.

She sat next to him. *Sometimes simply being beside each other is a comfort. At least for me.*

ARIA FOUND HERSELF THINKING of the conversation about how Fearghal would have left Blakeley and Burke and Jackson in the tunnel. How she'd expected something of Owen that he could not, should not, give. She glanced at him surreptitiously.

His eyes were half-closed, his expression unreadable but for the faint signs of weariness.

"May I ask you a question?" she whispered.

"Of course," he murmured. He blinked, as if coming back from a distant place.

"When I asked you about Fearghal leaving the men in the tunnel, you spoke of commanding the Fae." She blinked back sudden tears. "But you spoke of them, not me. I'm one of your Fae, aren't I?" Desperation filled her voice.

He turned to face her, his own expression startled. "Of course! I am your king. Nothing can break that bond but death, and I am not sure that death does, either." His blue eyes were gentle on her face, and he wiped a tear from her cheek with the cool pad of his thumb. "I spoke of them as separate from you because you grew up outside our covenant. You are not bound by the rules we are; I doubt you feel the guidance of El as we do, the sweet strictures on our lives and our thoughts. You have not sworn your allegiance to me, and without that, I have very limited authority over you."

"But… you're my king." The words were both a statement and a question. Aria wiped at her eyes, feeling the tears smeared in a thin sheen across her cheeks.

"Yes. Always." He smiled. "El did not exactly require me to bind myself to you in that way. I know it pleased him, but it was not required of me. It also pleased me. The weight of responsibility is heavy, but it is a burden I am glad to bear.

"You alone choose whether to swear your allegiance to me as subject. If you had been raised Fae, you would have sworn your allegiance long ago, when you were very young. You would have known when it was time, and you would have longed to do it. It is a choice both freely made and inevitable."

Aria sniffled and wiped her eyes again. Her throat felt tight with emotion. "All Fae? Even turned ones?"

Owen's expression saddened. "No Fae turns over this choice; rebellion, turning, occurs only afterwards. It is a deliberate severing of a bond that is meant to be lifelong, perhaps even eternal. Yet it does not completely sever; I do not reject the turned one. I never have! No king ever has." His voice, though quiet, rang with the purity of his words. "Now that we know turned ones can be brought back to El…" he let out a sudden breath, as if words failed him. "El is to be praised!"

The silence between them felt softer, more comforting than before. Aria felt her drowsiness rising again and leaned her head back against the wall.

Owen murmured, "Thank you for your apology. It taught me something I had not understood before."

She turned to him, fully awake. "How could I teach you anything? You're so much wiser than I am."

Amused affection glinted in his eyes. "Nevertheless, you have, and I thank you." He smiled, the light catching his straight white teeth. "Fae who deliberately offend have committed an offense not only against the other Fae but against El. It is rebellion and turning, from which we thought there was no return. I believe that if we were human, accidental offense would warrant an apology, but our understanding of courtesy is different. We have previously had little understanding of forgiveness.

"Our experience of El has not given us reason to forgive, or to understand the concept of forgiveness. For what reason would a Fae apologize? Inadvertent offense does not cause a turning from El, and if El is not offended by a Fae's accidental act or word, then what standing does another Fae have to hold onto indignation?

"Yet… you apologized to me." Owen paused, his expression distant for a moment, as he appeared to ponder his words. "I had forgiven Grenidor for his cruelty to me, yet the forgiveness was different. It was a decision to act as if the offense had not occurred, although I still bear the agony of it in my bones and in my flesh. I cannot forget it, yet I decided, with the grace of El, to act in grace rather than in justified anger or in hatred.

"I wished to please El. My understanding of El's grace was growing, and I felt that such a decision would please him, but I did not understand how or why. My decision had little to do with Grenidor himself, and only a little more to do with my leadership of my people. It was an act of worship, I suppose, a decision and an act meant purely for El.

"I made a similar decision in my reaction to you; I would not have been permitted any physical retaliation, but I was permitted to withdraw from you, never to speak to you again. I did not wish such a withdrawal; you were my subject, and I cared for you. Your apology was a recognition of the hurt you caused me and a request for forgiveness." The thin skin around his eyes crinkled as he smiled, his eyes bright and kind. "I had never been offered such an opportunity to grant forgiveness. I found my heart warm and filled with gratitude, even joy, that one of my subjects recognized an offense and wished to repent of it." His gaze held hers. "I think I understand the heart of El a little more than I did before. So I thank you. The hurt of

215

your words is soothed, and what remains is gratitude and love."

Aria felt herself trembling, and she twisted her hands together in her lap, unable to meet his gaze any longer. *Is that what El does? Is that what he demands of me? I can't be like Owen is.*

CHAPTER 17

FEICHIN APPEARED at Bartok's side as he blinked awake. "Lord Owen wishes to speak with you, if you will follow me."

"Of course."

"I thank you, Dr. Bartok." Owen smiled at his arrival. Then he said seriously, "I have been pondering many thoughts, and I would like your insight."

Bartok nodded assent.

"It troubles me that the bull figurine and bullets were smeared with the blood of Christians. I understand that humans kill for many reasons, but I see no reason why this horror would have occurred. I feel the evil in it; I can speculate that a dark one would have been the source of such an idea. But what does that mean?" He looked toward Bartok.

Bartok frowned as he thought. "We don't have a lot of detail about demons in the Bible, but we know that Satan led a rebellion against God. Demons can't really strike at God directly; how could they? But they can strike at what God loves, his creation. So the rebellion of Satan, and demons who follow him, is manifested through war and death and selfishness and disease and hunger and every other affliction. These things are a manifestation of the hatred they hold for God, who made us."

Feichin nodded solemnly. "It hates everything and everyone. It is beautiful and obscene, created to be wondrous and magnificent beyond words, then twisted into a mockery of itself. It hates what it was and what it is. It hates love and compassion and purity and selflessness." He met Bartok's gaze. "Most of all, it hates El."

Bartok frowned. "Which explains a little of why it hates Fae so much. You are obedient. It can't stand that. It hates Christians, too, because we are redeemed by the blood of Christ." Bartok smiled wryly. "So you two, Owen and Feichin, are particularly hated."

Feichin swallowed. "I understand."

Owen's expression was distant for a moment, and he nodded thoughtfully. "I have a question for Gabriel."

Feichin rose with disconcerting grace and jogged away, returning some minutes later with Gabriel. The rebel leader was tense, eying Feichin with poorly concealed wariness. Feichin gestured courteously to the space next to Owen, kneeling at Owen's side as if waiting for another command.

"He said you had a question," Gabriel muttered, jerking his chin at Feichin.

"The attempts to control the human population seem unnecessarily complicated. Can you speculate as to why the Empire has chosen such methods?" Owen asked.

Gabriel rocked backward, his expression shifting from irritated caution to interest. "I've been thinking on that, as well. The brainwashing seems far too complicated. It's probably expensive, and it's definitely a lot of effort. Political leaders have never needed such measures before. Threats of violence, actual violence, widespread surveillance, informers, elimination of political opposition, propaganda, secret police... tyrants have never needed drugs and wires in people's brains to control the masses. So why now?"

"And human sacrifice," Bartok murmured. "That's not something that an aggressively anti-religious government would invent without help."

Gabriel's eyes narrowed as he thought. "So who taught, or is teaching, them to do magic? Not fallen Fae." He glanced at the others.

"This 'dark one' is involved. I'm assuming that's a demon of some sort," said Bartok.

Gabriel blew out his breath thoughtfully.

Bartok said, "Well, we know it communicates with fallen Fae sometimes. We know from the Bible that demons can communicate and even possess human and animal bodies, at least occasionally. But there must be some constraints, particularly on how they can affect our minds. To have free will we have to be able to choose or reject God, so while we can't know the exact limits of what a demon can do, we can assume they can't seriously interfere with our free will. But what about another human?"

Gabriel sucked in his breath.

Bartok continued, "We know from Colonel Grenidor that it was manipulating him, and probably others in the Empire, too. Through brainwashing, a human *could* change or limit someone's free will. So maybe the demon is helping the Empire—maybe even created the Empire— *mostly* because it wants the brainwashing. It wants people to be unable to choose."

Gabriel's hands tightened into fists. He shouted, "Dr. Burke! Col. Grenidor! Lt. Col. Blakeley!"

The men joined them a moment later. Feichin slid backward, hidden from the humans, though he stayed close by Owen.

"You said someone was drugged, didn't you? On television?" Gabriel asked without explanation.

Dr. Burke nodded. "Yes, most of the Council." He frowned. "Why?"

"This whole conflict is about free will. Choice." Bartok met everyone's eyes in turn. "I think the demon is trying to subvert free will. It wants to prevent people from being able to choose. If so, it might intend to expand the Empire to the whole world. That would explain how the Empire rose to power so easily, and the use of magic, and…"

"That explains a *lot*," Grenidor said, his voice so low that Aria scarcely heard him.

Bartok glanced at him, and Grenidor added, "He… the demon… wanted me to use Christians."

At everyone's inquiring looks, he muttered, "For the sacrifice. He… It suggested animal sacrifices and said they would be adequate, but human sacrifices would be much more effective. I wanted results. It wanted worshippers and seemed particularly pleased by the idea of drugged worshippers. I suggested using animals for the sacrifices and drugging Christians to get the worshippers it wanted. I thought it was more humane than killing the Christians, but it panicked and threatened me." His voice cracked, and he cleared his throat. "I think that must be against the rules somehow."

Gabriel's eyes widened. "That's a dangerous play."

"I don't understand," Burke said. "Why is drugging Christians any different than drugging anyone else? And why are you talking about demons and God anyway?"

"I'll explain about God and redemption in a minute." Bartok said. He turned to Gabriel. "You're right. I can imagine that while martyring Christians would be permitted, drugging them and brainwashing them into demon-worship would not be. The Bible says 'Who shall separate us from the love of Christ? Shall trouble or hardship or persecution or famine or nakedness or danger or sword? As it is written: 'For your sake we face death all day long; we are considered as sheep to be slaughtered.' No, in all these things we are more than conquerors through him who loved us. For I am convinced that neither death nor life, neither angels nor demons, neither the present nor the future, nor any powers, neither height nor depth, nor anything else in all creation, will be able to separate us from the love of God that is in Christ Jesus our Lord.'" He smiled. "So be of good courage, men of God. You can be killed, but you can't be lost." He glanced at Aria, then away, a flicker of emotion in his eyes catching at her heart.

"You knew that text by memory?" Grenidor asked. He glanced at Gabriel, who looked away.

"The Bible is the word of God to humanity. It's one of the ways we can begin to know his heart." Bartok smiled. "I certainly haven't memorized it all, or even most of it, but it's comforting to have verses come easily to mind, and that passage has always been one of my favorites. It reminds me we aren't the first Christians to face adversity, even if it looks a bit different than it used to."

Gabriel had said nothing for some minutes, staring fixedly at a spot in the concrete in front of his crossed ankles. He finally muttered, "It explains more than you realize, Grenidor." He looked up, his eyes bright and hard. "We might as well have been drugged, too."

"What do you mean?" Burke bristled a little, though the comment wasn't addressed to him.

Bartok straightened, a faint smile on his lips, as he understood what Gabriel meant.

"I mean we've been wasting our time!" Gabriel's voice rose. "Our actions against the Empire have been almost entirely fruitless. If the Empire we're fighting is the tool of a demon in a scheme against the whole human race, well then, no wonder! We've been wasting our efforts fighting battles that make no difference. Our few victories don't affect his plans at all. He's tricked us into pointless plans and efforts.

"We thought we should wait until someone from the outside would offer assistance, or perhaps the people would realize what's going on and revolt. We imagined internal unrest was brewing, even though we never saw any signs of it. Our plan to hold out until the Empire makes a mistake, or someone comes to aid us, won't work.

"Doing nothing is exactly what the demon would want of us if he'd brainwashed us. Can you imagine how the forces outside the Empire would fare against a demon? It's absurd to imagine they could do anything for us. I doubt they even realize we need help. No external aid could prevail against a demon. And internal unrest? What unrest? There's nothing! People are complacent."

Grenidor spoke in a low voice, "He—*It*—once told me something about how he experiences time. It's not how we experience it. He sees the future as many possible outcomes. He said although he can't be sure which will happen, he has some insight as to which outcome is most likely. He lies, but he also sometimes slips little bits of truth among his lies to be more convincing. I think that was true, or at least something close to truth. I know he can be surprised; I think me surviving the meeting with Owen and Feichin and everyone surprised him. But he knew the meeting was going to happen, and who would be present, before I even thought about arranging it."

Kneeling just beside Owen, Feichin made himself visible, startling all the humans. Grenidor stared across the circle at him, his eyes wide, his hands clenched tightly in his lap. Blakeley cursed and scooted backward, his hand darting toward the sidearm he no longer wore. He froze, realizing the gun was gone. Beside him, Burke's reaction was more muted, a quickening of his breath and a sudden trembling.

Feichin said, "The dark one, or demon as you call it, gave me reason to believe that it wanted me to kill Aria. Since there appears as yet to be little reason for this, perhaps he wanted this because of something that may yet happen, something we have not yet experienced or foreseen. Or perhaps the moment the dark one feared may have passed already. She has, I believe, made significant contributions to the resistance. I heard of her role in rescuing Lord Owen from captivity; without her involvement, much of what ensued would not have occurred because Lord Owen would be dead." He glanced around the group, quicksilver eyes meeting each gaze in turn. "Lord Owen's understanding of our place in El's creation, especially our place in relation to humans, is changing. I wonder if the dark one wants to prevent something that will result from that new understanding."

Burke made a tiny sound of terror and closed his eyes, lips pressing tightly together. Grenidor cleared his throat and said, "I didn't realize you were still here."

Feichin's lips lifted in a thin smile, and he inclined his head courteously. "I have been here since you brought me to Lord Owen. I thank you for that, although what resulted was not what either of us expected." The light gleamed on his white teeth as his smile widened. "Perhaps the dark one had some inkling of this outcome, among the possibilities. Certainly my redemption will not have pleased him."

"No, I imagine not."

Blakeley muttered something in Grenidor's ear that Aria could almost make out. Grenidor shook his head, and Blakeley's shoulders relaxed almost imperceptibly. He kept a wary eye toward Feichin.

Gabriel cleared his throat, breaking the silence. "If the demon wants the whole world to fall to the Empire, then the stakes are a lot higher than political freedom here in this quadrant. Before, the potential gains didn't outweigh the risks of taking action. But now, the consequences of doing nothing are much higher. We can't afford to stand by and do nothing. Our inaction would result in... well, the most complete defeat imaginable." His voice rasped as he said, "Any risk is acceptable if we have some hope of making a difference."

Grenidor said, "It wouldn't have focused on you and the Fae so much, it wouldn't have spent so much effort trying to eliminate you or incapacitate you if it was impossible for you to make a difference." He blinked, as if surprised by his own words.

Bartok nodded with a faint smile. "Agreed." He glanced across the circle to meet Owen's eyes. "The demon is a lot older, smarter, stronger, and more strategic than we are. But we do not fight alone.

"I don't think inaction is an option. Fighting a human enemy is one thing. But if this is a battle against evil, not just the evil of men and our sin but a demonic plot against humanity, we can't stand aside, afraid of the risk. We *must* act."

Owen spoke, his voice low and melodious among the human voices. "Well said, Dr. Bartok."

Feichin edged forward and bent to speak into Owen's ear. After a moment, Owen looked up. "Excuse me." He stood and withdrew some distance away, where he sat with Feichin in seclusion.

FEICHIN AND OWEN spoke in low tones for a very long time, the sound of their words like the ripples in a distant brook. Aria wondered of what they spoke. Several times she found herself staring and had to look away. Feichin was still skeletal, his eyes silvery-blue in the shadows under his brows. The light caught a few glints of silver in his ebony curls and the white of his teeth between pale lips when he smiled, startled at something Owen had said.

Watching them, Aria could see their similarities; their dark hair, the lines of their jaws, even the way they inclined their heads in that faintly regal gesture of assent or acknowledgment. Feichin was older, but the deference he gave Owen was obvious.

Owen stood. "Come!" he called in a ringing voice. "Come."

The Fae followed him without question. The humans neither heard nor obeyed; the command was not meant for them. Aria knew that the Fae could keep their voices unnoticed, but she hadn't realized that even a loud voice could be concealed. Or perhaps Owen had not actually spoken aloud. She found that she was unsure.

Owen led them outside and a short distance into the garden. The air was icy but still, and a bright, cold light shone down. The sky was a perfect robin's egg blue. Aria took a breath so deep her lungs ached and held the air inside; she felt alive with a surge of joy unlike any in weeks.

Feichin knelt before Owen. The other Fae circled around, their faces solemn. Aria thought a few of them looked slightly confused, though she couldn't read their expressions as well as she could read Owen's.

"Speak, Feichin." Owen stood gazing down at Feichin with an expression of pride and affection.

Feichin remained on his knees, eyes downward as if he were looking at Owen's feet. But his expression told her that his thoughts were far loftier than the brittle grass beneath his knees.

"You know that I was once a Fae like you. Then I turned, unable to bear the pain and distress of captivity with a pure heart, as El commanded. You also know that Lord Owen told me how El offers grace and forgiveness through the man Jesus Christ, perfect son of El. I doubted such grace would be offered even to me, but I trusted Lord Owen's testimony, and I was redeemed.

"I know not exactly what I am now, except that in English I am a Christian. Perhaps I am a new kind of Fae; one who lives trusting in the grace of Christ rather than the mercy and justice of our older covenant.

"This knowledge of grace burns within me far hotter and far brighter than my hatred ever did. I cannot rest until other turned Fae also know that they can return to fellowship with El. They *must* know of grace!" His voice had risen until it rang like a bell, as clear and bright as the sunlight on his face. "I know not why El loves us enough to offer us grace, but I cannot doubt that he does. Not now. My restoration is proof of El's love.

"I have requested Lord Owen's consent to leave your company and bring the message of El's love and offer of grace to the dark places. The turned ones must know."

Aria sucked in her breath. *What is he doing? He's asking to leave us to go find vampires and talk to them? He'll be killed!*

Owen spoke, his voice lower and softer. "And I have given my consent and my blessing. It is a worthy mission. Such compassion is proof of El's work in Feichin's heart. Sing with me now, to give him strength and joy in the work, and to ask for El's blessing on him in the dark places. For where El is, darkness cannot remain."

Voices rose immediately, and the Fae clustered closer to Feichin. They put their hands on his shoulders and his head, and those who could not reach him put their hands on the shoulders of the Fae nearer him, as if to transfer strength and encouragement through their own bodies into his. He closed his eyes, and of all the Fae voices, his was the softest, but no less pure. When she focused on Feichin, watching his lips, she could hear his voice among the others, gentle and passionate and overflowing with hope.

Aria stood with tears in her eyes, unable to sing as the Fae could, wishing desperately she could sing for Feichin, too. *God, I can't make a beautiful sound to you. But if you listen to my heart, I'm praying for him. It's a dangerous thing that he goes to do, and he's so new to you. He's fragile. Do you see him? He's like a steel wire strung so tight it might snap at any moment, and yet he wants to go into the darkness carrying the tiny light of his salvation, as if it's enough to chase away the demons and the bloodlust and the fury.*

I know you exist, God. I know you're good. At least I know you love goodness. How could you not love Owen and Niall? And if you love Feichin, if you'll take

*him back and offer him such compassion after what he
did, if you'll fill him with your love... then you must
love me.*

*I want to be yours. I don't know how this works.
But please give me the grace you gave Feichin, the grace
that doesn't hold against me the things I've done or the
thoughts I've thought. The grace from Jesus.*

The song faded, but Aria didn't notice.

She found herself on her knees, bent forward
with her head buried in her hands. Her face felt
sticky with tears. *It's not sorrow. It's more like the
feeling of a broken piece of pottery repaired with pure
gold. The broken places in my life have been made the
most beautiful.*

She kept her eyes closed, trying to compose
herself. *I shouldn't be like this! This is Feichin's time. I
shouldn't make a scene.* But she couldn't help the
tears that kept slipping down her cheeks. Awareness of every selfish thought, every unkind word,
filled her for a split second, but then the feeling of
crushing guilt was gone, swallowed up in love so
great she caught her breath on a sob. Comfort
wrapped around her heart, overwhelming
warmth, love, compassion, and belonging.

She looked up only at a touch on her shoulder,
then another. Feichin knelt just beside her and
Owen in front of her, the other Fae surrounding
her.

Feichin spoke first, his thin face radiant with
joy. "You have found comfort in El's grace. I am
glad."

Owen's smile was even more brilliant, his eyes
catching the sun like sapphires. "And I, too, Aria."

"I'm sorry," she sniffled.

229

Feichin's smile deepened. "You have given me joy before I depart. That is a gift. I thank you." He stood gracefully, the quick strength of his movements at odds with his frail appearance. "I will depart now, Lord Owen, with your blessing."

Owen said something in Fae, his words like the reflections of moonlight on water. Feichin bowed deeply, and Owen put a hand on Feichin's head for a moment.

Feichin turned and jogged from the garden.

TINY SNOWFLAKES SWIRLED through the air, glinting in the sunlight and on the ground as the snow stuck. Aria spent an hour by herself in the garden, watching the dusting of snow accumulate on the brown grass and on the worn flagstones of the paths. She thought about God and the cross. Bartok had told her enough that she knew the cross was a disgraceful death, a criminal's death. She'd heard him read the accounts of Jesus's trial and execution in the Bible, but the accounts didn't have much gory detail. Now, thinking about redemption, she knew the cross had been a gory, bloody, horrible death. Nails and thorns and vinegar and grief that cracked the sky.

Death wasn't the end, though. Christ had conquered death and risen, alive again. As absurd as it sounded, it was true. *So what else is true? What else have I doubted that I should believe?*

She went to Bartok. He was speaking to a small group of humans, including Evrial, Eli, Levi, and Jennison. She sat near him and listened, not willing yet to interrupt him.

He was speaking, yet again, of God's grace and salvation. His face was alight with hope and compassion.

She studied the faces of those listening. Evrial listened, her expression that of familiarity and friendly skepticism. *She doesn't believe his words, but she can't stop listening. She loves him like a brother. His life is proof of his message, and yet she can't accept the explanation.* Levi was more openly grumbling, and Aria wondered why he didn't simply walk away. Eli kept his face cast down, so she couldn't read his expression. She thought he might be much like Gabriel; a man who knew the truth of God but was disillusioned, unwilling to place trust in a God who let tragedy happen.

No, Gabriel believes, and in his heart, he wants to obey. He's just angry. Eli also believes but isn't certain whether he wants to trust. He may decide he doesn't like this God. He'd be like Feichin was... one who believes but chooses not to follow. Or Lachtnal. The thought made her shiver.

Why do bad things happen, God? I believe you exist, but I still don't understand!

Jennison leaned forward, his solid frame tense and eager. "And all you have to do is ask? Why would God do that? If it's true, why would God let us into heaven if we're so bad? Justice isn't served by someone else dying for us."

"But it is! It's like..." Bartok blew out his breath as he thought. "Some of the church language has lost its impact through familiarity. We forget what it really means. We are guilty of sin. It's impossible to undo the sin, and we can't simply be forgiven in the way we normally use the word today, to overlook the offense. For justice, the penalty *must* be paid. Think of a crime, a violation of the law. A just judge, even one who is the father of the criminal, will not simply ignore the lawful penalty, even if his son is repentant. That would prove nothing other than that the law is of no consequence. But he *is* willing to pay the penalty himself, in place of his son. Even if the penalty is huge.

"There's a phrase 'covered in the blood' or 'covered by the blood' of Jesus. It's a figurative phrase, of course, because we weren't born when Jesus died. But think about what it means. We are covered in the blood of Christ. When God looks at us, he sees the blood of his perfect son—he sees the evidence that the penalty for our sin has been paid. It's like a receipt for something from a store that you've already bought. It's proof that it's already been paid for. You can't be made to pay for it again. Now imagine that someone else paid for it and gave you the receipt. You can walk out with that item. It's not stolen, it's paid for, but you aren't the one who paid for it." He looked down. "Is it fair? Not really. Not to Christ. But it's generous, and it's good, and it's love. Love greater than we can comprehend. How can we not want to serve a God like that?"

Levi grunted and got up. "If you say so." He grimaced and walked away. Bartok watched him go, sorrow in his eyes.

Jennison grunted, too. "Well, he may not believe you. But I do." He swallowed as if forcing a lump down his throat. "It's pretty unbelievable, I admit. But, if it's what makes you the way you are, I'll take it, too. If that's what God's like, I'll serve him, too."

Evrial watched, her eyes wondering, while Jennison and Bartok prayed together. She watched, and she listened.

Aria prayed for her.

AT LONG LAST, Bartok finished speaking with everyone. He'd prayed with several people, spent hours in conversation about sin, death, and salvation. He'd remained calm and polite, even when others grew frustrated by his answers. Now, the last one thanked him and turned away.

Aria thought Bartok would go find something to eat. He must have been hungry; he'd skipped lunch because he was praying with someone, and then he'd been drawn into another conversation. He hadn't protested when one man left to get dinner and another took his place, wiping the last bit of soup from his bowl with a bite of bread. Now it was long past nightfall, although the light never reached their underground refuge.

Bartok sighed and stretched his shoulders. He rubbed his hands across his face, pressing the heels of his hands into his eyes.

Perhaps he has a headache. I bet he does. He has to be hungry.

He stared at the floor in front of him for a few seconds, as if he was too exhausted to make a decision about what to do next. Then he closed his eyes.

He's going to pray again? The thought caught at her heart. *Hasn't he done enough for God today?* Even as she thought it, she realized the question was foolish. *No. There's never "enough." What God has done for us deserves everything we do and everything we are.*

Aria filled a plate, looped the strap of a thermos over her arm, and picked up an apple.

She sat down beside Bartok. He didn't move at first, his breathing steady and calm. His eyes were closed, and she took the opportunity to study his face. At first, she'd seen his face as sharp and slightly intimidating, his eyes set a little too deep to look entirely friendly. Virtuous, perhaps, but not obviously kind. Now she knew better. Long brown lashes brushed his cheeks. He was a little pale, but she thought it was probably the result of a winter spent mostly underground and a few missed meals rather than any real illness.

Bartok opened his eyes and turned to her, already smiling. "Good evening."

"I thought you might be hungry."

He glanced down, noticing the plate she offered. "That's for me?" His smile widened. "That's thoughtful. Thank you."

"I figured I owed you a meal."

"You don't owe me anything."

"Or a date."

He froze, then glanced at her. "I'll take one of those."

Aria grinned. "All right." She found herself unaccountably shy, discarding words one after another. "I meant to tell you yesterday. I... decided to trust God. I prayed like you said, like Colonel Grenidor did."

Joy broke over his face, fierce and beautiful. "Praise God!"

CHAPTER 18

DANDRA SAT IN A CORNER, a little apart from everyone else. Aria thought she looked lonely and sat down beside her.

"Are you doing all right?" she asked. "I know it's a lot to think about."

Dandra sighed. "It is." She picked at a thread on her worn trousers. "I haven't heard from my son. He was a missionary somewhere in the Empire; I didn't know it until recently, but he's been here a while, I think."

Aria frowned. "Do you think something happened to him?"

Dandra swallowed. "I think he was arrested."

"Oh." Aria didn't know what to say. Hadn't Gabriel mentioned that Christians were being held somewhere? Gabriel and Bartok had argued about a rescue.

Dandra brushed a silent tear from her cheek. "I'm sorry."

Aria put an arm around her shoulder. Dandra shuddered and leaned into her embrace. The older woman drew away after only a moment and said with a forced smile, "You've had an interesting few months."

"Very." Aria frowned. "I'm sorry, Dandra. Is there anything I can do?"

"I doubt it. Do you know anything about the arrests? Any names?"

"No." Aria frowned. "I wonder if Grenidor would."

She got up to find him. He'd withdrawn to a corner with Blakeley and Burke and appeared to be deep in discussion with them. She waited a few steps away, unwilling to interrupt.

He turned to her. "Did you need something?"

"We just had a few questions for you. Do you mind?"

He nodded to the others and followed her to where Dandra sat. She'd had her eyes closed, her hands clasped on her knees. Aria imagined she was praying, but she looked up when they approached, her expression that of wary hope.

Grenidor sat in front of her, his movements a little stiff. He stuck out a hand. "Paul Grenidor. You had a question for me?"

Dandra shook his hand with a skeptical frown. "You're Imperial Army?"

"I was. I'm not planning on going back." He cleared his throat.

"Do you know anything about the Christians who've been arrested?" Dandra asked.

Grenidor seemed to tense just a little. "I... yes. A little. Why?"

Dandra's voice was a little unsteady. "Have you heard anything about Oliver Highchurch? That was the name my son was using."

Grenidor stopped breathing. "Oliver High-church?" he whispered.

Dandra nodded, her pale eyes wide. "Do you know anything about him? Is he all right?"

Grenidor's shoulders drooped, then he met her eyes. "I'm sorry. He's dead. He died about a week ago."

"How did he die?" Her voice caught, and she stopped for a moment. "Was he tortured? Do you know of his friends? Any other names?"

Grenidor closed his eyes. It took long, uncomfortable moments for him to compose himself, his breathing ragged in the tense silence. When he finally spoke, his voice rasped. "He was tortured. He was executed in secret by gunshot. I don't know who his friends were, but I remember a few names. Myra Solomon. Angela and Devin Carlisle. Jennifer... Tate or Bates or something. And Louis something. No, Christopher Lewis. There were others, but those are the names I remember."

Dandra bent forward to bury her face in her hands. Her shoulders shook, but she made no sound.

Aria brushed at the tears slipping down her cheeks. "How do you know?" she whispered. "Couldn't he still be alive? Are you sure?"

Grenidor closed his eyes and turned his face away from her. She thought he didn't mean to answer, but finally he said, "No. He's dead." He took a deep breath. "I'm sorry. I ordered the execution myself, and I watched it done. It was fast."

Dandra looked up. "You did it yourself?"

"I ordered it done. I was there when the sentence was carried out." Grenidor's voice shook. "I'm sorry. It's one of many things I regret."

Dandra stared at him, tears streaking her soft face. "Get out of my sight," she whispered.

Grenidor sucked in his breath and stared at her, his eyes hard. For a moment, Aria feared he meant to strike her, but then he rose abruptly and stomped away.

Aria put one arm around Dandra's shoulders, feeling the older woman trembling as she wept. "I'm sorry," she whispered.

"Just go away."

Aria drew back, unsure whether to comply.

"Leave me alone. Please."

DANDRA SAT WITH HER FACE hidden for nearly an hour, and then she stared into space, not meeting anyone's gaze. Aria imagined that the air around her felt colder and more desolate; it was as if even the quiet sounds of people moving did not intrude on her grief.

Sometime in the afternoon, Owen approached her. He knelt beside her, and she looked at him with shadowed eyes.

"What do you want?" she whispered.

"I heard of your grief. I will sing for you if you wish." Owen's voice was so soft it barely reached Aria's ears.

"Is it gossip? Was he gloating about it?" Dandra's voice rose. "He was my son!"

"He regrets it." Owen glanced over his shoulder. Niamh rose immediately, as if summoned. Then he looked back at Dandra. "But your grievance is not primarily against Grenidor. It is against El, for El has permitted this sorrow. My sister Niamh has also grieved more deeply than many. She will sing with me."

Dandra blinked, focusing on Owen with reddened eyes. "What do you mean? Why do you talk of singing?"

"It is how we commune with El. You refer to El as God."

Niamh knelt beside Owen, her movement graceful and light. "You grieve because you miss him, yet you know he is with El. I also grieve. My husband was murdered by the Empire. My son lost his tongue. I know what it is to grieve. I know what it is to be so angry you cannot breathe." Her beautiful voice cracked, and she closed her eyes for a moment. She licked her lips and continued. "But in your grief and in your anger, do not hate. Do not judge them as unworthy of El's grace. Because we, none of us, are worthy of what El offers."

Dandra's nostrils flared, and she glared at Niamh. "Murdered? Was it a clean death? Or was it the torture they visited upon my son? I would have died for him! I have spent the last hours wishing I could have!"

Niamh's eyes flashed in a moment's anger, and she whispered softly, "They were testing a new technique to see if it killed us. They bound him in a chair with getlaril so that he could not move, and then they burned him alive.

239

"We do not die of asphyxiation as humans do. We believe breathing is a vestigial reflex for us; it is unnecessary but unavoidable. We also do not die of blood loss, though we feel the effects of it. I listened to him scream for hours, and I felt his screaming even after his voice was gone."

Owen put a silent hand on Niamh's shoulder, and she shuddered. Her voice dropped further, nearly inaudible. "Do not speak to me of anger, as if I know it not. I have experienced depths of fury you cannot fathom. Yet I have not ceased to sing to El. El is the only solace for grief such as this."

Dandra held her gaze for long, tense heartbeats. Then she bent forward and sobbed.

Owen's voice rose first, his eyes soft on his sister's face. Niamh was trembling, breathing hard as if fighting a thousand emotions. Still singing, Owen put one hand over Niamh's clenched fist. She turned to him and buried her head in the curve of his shoulder, her shoulders shaking.

Owen's voice rose alone, pure and perfect in the golden air. Aria glanced at the other Fae, wondering why they did not join his song.

Cillian's mouth was locked in a grimace of heart-pain so deep it might have been physical. Ardghal looked quietly furious, his lips pressed together. Sorcha had dropped her head, letting her pale brown hair fall over her face, hiding her expression. Her hands were twisted together in her lap. Aideen sat beside her, her head nearly touching Sorcha's, and appeared to be whispering to her.

Owen glanced at Aria and then away, just a split-second of his piercing blue gaze. In that moment, she saw a thousand things: a barren hillside

with three corpse-laden crosses, an olive grove, a
cave with a folded white cloth, a river running
over smooth stones, a mountain dusted with glittering snow. Owen dove from the top of a white
cliff into the deep waves at the bottom, emerging
long minutes later, dark curls plastered to his
head, nearly covering his eyes.

Aria blinked, and she was again in the basilica.
Owen sang, his eyes closed, the song weaving
upon itself. His chest rose and fell, as if the effort
taxed him sorely.

Niall crept to his side, putting one hand on
Owen's shoulder as if in support. Owen's voice
rose, his song wilder and impossibly beautiful. He
caught a breath, almost hiding his wince of pain,
the song never fading.

His song was a tapestry of sound that wrapped
around Aria and Dandra and Niamh, comfort and
peace and love, embracing the pain and giving it
up, letting it go like water.

Cillian's voice joined Owen's in a quiet harmony. Then Niamh's voice finally rose. Her voice
was unwavering, yet Aria could hear her tears in
it. Then, at last, the others; Ardghal, Sorcha, Lorcan, Aideen, even Aodhagan.

Owen's voice disappeared from the song. Aria
opened her eyes to see him collapse. Cillian
grasped at his arm, startled, but could not break
his fall. Only Niall was close enough to catch him,
small hands on Owen's shoulders shifting him
even as he fell, so that his head landed across
Niall's slender arm.

Glittering words in the air above Owen's body
said: *Sing. Sing for Dandra and for Lord Owen and for
my mother. Sing because El is good. Sing for love and*

241

joy. Sing for sorrow and pain. Even when our voices fail, we should sing.

THE GOLDEN LIGHT FADED. Shadows grew in the corners of the room, spreading slowly across the marble floor. Eli and Grenidor lit lamps and set them about on tables.

It had been hours since Owen lost consciousness, and he still hadn't moved.

"Is he all right?" Dandra finally asked. She'd gotten up to pace, trying to keep warm in the cold, still air, and she stopped close to Aria's shoulder.

Niall half-shrugged, not looking at her.

Beside Owen's shoulder, Cillian knelt, his forehead pressed against the cool stone floor.

Aria felt Cillian's singing, though it was inaudible to her ears. His voice felt stretched thin and hollow, made of pure sorrow, pleading to El for his brother to return. To heal.

Owen's soft breathing stopped, silent for one heart-rending moment. Then he gave a weak cough. Ever so gently, Cillian turned him to his side. Owen coughed again, a little more strongly, and spat a mouthful of blood onto the floor. His eyes still closed, he licked blood from his lips. He murmured something, his voice almost inaudible.

Niall sucked in his breath and shook his head.

Cillian snarled, "Speak not of such things, brother! It is not time yet."

Owen seemed to curl into himself. He made a soft sound that might have been either a groan or a word in one of the Fae languages, barely enunciated.

Cillian reacted as if he had been slapped; his pale face grew whiter and he bowed his head.

Dandra glanced at Aria, her eyes wide as saucers. "What happened?"

Owen's breathing caught again and then steadied. The tension in his shoulders eased. He was so limp he must have lost consciousness again.

Aria didn't realize she was crying until Dandra scooted closer, wrapping her arms around Aria's shoulders.

"I don't understand," Aria whispered, her face buried in Dandra's coat. "I don't understand." *I don't understand. Why is this happening to him? It's so unfair!*

She raised her head only moments later, brushing the tears from her cheeks.

Cillian remained on his knees beside Owen's motionless body. His face was hidden, but his shoulders shook as he silently wept.

Niall met her gaze, tear trails glinting on his own pale cheeks. His words made of light appeared between them. *He said I should choose my heir.*

Aria's eyes filled with tears again. "But he can't be dying! He was walking around before!"

Perhaps he is not. He feels he is. The pain is more than it was. Cillian spoke in anger and desperate love, though not in judgment. Lord Owen said, "Trust." I..." The boy looked away, brushing his cheeks dry with one trembling hand. He chewed his lower lip and finally looked back at them. *Cillian weeps because he feels he has no more trust for El. He trusts Lord Owen, and if Lord Owen dies... I am too young to lead. Yet Lord Owen has entrusted me with his authority as his heir. What am I to do?*

Niall caught his breath, hiding his face for a moment behind his hands. Again he steadied himself. *I trust. I trust El. I trust Lord Owen. And I will obey.*

Dandra was trembling beside Aria. "Who are they, Aria? They are so much more than we are. So much more than we could ever be."

Niamh appeared for the first time; Aria hadn't noticed her absence until now. She put a hand on Owen's shoulder and bent close to his face, inhaling his breath.

"Getlaril is coming out through his lungs; that is the cause of the blood." Her voice was low. "Blood in his lungs will not kill him, though the getlaril still threatens his life. Coughing to expel it may help his recovery."

"Or not." Cillian's voice was rough.

Niamh sighed, her expression defeated. "Or not."

"IS THERE NOTHING that can be done for him, Bartok? He's still in so much pain." Aria felt the tears in her voice threatening to overflow. *He could be dying! But I don't want to say that. If I say it, it makes it real. God, don't let him die!*

He frowned thoughtfully. "I doubt it, but maybe Colonel Grenidor knows something."

Aria trailed him toward Grenidor. Emotions warred within her, and the sight of his tired, unfriendly face made her heart ache.

"Owen is in a great deal of pain from getlaril in his body. Is there nothing that can be done for

him? No way to counter the effects?" Bartok said
without preamble.

Grenidor jumped at the doctor's voice, having
apparently been lost in his own unpleasant
thoughts. "Not that I know of."

"Nothing?" Bartok's voice rose a little, the first
sign of anger that Aria had ever seen in him. One
hand clenched into a fist, then relaxed. "That's
rather irresponsible, isn't it? To administer poisons
without a known antidote?"

Grenidor's face hardened. "What do you know
of—"

"I'm sorry," Bartok said, his voice tight. "I
shouldn't have spoken so harshly. You've been
forgiven for it, and I shouldn't throw it in your
face."

Grenidor blinked at him, his defensiveness
fading. "What then? You just forget about it?"
Skepticism filled his voice.

"No. We're not really capable of that, are we?
Humans, I mean. But I pretend, even to myself,
that I've forgotten. I never bring it up, never throw
it in your face, and try to leave it out of any internal debates when I question whether to trust you."
Bartok sighed heavily and flopped down in the
chair beside Grenidor, one long leg bouncing up
and down in tired jitters. "You don't know anything that might help?"

Grenidor shook his head and ran one hand
over his short hair. "We never thought about using
it internally. There was never any reason to need
an antidote."

Bartok sighed and glanced at Aria. *I'm sorry*, he
mouthed.

CILLIAN SANG OVER OWEN, his song sad and forlorn. Afterwards he wiped gray powder from the pale skin of Owen's back and one of his legs. Still curled on one side, Owen coughed at long intervals. Sometimes he brought up a little blood, sometimes he didn't. He did not wake.

Niall, Niamh, and Cillian took turns sitting by Owen. Sometimes they sang softly, but otherwise, they held their vigil in silence.

Early in the morning, Aithne, Feichin's daughter, crept to Niamh's side. They conversed in low tones beside Owen's limp body for almost an hour, and then Aithne's questions must have subsided. She sang, her voice like crystal.

Aria blinked, and saw a pale doe picking her way across a carpet of new-fallen snow. The doe raised her head and looked mournfully at Aria, deep brown eyes in stark contrast to the snow dusting her coat.

Owen coughed and moaned softly. Niamh wiped a tear from her eye and leaned close to him.

He blinked back to awareness, murmuring something to Niamh as he coughed again. She darted away, returning with the first aid kit. She opened it and pulled out a cloth bandage, which she handed to Owen. He coughed, spit out a mouthful of blood, then wiped the inside of his mouth with the bandage. It came out smeared with blood, the blood spotted with almost invisibly small dark specks.

"How do you feel?" Aria couldn't help moving closer.

Owen took a slow breath and let it out, along with another faint cough. "Perhaps better?" he murmured. He licked his lips and grimaced. "Tastes vile."

"Would you like something to drink?"

"Water, please."

Niamh helped him sit up. He leaned on her, stifling another cough. He murmured to Niamh, and she answered him, but Aria didn't know what they said. Questions, she imagined, probably about Dandra and the others.

CHAPTER 19

BLAKELEY, BURKE, AND JACKSON sat at the worn tables with Gabriel, Eli, Grenidor, and Bartok. Owen sat hidden against the wall some yards away, pale as marble, surrounded by Cillian, Niamh, Niall, and a few other Fae. Aria hesitated, indecisive, then finally sat by Bartok, though she wasn't sure she had any reason to be included in the discussion.

"I have to ask, Colonel. What made you try a getlaril solution?" Burke said.

Grenidor swallowed. "Do we have to talk about this now?"

Burke frowned. "Well, no, but I want to understand what we're dealing with here. I thought I understood our project, and now I'm not sure I know what we were trying to accomplish."

Grenidor's jaw tightened. "I went too far. Owen wouldn't give me the information I wanted, and time was running out. I wanted to know where Gabriel and the resistance were. And... something else."

"What else?" Burke frowned.

Grenidor sighed, and the sound caught at Aria's heart. He sounded so broken. "Some of the vampires had mentioned dark ones. They sounded afraid. So I tried to get Owen to tell me how to contact the dark ones. I didn't know what they were. I shouldn't have asked. Owen didn't tell me, then or later. But Feichin did later, and I wish he hadn't." He shivered and ran one hand over his short gray hair. "I talked to one, and it was the worst decision I've ever made. Owen was protecting me. Us. Humans."

Aria glanced at Owen. He made a tiny movement, as if he meant to rise and say something, but then stopped, only looking at Grenidor with compassion on his face. *I wonder if I would have seen that two months ago? I think the expression is so subtle I would have missed it before. But now it is obvious. Do I just know him better now, or have I actually changed? Or has he changed?*

"But why a solution? What made you think of that?" Burke pressed.

Grenidor shrugged, keeping his eyes down. "I knew getlaril was painful for them. I hadn't found any other method that got results."

"Any lasting effects?" Burke leaned forward. "I wish you'd consulted me or even Dr. Pyorski before you did it. What concentration did you use?"

Grenidor frowned. "Why are you so interested in this? What difference does it make?"

Burke rubbed the back of his neck thoughtfully. "Well, you know how we came up with getlaril as a restraint for vampires, don't you?"

Grenidor shook his head.

Bartok said quietly, "Yes, there are lasting effects. Is there an antidote?"

Burke frowned. "Well, maybe. At least for humans. Before I worked on the vampire program itself, I worked on the population behavior control and tracking program. What do you know about that?"

"Not enough." Gabriel and Bartok spoke at the same time.

"Basically, the Empire, or the Revolution at the time, wanted a way to control people's behavior. Not too much, you understand. Just enough to keep them calm and not cause trouble while the leaders got things settled." He frowned. "Well, that was the reason we were given. I think they got accustomed to a docile population." He grimaced. "I don't know if I'd work on the program now, but I did then. It seemed an innocent enough idea, keep people from causing trouble, keep them from asking too many questions, keep the violence to a minimum. We didn't want to affect people's behavior much; it wasn't meant to be a dramatic change. Just a slight dampening, I guess. Trackers were a given; leadership was insistent on knowing where everyone was. We didn't want everyone to get it. Political leadership, surgeons, and a few others were exempt; there were certain people in certain positions who needed to remain completely alert. Drugging a large population, even with best of intentions, was problematic. We couldn't mix it into the water or food because controlling the dosage was too difficult, and besides, we didn't want everyone affected.

"During the last years of the Revolution, the drugs even affected population growth. You've seen all the empty buildings, right? Some people left, but another contributing factor is that the birth rate fell precipitously for about ten years. The first drug combinations we tried had an effect on people's urge to procreate. They *could*; they just didn't care to make the effort. So we worked on dosages and different drug cocktails, refining what we had as well as looking for new solutions. Of course, getting the population into denser housing did have benefits; the surveillance divisions really liked that. But we kept working on the drugs."

"Last years of the Revolution? What?"

Burke shrugged uncomfortably. "We experimented surreptitiously before the Empire was the Empire, wherever Rev Forces had control." He gave a thin, mirthless smile. "We, my team and I, developed a drug that could be delivered as a slow-release metallic salt. Implanted under the skin, a tiny piece would dissolve over about twenty years at a predictable rate. The dosage was tiny enough that children and adults could receive the same implant with no danger to children from overdose and no decrease in efficacy even for larger adults.

"It was a beautiful solution. We used it as the shell of the trackers for the vast majority of the population. Some people, hand-selected by the program directors and political leadership, received trackers without the drug-shell; there were titanium-shell ones as well."

Gabriel said, "Wait, so the trackers actually *did* drug people?"

"Most of the time, yes. But guards, researchers, surgeons, etc.... We got the titanium-shell ones, with no effect on cognitive function." Burke sighed and then continued, "We called the metallic salt Crawfordium. It was kind of a joke, just a nod to the researcher who discovered it. He wouldn't ever tell us how he discovered it either, which really ticked off some people.

"We tried it on a vampire to see if it would have the same effect as on a human; maybe it would make him more docile, perhaps even controllable. But he reacted completely differently, exhibiting pain and other symptoms. Given how aggressive they could be, how dangerous... it wasn't the result we were hoping for, but it was useful. Later we realized it impeded their use of magic, too. It was the perfect material for cell walls and other restraints. They called it getlaril, and we gradually adopted the term."

Bartok leaned forward. "Then you must have an antidote! No attempt at wide-scale drugging would have been approved without some kind of antidote."

Burke rocked back, as if surprised by Bartok's intensity. "Well, yes, more or less. Once the salt is absorbed in the body, it can't be entirely removed. It is excreted over about twenty years. You can decrease the amount in the body by removing the remaining bit of getlaril, but whatever was absorbed remains in the body until it is excreted naturally. Years, at least, even after the source is removed. *However*," he said, "you're right. We can neutralize it, if necessary. Heavy doses of vitamin

C render the acid biologically inert. The salt bonds to part of the ascorbic acid. You have to keep taking the C until the drug is excreted, but it works. It's basically like 'undrugging' the subject. I think we decided that a dose of about four grams a day for the first few days, then twenty-five hundred milligrams a day until the getlaril was dissolved and excreted. Years."

Bartok raised his eyebrows. "That's a lot. You didn't have negative responses to that?"

Burke shrugged. "We didn't test it extensively on humans, but we didn't see any. Overdoses of C are well tolerated, though."

"How fast did it work?"

"Injected C worked in about twenty minutes, I think. The oral dose worked in maybe an hour or two? Something like that."

Bartok stood. "Right then. I'll be back."

"What are you doing?" Burke looked up.

"To get some vitamin C."

Burke blinked. "Why?"

Grenidor buried his face in his hands. "Just… keep talking, Burke. Blakeley and Jackson, jump in if you think there's something else we need to know."

Bartok turned in Owen's general direction, though he didn't seem to see them yet. "Lord Owen?"

Cillian stepped forward; he must have hidden Bartok because Burke and the others blinked, then looked around nervously.

The young Fae drew Bartok forward to meet a group of waiting Fae. "Dr. Bartok, my brother Lord Owen suffers greatly. Please tell us how to find this substance that may help him."

"I should go."

"We are faster and can cover more ground. Besides, you are needed here." Cillian's voice shook with emotion. "Please, Dr. Bartok. Tell us how to help him."

Bartok nodded acquiescence. "I'll write it for you." He shoved a hand in his pocket, looking for a scrap of paper, then smiled at Niall's proffered notebook. "Vitamin C comes in a number of forms and concentrations. Pharmacies may have it as a supplement. It will say Vitamin C on the bottle. It's also sold as ascorbic acid in grocery stores for canning; no one cans food much these days, but you might find it in one of the small ethnic shops as a powder or tablets. You can also get some natural foods high in vitamin C; look for red or green Bell peppers, cantaloupe, citrus fruits like oranges and lemons, even pineapple. It's hard to find those fresh, though, and he needs a lot. Better to look for powder and pills if you can." He hesitated. "May I see him?"

Cillian frowned uncertainly, but nodded. He moved aside, revealing Owen slumped against the wall. Bartok knelt in front of him, Aria at his side.

Owen's eyes opened, and he straightened a little. "Thank you for your assistance, Dr. Bartok," he murmured. He coughed, his body tensing almost imperceptibly as if fighting pain. "Is there any danger to my people if they search for this substance?"

"Not that I am aware of, aside from the usual." Bartok looked closer. "Can I look at your eyes for a moment?"

Owen met his gaze, bright cold blue and warm brown holding steady.

"Are you dizzy?" Bartok asked.

Owen blinked slowly, then one corner of his mouth lifted in a faint smile. "No more than yesterday."

Bartok's eyes narrowed slightly, and he nodded. He turned to Cillian. "I'll do what I can. Be careful."

Cillian nodded.

"Stay, Cillian," said Owen. "I wish to speak with you."

"Send the others?" pleaded the younger Fae.

Owen nodded. Cillian gestured, and a dozen Fae sprinted away. Cillian knelt beside Owen, eyes solemn and expression attentive.

CHAPTER 20

GRENIDOR PACED ALL MORNING. He spent an hour with Bartok, learning about God and what he was to do with his new life. The idea of redemption seemed fantastic and unbelievable. The sense of peace that had overwhelmed him in the tunnel had faded, leaving him tense. Guilt pressed upon him again.

Finally, he sat beside Bartok. He leaned forward, burying his face in his hands. "I don't feel saved. I don't feel like I'm good. I want to be different, but I think I'm just drowning." The words were nearly inaudible. He wasn't sure whether he wanted even Bartok to hear.

"You're not good. That's not the point." Bartok leaned forward too, resting his elbows on his knees. "I mean, sure, we should try to walk in the light of God, live according to God's will, but we fail. We all fail. You're not uniquely bad in that.

The point is that when God looks at you now, he doesn't see your failures. He sees that you've been forgiven."

Grenidor frowned into the shadows between his hands.

Gabriel called, "Bartok? We need you for a minute."

Bartok gave Grenidor a reassuring thump on the shoulder as he stood. "Pray about it."

"I don't know how to pray."

"Just talk to God, silently if you want. Listen, too. I'll be back."

CHAPTER 21

BARTOK'S LONG LEGS carried him to their group in a moment. "What do you need?" He frowned at Gabriel.

"Dandra's concerned about the Christians who've been arrested. We're considering a rescue mission and determining if we have enough volunteers. Evrial will go, Jennison, maybe a couple of others. I'll go."

Bartok sighed and rolled his shoulders. "What's the plan?"

"We don't have one yet. I thought we'd ask Grenidor if he knew where they're being kept. We don't even know that." Gabriel looked down at his hands. "How is he?"

Bartok half-shrugged. "He's... all right. A bit shaken up." He hesitated and continued, "He could use some prayer."

Gabriel ran a finger over a wrinkle near the knee in his pants. "I guess so." He sighed. "You want to pray?"

Bartok held his gaze for a moment and then nodded. He bowed his head, and for a moment, everyone was still. He prayed for wisdom for Gabriel, for peace for them all, for the men and women of their party who had not accepted Christ, for Grenidor to find peace in the love of God, and for their group to find courage.

Aria, sitting beside Bartok, snuck a peek from beneath her eyelashes. Gabriel scowled, his eyes closed, as if he wanted to do anything but pray for Grenidor; yet at times, his lips moved in silent prayer. *He's so torn. I wonder what happened between them.* Bartok's long fingers were laced together, his right thumb rubbing along his left in an unconscious rhythm. His voice was low and intense, and Aria found her attention snapped back to the prayer as he mentioned her name.

"—be brave, Lord, and give her peace as she walks between two peoples and two worlds." He stopped, as if suddenly considering his words. "And give me courage, because I need it." He hesitated again, the silence drawing out. "Amen."

He didn't look up immediately, merely studying his hands. Then he rubbed his hands across his face. He looked up. "Do we have enough people?"

Grenidor interrupted them. "Excuse me…"

Gabriel raised his eyebrows.

"Is there a way to get a message back to someone? Blakeley wants to check in with the guard they left to see what kind of a pursuit we should expect. I'm surprised we haven't already had to move." He glanced away, as if he didn't want to meet Gabriel's eyes. "And to make sure he's all right."

Gabriel frowned. "Not easily. Unless the Fae want to do it..." He glanced at Aria.

Aria licked her lips and frowned. A movement caught her eye, and a moment later, Cillian knelt beside her.

"You ask whether we will carry a message for you?" His voice had a dangerous edge. "As if we are in your service?"

"No!" Gabriel shook his head hurriedly. "Only if you want to know what kind of pursuit we should prepare for."

But Cillian had already raised his head, as if listening. His gaze flicked back to rest on Gabriel again. "I spoke out of my authority. It pleases my brother Lord Owen to offer this service, provided Colonel Grenidor will vouch that the guard is unlikely to initiate violence with the messenger."

Grenidor swallowed. "I don't know the guard. Only Blakeley does."

Cillian turned away and stalked toward Blakeley. "And you? Will you speak for the guard? Will a messenger be able to speak with him?"

Blakeley startled, his hand going to his holster before he deliberately clasped his hands behind himself in a parade rest position. "He's a good kid. I think he'd listen if you didn't scare him too badly first."

Cillian's teeth gleamed as he smiled. "Then, provided you have an address, I will take the message to him at home."

They didn't have an exact address, but Jackson said Rink would get off late shift at three in the morning. He'd walk north and catch the bus at the corner.

"He's about my height, blond, big shoulders. He's not dumb, but he has a face that makes you think he is." Jackson's description made Aria smile, but Cillian merely looked confused.

"Will you be able to find him?" Jackson asked.

"Yes. Blond, big shoulders, will board a bus on the corner north of the Eastborn main entrance."

Jackson looked equally confused. "You'll ride the bus?"

Cillian frowned. "Should I not? They will not notice me. I can ride on the outside or run beside it if it seems safer."

Jackson blinked. "If you say so."

Cillian tilted his head and studied Jackson, as if gauging his honesty. He opened his mouth, but then closed it again without saying anything. He stepped back. A startled expression crossed Jackson's face as Cillian hid himself.

OWEN SAT AGAINST A WALL, one leg stretched out in front of him and the other bent. At long intervals, he coughed. Sometimes, he brought up a little blood, which he spat into a handkerchief. His face was white as marble, and the blood on his lips stood out in horrible contrast before he wiped it away.

Aria had woken from disturbing dreams to find herself staring at the ceiling. The intricate design was almost lost in the darkness, and she narrowed her eyes, picking out glints of gold and white amid the deeper shades. She sighed and turned to study Owen surreptitiously. Niamh sat beside him, her face showing silent sympathy. Niall was curled near Owen's outstretched leg, asleep. She turned her gaze back to the ceiling, one side faintly lit by the moonlight coming through the rose window. A few weeks ago, she wouldn't have been able to see even that much; her eyesight was definitely improving.

Cillian returned in the small hours of the morning. He jogged to Owen and spoke in a low voice. Aria couldn't make out his words, but she saw Owen's nod. He glanced at her, as if knowing she watched, and smiled faintly.

Without words, she felt the gentle brush of his presence, his comfort and reassurance. She sighed and pulled the blanket up a little higher.

IN THE MORNING, Aodhagan sat in front of her and motioned toward her head with a tentative, hopeful expression.

"You want to share memories with me?"

He studied her face, unsure what she meant but obviously trying to understand. He touched his own temple and then motioned toward her again.

She nodded.

His small hand was cool on her temple, and a moment later she looked through his eyes.

Aodhagan sat on a rock in the middle of a river only a few feet from the top of a thundering waterfall. Beside him, his—their—father stood shirtless in hip-deep water. His dark thistledown hair and his lean, coffee-brown body glistened with droplets that shone like diamonds in the brilliant sun. His wild, joyous eyes gleamed gold. He spoke, his voice barely audible over the roar of the falling water.

The infant Aodhagan shook his head. In his memory, she felt him make a tiny whimper of suppressed fear. Their father smiled and bent to kiss his forehead, then stepped closer to the waterfall. Another step and he was at the very edge, the water catching at him, nearly pulling him off the edge. He waved and leaped into the spray, disappearing from view.

Aodhagan craned forward, then slipped on the wet stone and nearly fell into the water. He cried out in terror, clinging to the rock.

A minute later, their father appeared on the riverbank, drenched, his hair a bit more chaotic than usual, still defying gravity. He grinned, all wildness and joy, like a spirit of the woods. He waded into the water and held out a hand to Aodhagan.

The tiny boy took it, clinging to his father like a second skin. In his memory, Aria felt the strength of their father's muscles moving beneath his cold skin, the love that flowed through Aodhagan's grip and their father's arm around him. Their father spoke into Aodhagan's ear, and though she couldn't understand his words, she knew they were kind. He spoke encouragement and reassurance.

Their father took Aodhagan to the edge of the waterfall and leapt off.

Aodhagan shrieked in terror as they fell, his voice cut off in an instant as he clapped his mouth shut against the rushing water. Aria heard Aodhagan's heartbeat in his ears as if it was her own, his terror barely beginning to edge into exhilaration when they plunged beneath the icy water at the bottom. Their father's strong arm didn't lose his grip as he surged through the churning water to the surface and then to the shore.

The memory shifted. This time, Aodhagan leapt off the top of the waterfall alone. He screamed with joy, his tiny arms and legs flailing in the air. Although he looked like a human baby, he swam with confidence toward the shore. Their mother waited, Aria's tiny figure cradled in her arms.

The memory faded, and Aria blinked back to the present. Aodhagan smiled at her shyly.

SUNLIGHT FILTERED DOWN the cold concrete stairwell, gilding the dust motes in the air. Aria sat against the wall near the bottom.

Evrial peeked around the door. "You want company?"

Aria shrugged. "Sure."

The older woman slipped around the door and settled beside Aria with a sigh. "You all right?"

"Mostly."

There was a gust of wind above, sending a chill through Aria's coat.

Evrial shifted. "Aria, we need to talk…"

"What?" Aria turned to study the older woman's expression. "Have I done something wrong?"

"No. Not exactly. Not on purpose." Evrial glanced at her. "So how are things with you and Tobias?"

Aria blinked. "Bartok? We're friends. We talk sometimes." She smiled a little. "What does that have to do with anything?"

Evrial rubbed a hand along her trouser leg, letting her thumbnail catch at the worn seam in the fabric. "This is a small group. You know that. We're isolated and often tense. Sometimes we're very depressed, with occasional moments of excitement. Most of the group, excluding Gabriel and myself, are rather young, although I suppose you're even younger. They're full of... energy, if you know what I mean. There are complicated group dynamics, with more emotions running under the surface than you might see at first." She rolled her shoulders as if rolling out tension. "Everyone has a gun. We're often in situations where it would be bad to be unhappy with life, or with someone else, or with someone else's life. It's important to keep the ship sailing on an even keel."

The older woman glanced at Aria. "Do you know what a loose cannon is?"

"It's dangerous?" Aria offered.

Evrial nodded. "The term dates back to the days of sailing ships. The cannons were tied down with ropes that let them recoil and also let them be drawn back inside the ship to reload by stuffing the powder and balls down their muzzles. They were on wheels, so they could move as needed, but tied so they couldn't roll around when the ship tossed to and fro. They were heavy, as you can imagine. A loose cannon could do a lot of damage. Kill people. Even tip the ship over.

"The people who have been in our group a long time know how the group works. They know the rules. Attachments form. Attachments break. People have liaisons, or don't, for their own reasons. We all know how to keep the group cohesive and the ship on an even keel.

"But you don't know the ropes. You aren't tied carefully like the rest of us. You roll. You're rocking the boat." Evrial turned to meet Aria's wide eyes.

"But I'm not doing anything! Am I?" Aria's voice shook. "What am I doing wrong?"

Evrial sighed heavily. "Everyone likes Toby Bartok, and everyone respects him. He's a good man and a good doctor. He's been approached by a few women, but he's never reciprocated any advances, much less initiated any of his own. This works out pretty well, except perhaps for him. Some women mope around a little when they don't make any headway, but they don't see anyone else doing much better, so they can tell themselves that it's not them, or that maybe someday they'll succeed. The men don't mind because he's not competing with them. Since he's the doctor, this avoids a lot of complications." She clasped her hands in her lap and looked down at her fingers woven together.

She continued, "So now you're interested in each other. Everyone notices. Most of the women are happy enough for him, but there's an undercurrent of... not jealousy, exactly. Maybe protectiveness, colored with a little envy. Why should you catch his affection when they didn't? You're pretty and nice enough, but you're not one of us. Not yet.

"If it all goes well between you, that's fine. They'll come around. But you don't know the rules, the ropes that keep the cannons safely in place." She met Aria's gaze. "If you break his heart, there will be hard feelings. Some who'd given up will rush to comfort him, hoping to catch him on the rebound. Maybe that's all right if there's only one, but there might be more than one and that means competition, and perhaps breaking other relationships... the loose cannon, breaking other cannons loose. It's chaos. I care for the tensions and the heartache, but I care more about the danger they might bring. Do you understand?"

Aria swallowed. "But we're just friends."

"Oh, you simple girl!" Evrial's laughter faded, and she sighed. "I didn't realize you were so inexperienced. His feelings are obvious to everyone. But you wouldn't know how he acts with other women, so you don't see the difference. It's amusing, I suppose, that you don't realize your interest in him." Her eyebrows drew together. "Maybe that's good. Maybe your naiveté will help others accept whatever happens. It's better than having them think you deliberately, effortlessly took what they wanted and could never attain. Just remember your actions affect everyone. Be cautious."

"I will." Aria's voice shook.

CHAPTER 22

THE RESISTANCE HAD ESTABLISHED sentry points some distance outside of every entrance to the basilica. The aboveground entrances were relatively easy to watch, but the basilica basement was connected to the network of tunnels beneath the city. The camp had been much more secure after the Fae had begun keeping watch as well; their hearing and eyesight were far more sensitive, and having the Fae spread among the tunnels helped reduce the incidence of vertril converging on their location. Prior to the Fae joining them, the sentries had stood watch in pairs, in case of vampire attack, but that was deemed unnecessary now.

Before beginning watch, the sentries let their eyes adjust to the darkness in staging zones within the tunnels but close by the camp. Bartok's routine was to drink a cup of hot water or tea if it was available and take a short nap if he needed sleep before a round of exercises to get his blood flowing. Tonight he shivered within his heavy coat and wiggled his toes against the cold. The tunnel had been deathly silent but for the distant scuttle of rats at long intervals. He stood against the wall and let his eyes close for a few moments, then opened them again, squinting at the almost imperceptible concrete of the wall across from him.

"I heard you talking earlier. I have some questions. Do you mind?" The voice was unfamiliar; the man stood some feet away, the darkness far too deep to see his face.

"No, but I'm about to go on watch."

The man's voice carried a smile. "Seems quiet enough."

Bartok shrugged one shoulder. "All right. There are sentries farther out, and I'm not on duty yet."

"Thanks." The man stuck out a hand and shook agreeably, finding Bartok's hand without any difficulty in the darkness. "Here." The smell of coffee was comfortingly familiar as the man handed him a brimming mug.

Then he settled with his shoulders against the concrete wall beside Bartok, his posture relaxed. "I heard you talking earlier about the Fae and God and all the rest. It seems you've thought about these things a great deal."

"I've studied the Bible off and on since I was young. I'm a Christian; how better to know the one I worship than to study his word? But the Fae are new to me; I'm still thinking about their place in God's creation."

The man made a thoughtful *hm* sound. "I once worked for a group that delivered the Word to those who needed to hear it. I believed the message, but I confess I never really understood it. Looking back, I don't think many of us did. You seem to have some insight, and I wonder if you'd answer a few questions."

"I can try."

"My first question is about angels."

Bartok blinked. "Angels?"

"Yes. They are mentioned in the Bible. My question is whether you believe angels can be redeemed as humans are."

Bartok frowned. "Well… we don't really know. Scripture doesn't specify."

"What do you think, though? You are a wise man. Surely you have an opinion."

"I have no way to know. Angels rejoiced and were baffled by God's plan of redemption for humanity. I've always wondered whether that meant that the concept of redemption, perhaps even of forgiveness, was unknown to them, a miracle they can comprehend no better than we can."

The man grunted. "Perhaps you are right. But what does that mean now?"

"Angels know God exists. They know he is holy and righteous and wise and powerful and perfect. They have seen him act in justice and mercy and grace and majesty. If redemption is offered to them, I would hope that they would not intentionally sin in order to experience grace. Even if their relationship with God is completely different than that of humans, they honor him by obedience, not by disobedience. We are commanded not to sin in order to magnify God's grace, and I'd think that command would apply to angels, as well."

Silence drew out, cold and desolate. Finally, the man said, "Perhaps. I believe at least some angels were created as servants. Should a servant aspire to be a son?"

Bartok hesitated. "Perhaps the analogy holds, but I doubt it entirely encompasses God's purpose for angels."

The man's sharp bark of laughter echoed in the tunnel as he murmured, "Indeed. Who can know the mind of God?"

Then he sobered, and said, "My other question is related to the Fae. The first Fae, specifically. Their physical differences may have been, *must have been*, bestowed upon them as a gift. To be stronger and faster, to heal more quickly, to see more clearly, and hear more acutely... these abilities set them apart.

"Imagine, for a moment, that you are a blind man, living contentedly among the blind. Your family and friends are blind. Your world accepts blindness as normal. You rarely feel the lack of sight, and when you do, you have no words or concepts for the sense you lack.

"Imagine that suddenly you are given the gift of sight. You perceive the world differently and have powers your friends and family do not have. The world would not understand you or your new sight.

"This would change your life, would it not? Some of those changes might be difficult. Relationships would change. Some who were friends would desert you, even fear you.

"So, Bartok, were the ones given sight in such circumstances blessed? Or were they cursed, given

271

a misfortune that carried throughout their generations?"

Bartok let out a long breath, and the sound of
the blood pulsing in his ears seemed suddenly too
loud. He ran one hand through his hair, his fingers
warm from the hot coffee mug. "But I'd be seeing
more of what's true. Seeing the truth is not a bad
thing. What they felt while blind was true, but incomplete, perhaps even misleading. I think sight
would be a blessing. Not all blessings are painless.
Would I choose it if it were offered to me?" Bartok
paused, feeling the cold air sting his lungs. "I
think, if God offers you more to work with, you
should take it, and you should use it as well as you
can. There's a verse in Luke that says 'From whom
much is given, much will be required.' That verse
has both pleasant and unpleasant aspects, but it's a
poor reason to say 'Don't give me much; I want to
have an easy job!'

"Yes, it might be hard. But if God were to ask
'Are you willing to take on a hard but important
job for me?' I like to think I would say yes. We
know that, in all things, God works for the good of
those who love him and who have been called according to his purpose. Maybe that good isn't in an
easy life, but a life of sacrifice for God's purpose."

The man murmured, "Well said, Dr. Tobias
Bartok." His steps echoed as he walked away.

Bartok almost called him back, but let him go
without comment. He swirled the last bit of coffee
in his cup and drained it, then placed it on the concrete beside his right foot.

Only a few minutes later, the man returned.
"Pray for me," he said without preamble. "Please."

Bartok nodded. "All right. Would you like to talk about something troubling you?"

The man hesitated and responded carefully, "I am facing a difficult decision. What I want is… I am not sure that what I want is best, or whether it is possible, at all. The consequences of an incorrect choice would be…" he shuddered "…beyond words." He shifted; Bartok had the sense the man was facing him, but in the darkness Bartok couldn't see him, much less read his expression. "The prayer of a righteous man avails much. I have great need of your prayers."

Bartok smiled. "Thank you. Shall we now?"

"You're going on watch." The man's voice carried the hint of a sardonic smile. "Later is fine. Thank you."

"Wait a moment. I don't think I know you. Are you new?" Bartok asked.

"Call me Dragomir." He shook Bartok's hand agreeably; then he disappeared into the darkness.

Bartok blinked to sudden wakefulness. He licked his lips, tasting no coffee on his breath. He looked around, then down at the ground where he had placed his coffee cup. There was nothing there. He shifted his shoulders, feeling the stiffness of sleep fading into the familiar alertness of watch.

CHAPTER 23

"LIEUTENANT RINK SAYS that you are still in good graces at Eastborn and no pursuit is forthcoming as yet. You, Lieutenant Colonel Blakeley, and Captain Jackson are said to be at an offsite project."

Blakeley and Grenidor blinked at Cillian and then glanced at each other. Blakeley frowned. "Are you sure? I didn't expect that."

Cillian stiffened almost imperceptibly. "Do you wish to know his words verbatim? I can repeat them all for you if you do not trust my summary."

Blakeley opened his mouth but Grenidor spoke first. "No! No, that's perfectly fine. If you're confident that's what he meant, I'll accept it."

Cillian's nostrils flared in suppressed anger, but he said nothing else.

Aria studied him from across the table where she sat beside Bartok. The young Fae looked tenser

than usual, and she imagined that Owen's suffering weighed on him.

Grenidor took a deep breath. "Then I could go
back."

Gabriel, who had been listening to Eli speaking
nearby, turned to him abruptly. "What?" He took a
step closer. "Tell me I misheard you. You've no
reason to go back to the empire unless you mean to
betray us already."

Grenidor's chair overturned as he shot to his
feet. "I would not do that!"

"Oh, wouldn't you?" Gabriel's voice dropped
dangerously. "Then why do you want to go back?"

Grenidor swallowed, and Aria felt a rush of
pity for him. He'd been so sure, moments earlier.
Now he looked tired, and perhaps a little frightened, though she wasn't sure if she was reading
that into his expression because *she* felt frightened,
or because he actually was frightened.

"You wanted a way to rescue the Christians,
right? It's my fault they're being arrested. I'll try to
get them assigned to me as..." he hesitated, "I've
used humans before in my experiments. Fletcher
might let me have them."

Aria's attention snapped to Owen. Niamh was
helping him stand. He swayed a little, leaning on
her arm. Then he shrugged into strength as if it
were a coat he wore; his shoulders straightened,
his posture became proud and graceful. He
stepped forward, leaving Niamh's support.

"You risk your life, Grenidor. For guilt?" He
slid into the chair beside Grenidor.

Grenidor started in surprise. It was the first
time he'd seen Owen in days. "I thought you were

275

angry or something. You disappeared. I didn't know if you were still here."

"I never left." Owen glanced at Gabriel before focusing on Grenidor again. "Why risk yourself?"

Grenidor's mouth twisted. "Better me than Blakeley. It's my fault. Seems like the least I can do." He ran one hand over his hair as he thought.

"What about the trackers? How will you explain that yours was removed?" Gabriel frowned at him.

"I doubt I can hide the fact that I hoped to meet with the vampires. Fae, I mean." He glanced at Owen and swallowed, as if expecting anger. "So, I can say, truthfully, that they wouldn't meet me while the tracker was in place."

"And do what?" pressed Gabriel.

Grenidor ran a hand over his short hair. "There's an access to the old Metro system near Eastborn. Not the one I think you went through before." He glanced at Owen again. "Two blocks east. Do you know it?"

"Yes."

"If I can, I'll take them there. Someone will need to meet us because I don't know the tunnels."

Owen studied Grenidor. The light caught the salt and pepper stubble dotting his jaw, the lines of long-held frustration around his mouth and eyes.

"Agreed." Owen inclined his head.

Gabriel's frown deepened. "All right. Suppose I go along with it. What do you need from us?"

"Nothing else, I think." Grenidor sat back, rubbing both hands over his face. "I'll go tomorrow morning around ten o'clock."

Gabriel stepped away, leaving him to his thoughts.

CHAPTER 24

GRENIDOR SAT FOR LONG MINUTES in silence, his face buried in his hands. What had he gotten himself into?

His thoughts whirled. He thought of Oliver Highchurch, the man whose death he'd ordered. Whose brains he'd seen spattered on the execution room wall. The Justice Room, they called it. But it wasn't just. The feel of blood and brain and tiny shards of bone between his fingers haunted him. Nausea rose in a sudden wave. He'd smeared the gore between his fingers and across the back of the idol. *The idol.* A horrible little figure that held no power and yet the power to consume his soul. *Edwin.* Such an innocuous name for such a horrible monster. He caught his breath on a silent sob.

Owen's voice broke into his thoughts. "Colonel Grenidor, are you well?"

"Yes." He swallowed, hating the terror that made his voice squeak. "Yes. Thank you." That was better.

Owen's presence beside him was oddly comforting. He forced himself to raise his head and look at the Fae ruler. Owen regarded him with those cold blue eyes, a faint smile playing around his lips.

"Do you want something?" Grenidor finally asked.

Owen tilted his head, his gaze never leaving Grenidor's face. He said in a low voice, "You smell of fear. I thought you might wish to discuss your thoughts. Perhaps I can offer some reassurance."

Grenidor swallowed. "It's that obvious?" He looked down at the table, spreading his hands flat across the cold surface. "Well, Edwin has made it clear that he hates me. He has plenty of dirt of me, both real and fabricated. He could destroy me easily. I'm trying to figure out why he hasn't, and trying to avoid playing into his hands further."

"Fabricated?" Owen lifted one eyebrow slightly.

"He showed me videos of me torturing the Fae girl, Feichin's daughter."

"Her name is Aithne," Owen murmured.

"Yeah. I never did what the videos showed." Grenidor cleared his throat, feeling it tighten at the memory. "I did plenty of other despicable things, but I didn't do those things. He once mentioned making those public." He blew out his breath as he thought. "But only I saw the videos. He also only spoke to me after he was invited to. I was stupid."

Owen's eyes, usually so cold, seemed unexpectedly sympathetic. "I had hoped to spare you

278

that." He sighed softly, and then coughed. He closed his eyes and swallowed.

"I don't know why he hasn't destroyed me yet. Maybe he's only hoping to lure me back to the Empire so my destruction can be more public. Maybe it's more satisfying that way. I get the feeling he likes public humiliations." Grenidor's voice caught.

"There are rules that govern our interactions with humans. There are also rules that govern the actions of other beings, like Petro and perhaps this Edwin. Whether he acknowledges it or not, whether he obeys El or not, he is subject to El's authority. Perhaps, despite his power, he cannot, or will not, or prefers not to break certain rules."

"Petro?"

Owen blinked and shook his head, as if shaking away dizziness. "Forgive my mention of him. He is not relevant to this discussion."

Grenidor frowned. "All right. So far as I know, Edwin only showed me the altered or fabricated videos. Maybe he can't show them to anyone he's not already dealing with. But I doubt he'd make threats he couldn't make good. Maybe he just doesn't want to, for whatever reason. He still has plenty to destroy me with, if he wants to. He wouldn't have to falsify information or fabricate evidence. Maybe he just wants to tempt me into exposing myself."

He glanced at Owen. *What do I hope for from him? He's already been more kind than I deserve.*

Owen coughed softly, his gaze distant for a moment, then he licked his lips, the motion leaving a reddish tinge of blood on the pale skin.

Grenidor stared at him, appalled. "Are you—"

C. J. BRIGHTLEY

Owen's eyes focused on him again with sudden intensity. "Am I what?"

Grenidor's words faltered. "Nothing." He cleared his throat again. "How is Niall?"

"He is well." Owen's expression seemed to be one of gentle confusion.

"And Feichin?" Grenidor's voice shook a little. He didn't know what he wanted. He hadn't seen Feichin since the night the vampire—no, the former vampire—had advised him that he should accept God's grace. *What an utterly bizarre conversation. Bartok, and I, and Feichin like a walking skeleton. He had every reason to hate me.* Grenidor glanced up at Owen and then away. *As does Owen. Yet he doesn't. Is that what the Slavemaster does? Or El, I suppose I should call him. Perhaps he doesn't like to be referred to as the Slavemaster. Or perhaps Feichin is lurking in the shadows, waiting for his moment. How could he forgive me? I haven't forgiven myself.*

Owen's lips lifted in a smile. "Feichin is serving El in a way new to us."

Grenidor forced his thoughts back to the Christians. He didn't know them, didn't care about them as individuals. But letting them die because he was too scared to try to save them was unthinkable. He had many flaws, but cowardice wasn't one of them. *Isn't it, though? What have you been, these last months, if not afraid?*

"Edwin may prefer to act through human agents. If so, this might be the opening he's been waiting for. But I'll risk it. I couldn't live with myself if I didn't at least try to save them."

Owen's gaze rested on his face for a long, silent moment. At last, he said, "As you wish. We will sing for you before you depart."

Grenidor couldn't speak around the sudden lump in his throat, so he nodded.

Owen rose and stepped away, disappearing within three steps.

CHAPTER 25

ONCE HE WAS HIDDEN, Owen's facade of strength
failed. He took one more step before pitching forward. Niamh caught him, his head lolling against
her arm as she let him down gently. He coughed,
and she helped him turn to the side to spit blood
on the cold stone floor. Niamh wiped blood from
his lips with the end of the bandage, her white
hands trembling.

"Niamh," he breathed.

"I'm here, my brother." Her voice cracked, and
she bent down so that they breathed the same cold
air. She pressed a kiss to his temple. "I'm here."

Aria crept closer, knowing that their conversation was private but unable to tear herself away.
Tears streamed down her cheeks unheeded.

Owen murmured something indistinct.
Niamh's silent tears fell on the side of Owen's face,

slipping down the line of his jaw and across his lips, glimmering like diamonds.

With excruciating care, she lifted his head and slid her leg beneath him, so that his head rested in her lap. His breath rasped in a faint moan, but he said nothing else. After a moment, she began to sing, the intricate melody nearly inaudible.

A few tears slipped from beneath Owen's eyelids.

Aria fell to her knees beside Niamh. "Please," she whispered. "Is there anything I can do?"

Niamh shook her head, her eyes closing in grief.

"May I ask? May I ask what he said?"

Niamh started to shake her head again, but Owen gave the faintest nod, his eyelashes damp on his cheeks. Niamh studied his face for a moment; then she let out a tremulous breath. She murmured, "He... he wished to go to El. He has endured much and wishes for this trial to end. But he will obey." Her voice broke. "I would bear it myself if I could."

Owen murmured something, and she caught her breath, her face white and horrified. "No, my brother. No. Please do not think it." She bent, her tear-filled eyes wide, searching his face. "Rest, now. Please."

She sang, and gradually the tension in Owen's body dropped away until he lay unconscious, his left hand curled by Niamh's knee, his head resting on her slim thigh. Blood crusted the corner of his mouth; the salt of tears had dried in his eyelashes.

At long last Niamh's voice faded, and she closed her eyes in exhaustion. Aria put her arm tentatively around Niamh, and the Fae woman leaned her dark head against Aria's shoulder. She whispered, "He asked me to forgive him for his weakness, Aria. For his weakness! As if he had failed me by becoming my little brother again, only for a moment, instead of my king."

Niamh bent forward, letting her hair fall over her face. "I am not strong enough to watch him suffer so. Will there ever be joy again?"

WAVES CRASHED OVER Owen's dark curls.

He sank beneath the waves, the filmy cloth of his shirt floating upward in the water. His hair spread around his face like a cloud, and he kicked upward, only to be driven beneath the surface again.

He opened his mouth, releasing a cloud of bubbles.

Inhale.

Exhale.

Inhale.

The Fae king breathed water, looking faintly surprised by the phenomenon. Bare feet and arms pale as marble, white as death, eyes like the ocean depths.

Beneath the surface, he swam with long, strong strokes, no longer needing to surface for air. He was one with the water, movements fluid and rhythmic as the waves that swept the water into froth far above his head.

Time was irrelevant; he swam for minutes or perhaps hours before dark stones appeared from the depths below. The water grew shallower. The waves grew rougher.

The pounding waves took him, carried him into the air, then down to the rocky sea floor, then up again, down farther up the stones, dragging him over the sand, pebbles, and boulders, tumbling his bruised body through frothy water and stone.

He staggered up the shore, bleeding from a thousand small abrasions and a few larger gashes. Sand stuck to his cheeks and glittered on his eyelashes. He coughed, retched, brought up seawater pink with blood. Black hair plastered over his face, he fell to his knees, pressed his face to the wet sand, and began to sing.

CHAPTER 26

GABRIEL SAT DOWN across from Grenidor. "I didn't hear all of your conversation with Owen, just enough to know you're worried. I can't blame you." He scratched at a mark on the worn table with one fingernail, not meeting the other man's eyes.

Grenidor grunted. Aria, watching from a few feet away, wondered whether Grenidor realized how unfriendly he looked.

The rebel leader sighed and crossed his arms. "It may not be much comfort at the moment, but even if the demon can kill you, he probably won't right now."

Grenidor snorted. "And why not?"

"Well, you don't belong to him anymore." Gabriel looked up to face him squarely. "That's part of being saved. What did you think happened in the tunnel?"

"I don't know." Grenidor sighed heavily, as if all the animosity had been suddenly drained from him. Now he merely looked tired and sad. "Can he take me back? I don't want to go back. But it's a war, isn't it? Between the Slavemaster and *things* like Edwin."

"No. Perhaps he wants to. I don't..." Gabriel frowned and blew out his cheeks as he thought. "Bartok and I disagree on whether you can be saved and then choose to eject God from your heart and become unsaved again. But if you're not planning on doing that, then no. Your soul is safe.

"That doesn't mean your body is safe. But, while he hates you, he may hope to win you back and kill you then, while you belong to him. Perhaps even demons don't fully understand what happens."

Grenidor blinked. "Really? I'd think they'd know everything."

Gabriel snorted. "Then they'd be like God. They may know more than we do, and they may know different things than we do, but they don't know everything." He tilted his head. "What happened to you after I left the army?"

The question earned him a grunt and a glare. Finally, Grenidor muttered, "I don't want to talk about it."

"Whatever happened... Is that why you're still a colonel?

Grenidor snorted. "No, I refused the promotion. It would have taken me away from HHIREP."

Niall appeared beside Gabriel. *May I join your conversation?*

287

Grenidor smiled, his relief obvious. "Yes. I'd wondered how you were." His eyes flicked up and down Niall's slim figure. "You're all right?"

Yes. Thank you. The young Fae hesitated and then sat down beside him, half-turned in the chair so that he faced both men. *I heard what happened in the tunnel. I am glad that you have found El. I regret that I was not present to share that joy.* He studied Grenidor's face, then his lips quirked in a slight smile and he bowed, though remaining seated.

"Thank you." Grenidor's throat felt tight, but he cleared his throat and said, "For... before. For coming to see me."

Niall's smile widened a little. *You are welcome. I believe, and I have spoken to others who are wise, and they* Then his smiled faded. *agree. We think, we trust, that you will succeed in your mission tomorrow morning.*

If the dark one meant to destroy you in the tunnel, he would have done so and let his action speak for itself, presuming he could have, which is not necessarily true.

He means to use fear. He wishes for you to be afraid, perhaps to think that every challenge and every danger you face is a result of his opposition. He wishes to keep you from acting in faith.

"Well, I'm terrified." Grenidor smiled grimly. "It's working."

No, it isn't. Because you're acting in faith anyway. Niall tilted his head, as if listening to something, or perhaps merely studying Grenidor's expression. *So far as we have been able to ascertain from what you have said, the dark one seems to avoid actions that are unmistakably supernatural. He prefers not to be noticed. We are...* Niall's gaze grew distant for a moment. *We are unsure what this means, but Dr. Bartok may be able to explain. He is wise. Perhaps also Gabriel can offer some wisdom?* The boy turned toward Gabriel with a hopeful look.

"Bartok's not back yet?" Gabriel's voice made his worry obvious.

He is here, but he is praying now. I do not wish to interrupt him. Niall glanced away. *I regret that I cannot offer more assurance, but we have never sought to know or understand the dark ones. We turn toward El; our faces and our hearts are… hidden… in the protection of El.* He stood abruptly, a flash of some unreadable emotion crossing his face. *Excuse me.*

CHAPTER 27

SIOFRA JOGGED into the station and knelt in front of Bartok, waiting silently while he continued to pray. Niall was at her side in a moment, a question in his eyes.

"I found some powder as he described," she said softly. "How is Lord Owen?"

Niall answered in his neat English writing, the letters gleaming in the air. *It is difficult to tell. He slept some, but I think the pain troubled him even in sleep. When he is awake, he controls himself so well, but asleep, you can hear it in his pulse and in his breathing.*

"Is it dishonesty to conceal pain so well? Or it is merely courage that should instruct us all? I have not suffered as he has, so I cannot tell." Siofra bowed her head. "This is the least of the many questions which trouble my heart."

He does not lie. Niall frowned faintly at the suggestion that the Fae king was dishonest. *I think we*

have not understood very much about love and courage.
We have seen one aspect of obedience clearly, and yet
remained ignorant of the most significant matters. Have
you asked El for the grace of Christ?

"I have not. I have yet one question for Dr. Bartok and Lord Owen, and then I will decide."

Deep in prayer, Bartok only now heard Siofra's soft voice and raised his head. "I'm sorry; I didn't realize you were waiting for me. What do you need?"

"I have found powder as you described." She proffered a tin with a plastic lid over a metallic paper seal. "Will it help Lord Owen?"

Bartok studied the label on the tin. "Yes. I'll get it ready now."

Several minutes later, he was scribbling in a notebook, calculating how much powder to add to a thermos of water beside him. He measured the powder, then screwed the top on the thermos and shook it vigorously. "Where is he?"

Siofra gestured politely.

The Fae leader was sitting against a wall as before, one leg stretched out before him, the other bent. His hands were slack in his lap. His eyes were closed.

Niamh knelt, her face bowed to the ground beside Owen's hip. Her hair brushed the back of his hand, black against his stark white skin. Aria sat at his other side, her face pale and worried.

To Bartok's evident surprise, Owen looked up as he approached. He straightened a little, giving Bartok a kind smile, then looking toward Siofra. "I trust you were undetected," he murmured.

"Yes. It was my honor to serve you, Lord Owen." Siofra bowed gracefully.

"How do you feel now?" Bartok knelt beside Owen and studied his face. "Still dizzy?"

"Better, thank you."

Aria, Niamh, and Cillian all turned to him. "Better?" Aria's voice squeaked.

Owen shrugged one shoulder slightly. "Than this morning."

Bartok set down the thermos. "It's a powder dissolved in the water. Can you drink it?"

"Probably." Owen murmured. His eyelids drifted closed, and he swallowed before forcing his eyes open again. Hand shaking, he wrapped his fingers around the thermos, lifting it to take several swallows. He made a strange noise deep in his throat and nearly dropped the thermos. Bartok steadied it.

"Tastes odd," Owen breathed.

Bartok nodded sympathetically. "I can imagine it would." He hesitated and then asked, "What exactly does it feel like? Generalized pain? Muscle or joint pain? Nausea?"

Owen licked his lips. "How much detail do you want?"

Bartok blinked. "Well, I don't think anyone can accuse you of malingering. I'm a doctor. I'm curious. You don't have to answer."

Owen gave a minute shrug and glanced at the other Fae before answering. "Getlaril blisters our skin. Dilute getlaril throughout my body feels as if every individual cell is being blistered at once. Also, there is aching and cramping. Some nausea and other discomforts."

Bartok hesitated and nodded. "I'm impressed that you're walking around at all."

Owen made a tiny sound as if he had meant to laugh, but it turned into a cough. "I haven't much. I do not wish to let my pain take me from my people. They have suffered enough. But the pain is tolerable. I have come to terms with it." He raised the thermos and drank again, the pale skin of his neck moving smoothly as he swallowed. Then he blinked, as if he were pushing back dizziness, and drained the thermos.

Everyone studied Owen intently; the Fae king's expression was tired and distant. He coughed.

Cillian frowned. "What do you expect to happen?" he asked Bartok.

Owen made a subtle motion with one hand and Cillian fell silent.

"He smells different," Niamh said.

Owen took a deep, slow breath, and let it out just as slowly. He straightened as if a weight long-carried had been removed from him. "I thank you, Dr. Bartok." He looked up with a brilliant smile. "The pain is not entirely gone, but it is much lessened and still fading."

BARTOK STUDIED OWEN. "You'll need a dose of vitamin C every day for years. It's water soluble, so it metabolizes quickly."

Owen nodded, blinking as if his vision was still clearing. Niall, who had been watching silently from just behind Cillian, shifted, and his glowing words appeared in the air. *Will you speak with Colonel Grenidor? I believe he has questions about the dark one.*

Bartok rose, his movement a bit slower than usual. "Of course."

Dr. Bartok, I apologize. I did not consider how tired you must be.

"It's fine, Niall." He smiled down at the Fae boy. "I should talk to him anyway."

Bartok slid into the seat beside Grenidor. "I heard you had some questions," he prompted.

Grenidor sighed. "Nothing specific. I was wondering why Edwin didn't destroy me in the tunnel. Niall and Owen said they thought he wanted to be undetected, so he might not do anything too obvious." He absently rubbed one hand over his short hair.

Bartok stretched out his long legs and yawned. "Anything else?"

Niall stepped closer with a slight bow. His words appeared in the air. *Colonel Grenidor, please refer to Lord Owen with his title, not merely his name. I know it is strange to you, but to our ears, it is a mark of profound disrespect. I think he deserves your respect and gratitude.*

Grenidor froze for a moment, then grimaced. "Please convey my apologies."

I will. Niall inclined his head.

"Mine as well. I believe I have addressed him, or spoken of him, without his title." Bartok looked chagrined. "I didn't mean any disrespect."

Niall looked a little startled, and he smiled, warmth shining in his eyes. *I will, Dr. Bartok. But what you have told us and done for us far outweighs any accidental discourtesy. You have our gratitude.* The boy bowed and stepped into the shadows.

Bartok blinked and shook his head, looking back at Grenidor. "You were asking about the demon? I'm not an expert on demons... I don't think anyone is. But we do know a few things. Satan is called the Father of Lies. He and his side work by lies and deception, as well as in other ways. They lead you astray. They like to work through manipulating humans because making themselves obvious through their own actions is risky for them. It brings attention to the spiritual world. People question whether God exists rather than discounting God entirely. Demons don't like people choosing sides with full disclosure.

"An imperial investigation of you would involve taking a close look at the evidence. Lies inevitably leave loose ends and inconsistencies. Perhaps he fears that an investigation would cost his side more than it would gain."

Grenidor blinked at him. "How?"

Bartok shrugged. "It's just a guess. But I doubt you're the only one he's been manipulating. Maybe an investigation could shed light on someone else he is still using."

Grenidor traced a scratch on the table with one finger. "I suppose it doesn't matter. I'm going to do it anyway."

"Good." Bartok smiled kindly. "I wouldn't dream of minimizing the danger. But there are worse things than death. You belong to God now, and nothing, *nothing*, can change that. No power of hell or scheme of man can ever take you from God's hand."

"Thanks."

Beside Aria, Owen shifted, his eyes drifting closed. "That's poetic. I like it."

BARTOK HAD SPOKEN to every human member of the resistance about salvation. Some had trusted God. Others had not.

Dominic cursed Bartok thoroughly for trying to get him to believe in "that God nonsense." Bartok blinked at his vehemence.

"Just because it works for you doesn't mean it works for me. You're a smart guy, Bartok. How can you believe that a man actually rose from the dead?"

"The Bible says—"

"I don't care what the Bible says. Who knows how many times it's been translated and retranslated? It's like playing that kids' game where you whisper in each other's ear; you whisper 'I like cookies' and what comes out at the end is 'ketchup is green' or something stupid. I don't buy it, Bartok. I don't know why you do, either."

"Actually, the translations are extremely good and based on very early copies. Lots of different copies have been compared for any inconsistencies. Scholarship on the authenticity and reliability of the text is much better than that of any other ancient document, like Beowulf or the Odyssey or—"

"It doesn't matter!" Dominic threw up his hands. "So what if the words are original? It still doesn't make it true! So there were con artists back in the old days? That doesn't tell me anything about some spiritual life!" He held up a hand. "Don't tell me, don't tell me. I don't care. I don't want to hear about it anymore. I'm glad it makes you happy, but it's not for me."

Bartok sighed. "All right."

He headed to his bedroll. He removed his shoes and massaged his feet for a minute, then splashed a bit of water on his face. Then he knelt with his face to the floor.

DESPITE THE LATE HOUR, Aria found herself far from sleepy. *Perhaps I don't need as much sleep as I did before.* She glanced toward Owen. After receiving the vitamin C, he had slept for several hours, waking refreshed a short time ago. Now he sat on the floor surrounded by Fae. For a split second, he looked up and met her gaze, his eyes a flash of brilliant blue.

Come.

She blinked at the command, unsure whether it was in her mind or her heart or audible to her ears. She rose, with a glance at Bartok's still form.

Owen must have been finished with his conversation, because as she approached the Fae made room for her. "You have said you wish to learn megdhonia. Is now an acceptable time to begin?"

"Yes!" She couldn't help her breathless excitement. "Oh, thank you!" Then concern rose, and she asked, "It won't be too tiring for you, will it?" *Perhaps I could have phrased that more diplomatically.*

His eyes shone with gentle amusement. "No. This is a child's exercise and not remotely taxing."

Aodhagan sat close by Owen's shoulder, and he murmured something to Owen with a long, respectful bow. Owen responded with a smile.

"What did he say?" Aria asked. *Perhaps I shouldn't have asked. It might have been personal.*

297

"He thanked me for fulfilling the duty of his father and mother, who have gone to El. That you have never learned megdhonia has grieved him, and our attempt is some solace for his grief."

Aria swallowed. "*Our* attempt? What are we going to do?"

Owen's eyes sparkled. "A simple exercise. Sit, please." He motioned toward the floor in front of him, and she sat at arm's reach. The other Fae circled around her, their presence silent but oddly reassuring.

"We will try this exercise first. It isn't difficult, but it will take concentration, at least while you are learning." Owen's voice was soft, but she could feel the power in it. "Close your eyes."

"Why?" she whispered. With her eyes closed, she felt strangely vulnerable.

His voice held a tinge of amusement. "So you aren't distracted. This is an exercise, nothing more. This skill is something like a child tracing the alphabet to learn the shape of the letters. It is of little practical use on its own."

As he talked, she felt something brushing against her mind, or something close to her mind. *My soul? Can you feel your soul?*

"It is a required precursor to many other uses of megdhonia. It is also a test to see whether you can be taught to use megdhonia at all."

"I feel something."

"Good. Now, breathe in the power that El has given you. Give thanks for it. And let it go. It was never yours; it was only given to you for a time."

At first, she felt only a faint, undefinable tug, but then she felt power, and weight, and authority.

"What is that?" she whispered.

"I am with you." His voice was soft. "Do you feel it?"

Peace. Kindness. Solemn joy. Love. Authority. Owen's unmistakable presence lessened a little, and she felt the undercurrent of power that threaded through his voice guiding her.

The effort felt a bit like breathing very thick air, air with substance and resistance to it. Instead of her lungs making the effort, it was her mind or her soul or something else not easily defined.

She finished the exercise feeling exhausted, though she wasn't sure why. She wasn't breathing heavily, and her muscles didn't ache, but she felt drained. The exhaustion was accompanied by a sense of exhilaration, even exaltation, that made her sigh in satisfaction.

Owen smiled at her, the corners of his eyes crinkling. "Very good."

Only then did she realize that Cillian, Niamh, Ardghal, Aideen, Aithne, and the others around her had been singing softly. The last notes of the song wrapped around her shoulders with a feeling of comfort and encouragement.

They were all smiling.

CHAPTER 28

OWEN GESTURED for Grenidor to sit. One by one, the Fae around him became visible. The number of them, the danger, set his heart racing. He'd known they were there, or at least suspected, but he'd been able to pretend to himself that it was only Owen and Cillian and Niall who stalked the shadows. *And Feichin.* Terror was a now-familiar copper taste in his throat.

Over twenty Fae surrounded him, pale and slim and unnaturally beautiful. Aithne, Feichin's daughter, stood close by Niamh, as if for support. Besides Cillian, those were the only names he remembered; that realization suddenly shamed him, and he dropped his head.

Owen's voice rose first, strong and pure. Moments later, the others joined him, one by one, like golden threads in the air.

Grenidor could not have told how long they sang; it might have been ten minutes or ten hours. His cheeks were sticky with tears, but he wasn't crying anymore. The song was comfort and courage; there was no need to weep.

Owen knelt before him. "Go with El. We will await you at the place you said."

"Thank you," Grenidor whispered.

He should have stopped then. It was a good moment to depart, to lift his chin and walk off into the danger. *Be brave, Pauly.*

But his courage suddenly fled, and he muttered, "I don't even know why I'm doing this. It can't possibly work."

Owen let out a soft breath, and Grenidor was startled to see a smile flash across his face. "I do."

"Why?"

"Love. You have asked El into your heart. How else can you act but in love?"

Grenidor flushed. "I'd call it honor. Love is for women."

"Did El save you for honor? No. It was love." Owen's smile deepened. "You should not be ashamed of it."

GRENIDOR EMERGED from the abandoned Metro stop into sudden spring. True, the wind gusting at him was still cold, but it carried a hint of green things growing in some distant place, beyond the cars and buildings. The sunlight was more golden, the sky a slightly deeper blue beyond the wispy white clouds.

He took a deep breath before he began walking. *Fletcher could turn me in. Or he could arrest me.* He tried to pray but didn't know what words to use. *I don't know why you saved me, but I believe you did. I know I don't deserve mercy. But for the sake of the prisoners, please let this work. Please, God, let this work.*

He flashed his badge at the guard, who nodded him forward to the turnstile. He swiped the badge, expecting an alarm, but the machine merely beeped and let him through.

His steps echoed in the mostly empty lobby. He turned left to the bank of elevators and pressed a button, trying not to tap his foot. Up four floors. Fletcher had an office in the building's SCIF, the Sensitive Compartmented Information Facility, which took up most of the fourth and fifth floors. Entering meant Grenidor had to swipe his badge again, enter his PIN, and sign on the visitor's log at the front desk under the watchful eye of the receptionist.

Despite the security, Fletcher's office had a coveted window and a view of the river, if you stood in one corner and craned your neck to see over the buildings. Grenidor had been there before and walked briskly down the hall, reading each nameplate.

Mark Fletcher, 408. The door was partially open, showing the corner of Fletcher's desk and the chair he had for visitors. Grenidor took a deep breath before he knocked on the doorframe.

"Come in." Fletcher spoke without looking up. The center section of his u-shaped desk held his computer. As Fletched faced the computer, the door was to his left and the window was to his right. The glass had a distinct green cast from the high-end, mirrored, security glass, a requirement for all windows in the SCIF.

Grenidor stepped in and closed the door behind him. "Mark. How are you?"

Fletcher looked up, surprise on his face for a moment before his brows lowered. "Paul." His voice was cool. He glanced back at his monitor and locked it so Grenidor could see only the screensaver requiring authorization. "Did you like that execution?"

"Like it?"

Fletcher's nostrils flared. "Yeah. Did you like it? Because I thought I was on board with this. I thought you did good work. Then I read the interrogation transcripts and now I feel like you set me up for something. Those weirdos may be religious freaks, but they weren't security risks. It makes me wonder what your problem is." He clenched his hands and leaned forward. "So why are you here?"

Grenidor licked his lips. "I'm here to make a request about the Christians."

"I'm not happy about the executions. I've diverted some manpower away from the Christians. We have bigger problems. There were three vampire attacks in the last week in Anacostia, and your program hasn't given us anything useful in months."

Grenidor laced his fingers together, unwilling to meet Fletcher's gaze. "Well, that's what I've come about. You're right. The Christians are no threat to the empire. I was mistaken. My source was biased. They should be released, or deported if necessary."

"WHAT?" Fletcher roared. "You're a piece of work, you know that? I had my boys pulling out fingernails and now you say 'oops'? These things can't be fixed, Paul!"

"I had reasons!" Grenidor heard his own voice rise in defensive anger and consciously lowered it again. "But they were based on flawed intelligence. I'll write it up formally if you want. I wanted to let you know as soon as possible before any others were executed."

Fletcher breathed heavily, staring at him across the desk. He clenched one fist and bumped it on the heavy wood surface as if considering whether to smash it into Grenidor's face. "It's not that simple," he said at last. "They did, technically, break laws that carry the death penalty. Proselytizing has always been a capital offense. It's just that no one cared until you brought it up. As long as they didn't cause trouble, there wasn't much reason to go hunting them. But now they've been arrested. We have confessions. We don't have much choice."

Grenidor's mouth was suddenly dry. "You don't?"

Fletcher shook his head. "No. We don't. I don't. And the hunt is on, Paul. I can dial it back a bit more, but I can't take them entirely off the radar. Not even on your say-so."

Grenidor blew out a soft breath. "Could you have them sent to me? I could use them."

Fletcher's eyebrows climbed. "For experiments?"

"Something like that."

Fletcher studied him. "I'd rather their blood be on your hands than mine. But... I'm already responsible. I've heard rumors of what you do. I'm not sure I believe everything I've heard, but maybe a quick execution is better than whatever you have planned."

Grenidor licked his lips and flattened his hands on the table. "It's a simple set of tests, not painful. But there is some risk they might escape the Empire."

Fletcher froze for one long heartbeat. Then he sat back, his eyes never leaving Grenidor's face. "That's dangerous."

"I don't know what you're talking about."

The rhythmic sound of Fletcher's fingers drumming on the desk kept pace with Grenidor's racing heart.

Fletcher stood abruptly. "Right then." He lowered his voice as he stepped around his desk toward the door. "If I were in your position, I hope I'd do the same."

Grenidor followed him out of the SCIF, dutifully signing out at the front desk, and to the elevator, where Fletcher pushed the button for B3, the third basement level. They rode in silence, hands clasped behind their backs in parade rest. For Grenidor, the position was reassuringly familiar; it kept him from nervously tapping his fingers against his leg.

Fletcher led him through the security checkpoints to the cells. Grenidor tried to keep his face schooled in an expression of professional disinterest, but he found himself grimacing. Disgust, empathy, horror… the emotions blended together so that he couldn't have explained it, even if Fletcher had asked.

Fletcher didn't ask; he only gave him a cool look and then turned to the first cell.

The cells had multiple locks, requiring a swipe of Fletcher's badge, a key code, and a physical key. The fronts were clear bulletproof glass, affording the prisoners no privacy. Each cell had a hard metal bench, a toilet, and a tiny sink. There was no bed and no blanket. The first prisoner was a man of about Grenidor's age, perhaps a year or two younger. He sat on the bench with his hands clasped between his knees. He wore a short-sleeved orange shirt and thin pants of the same color. His feet were bare. Even from the corridor between the cells, the chill bumps on his skin were visible. Grenidor still wore his thick wool coat over an undershirt and his BDUs; even with the layers, the basement was chilly.

Fletcher swept into the cell, Grenidor following in his wake.

"Show your hands," he barked.

The prisoner raised his hands compliantly, showing the handcuffs already around his wrists. Fletcher checked them, then shoved the man out the door and into the corridor, where he linked the man's cuffs to a chain on the wall

"Want their ankles cuffed too?"

"That won't be necessary."

Fletcher moved to the next cell. This prisoner was younger and thinner. Perhaps the cold bothered him more; he had hunched into the corner of the cell, as if the concrete walls would offer some comfort. At the first sound of the lock, he straightened, squaring his shoulders and schooling his features into a neutral expression.

"Show your hands."

The young man complied. "I'm not going to fight."

"Did I say to talk?" Fletcher growled. "Stand up." He guided the young man out into the corridor to stand beside the other prisoner. He chained their hands together and the second man to the wall.

Down the hall they went, collecting prisoners. Grenidor followed, the two men acting in concert. Fletcher opened each cell, checked the prisoner's bonds, and handed the prisoner over to Grenidor. Grenidor chained them to each other forming a line.

Twelve men, ten women. The youngest two were perhaps twenty, the eldest a woman who must have been nearly seventy. They had all been beaten to varying degrees. The old woman had bruises in the shape of handprints on her arms, as if someone had shaken her. She'd bitten through her lip and it was grotesquely swollen. One of the younger men, somewhere in his mid-twenties, had been beaten so badly he could barely walk. Blood crusted one side of his head and he curled gingerly to one side, as if protecting internal injuries. Fletcher shot Grenidor a dirty look when he hauled him out of the cell and chained him to the others.

Grenidor let out a soft breath, staring at them. Some of them looked back at Grenidor; others stared at the tile floor. One looked furious, though he didn't say anything. Others looked defiant but not angry, merely uncowed. One of the younger women coughed and then coughed again, harder, leaning against the wall. Her nose began to bleed. The thick, dark blood ran into her mouth, and she grimaced, still coughing, and wiped it clumsily on the sleeve of her shirt.

"This is what you want, right?" Fletcher asked.

"It's all of them?"

"Yes."

"That's all I need. Thanks, Mark."

Fletcher handed an electric shock wand to Grenidor. "Here. Use it on just one prisoner like this. Just hold the end of the chain if you want; or don't, it doesn't really matter. They can't run. If they try it, the whole chain is wired. Just push this button here and the entire line will light up. The safety's on." He thumbed the cover over the button.

"Is it lethal?"

"Not usually. It's a bit stronger than a standard TASER; the older ones might not survive it." He glanced at Grenidor as if evaluating him.

He kept his voice loud. He wants them to hear, so I don't have any trouble.

"Got it. Thanks."

Fletcher nodded curtly, then swiped his badge and keyed in the code to release the prisoners from the wall. "Come on."

Shame washed over Grenidor as he stepped forward, the chain in his hand. He followed Fletcher to the freight elevator, the prisoners crowding in first. Grenidor and Fletcher stood just inside the door, the electric wand ready. The prisoners made no move to initiate violence. The young woman with the bloody nose coughed again, trying to stifle it. She sagged against the woman next to her, who tried to support her with bound arms. The other woman murmured something, perhaps a prayer.

Fletcher walked them to the service entrance. Out of earshot of the guards, he muttered to

Grenidor, "If you're serious about this, you might have redeemed yourself."

"I am redeemed, but I didn't do it myself."

Fletcher gave him a sharp look and his eyes widened. He hesitated and nodded. "Maybe so. Good luck. You'll need it."

GRENIDOR LED the line of prisoners down the street. The young prisoner in the worst shape was painfully slow, staggering almost drunkenly, though he stayed on his feet.

Though the walk was only three blocks, it felt horribly exposed. The sun was brilliant, the buildings around them full of windows. Traffic was light and no other pedestrians were visible, but Grenidor felt sick with nerves.

"Here." He stopped at the manhole cover. He rapped the electric wand on it sharply three times, then twice. A moment later, it lifted and moved aside.

"Climb down." He unlocked the first prisoner's handcuffs.

The man looked at him in disbelief. "Climb down?"

"Yes, and do it quickly!"

The man blinked and then clambered clumsily down the ladder. Then the next, a woman. Another man.

Owen slipped out of the tunnel. He stepped to the most badly beaten prisoner, who was swaying, barely conscious. Owen's eyes were gentle as he touched the man's shoulder.

The Christian blinked; then he straightened, looking around in disbelief. His eyes widened when he saw Owen. "I… what did you do to me?" He moved his shoulders gingerly.

Owen had already moved on, touching each prisoner and healing their wounds. The effort drained him; by the time he reached the last, his hand trembled with weariness.

"Get in, Grenidor. I'll follow you." Owen waited a moment, then climbed into the tunnel himself, pulling the cover over them.

Grenidor breathed a sigh of relief.

The ladder descended some thirty feet to a large room where several tunnels joined. Old electrical boxes and discarded machinery lined the walls. Fearghal and several other Fae immediately pressed close to Owen, offering their strength to replenish what he had used in healing the prisoners.

"Who are you?" The question came from one of the Christians, a man of perhaps forty, broad-shouldered and strong. "What is happening?"

CHAPTER 29

ARIA WAITED with Owen, Niall, Cillian, Niamh, and several other Fae, as well as Bartok, Gabriel, and Eli, at the rendezvous. Electric lanterns cast harsh shadows on the walls. Everyone was armed, the humans with pistols and rifles of various makes, and the Fae mostly with long daggers. Owen wore his swords on his belt. Niamh and Cillian carried pistols in addition to their blades. Gabriel, Eli, and Owen carried radios.

While they waited, Bartok slipped his hand into Aria's. His movement was careful and gentle, as if he were letting her decide, moment by moment, whether she enjoyed the touch.

God, don't let me mess this up. I don't want to lead him on if this isn't going anywhere. Then, even as her thoughts formed, she knew. The butterflies in her stomach, the odd floating feeling, the uncertainty... they all disappeared. She gripped his hand more firmly, wrapping her fingers around his hand. It was warm and strong, his palm slightly callused. Her fingers fit perfectly against the slight hollow between his thumb and his forefinger, her thumb grazing the knuckle of his thumb. He shifted, looking down at her, and she smiled up at him. He grinned, and she knew he understood.

"What's happening?" the oldest woman asked.

A growl echoed in the tunnel, and Aria's heart skittered erratically. The lantern light caught the shapes of vertril running toward them through one of the tunnels.

Three. Four. Ten.

Aria's heart thundered.

"Stay here! We'll lead them away!" called Owen.

The Fae bolted, scattering among the unoccupied tunnels.

The humans pressed themselves up against the walls in wordless fear. Time seemed to slow as the vertril approached. Out of the corner of her eye, she saw the men pulling the women behind them. Someone screamed.

The growls became a roar, dozens upon dozens of snarling monsters, the sound reverberating in the tunnels until Aria nearly screamed.

The vertril ignored the humans completely, racing past them in pursuit of the Fae, who were already out of sight. She imagined Owen dancing before them, graceful, teasing, and dangerous.

One of the last beasts passed so close to Aria she might have touched it. A few steps away it stopped and turned back to her.

It growled.

Another one turned back with a vicious snarl, coming to stand beside the first. Their eyes fixed on her.

It knows I'm Fae! How could it know? God help me!

She stepped away, dropping Bartok's hand. Another step.

I have to lead it away from them. If it kills me, it kills me, but I can't let it kill them too.

Another step. One vertril growled and took a step forward, then another, its head tilted as if it wasn't quite sure whether she was Fae or not. Prey.

It leapt at her.

Bartok was suddenly between her and the beast. He fired two shots directly into its open mouth. Blood and bone and saliva caught the lantern light as it crashed into Bartok.

The vertril's momentum knocked him off his feet. His head cracked against the concrete floor. For a split second, he was still, the dead beast a crushing weight over his chest and neck, its mangled head dripping blood into his hair.

Bartok wheezed against the weight on him and the pain of the fall, and slithered out from under the vertril, rising dizzily to one knee.

The other vertril leapt at Aria.

Bartok lunged upward, catching at its fur and one leg.

It turned on him, its massive jaws crushing his arm in one quick bite. Then it let go, burying its teeth in his side. It shook him like a toy.

Bartok's body slammed against the concrete wall and floor, the sound of bones breaking lost in the horrible snarling.

Aria screamed. "NO! Leave him alone!"

The beast stopped and stared at her, Bartok's broken body falling from its mouth. It growled, head tilted, oddly tentative for a moment.

"Go away!" she cried, weeping.

The vertril lowered its head, the tunnel rumbling with a soft growl. It tilted its head to the other side, as if showing her its throat, and backed up... one step, then another.

Aria fell to her knees beside Bartok.

The vertril stared at Aria, ignoring the humans completely. It didn't notice Grenidor approaching it. He shot it three times in the head, and it collapsed in a heap, one paw twitching spasmodically.

Aria's tears fell on Bartok's broken face. He was unrecognizable, blood and bone and tattered cloth. His chest, or what there was of it, rose and fell unevenly. He gasped, a harsh sound in the terrible silence.

"God, save him. Help him!" She tried to sing, but no words would come. *Sing! God, I'll do anything. Please let him live!* "Stay with me. Hold on!" Her voice cracked, her song made of sobs.

Bartok made a soft, wordless sound of agony, and her tears fell harder.

"OWEN!" she screamed, but she knew it was too late.

THEN OWEN WAS ON HIS KNEES beside her, both hands pressed to Bartok's chest, blood pulsing between his pale fingers. Bone glinted in the lantern light, white and red and horrible.

Owen sang, though perhaps Aria heard him not with her ears but only with her broken heart.

Owen bowed his head until it rested upon Bartok's right shoulder. The Fae's breath quickened with effort.

Aria held her breath, hope beating wildly within her. *God, save him. Help him. Heal him. Please, God!*

Time lost meaning.

ARIA SMELLED BARTOK'S SWEET-SALTY BLOOD. Tears streaked down her cheeks unnoticed. Grenidor's hand rested on her shoulder for a moment.

Sobs ripped out of her. She bent forward, Owen's elbow just beside her ear. She wept, able to hear nothing but her own heartbeat and Owen's song.

Behind her, the Christians were huddled together, praying. Several were weeping.

"I love… I love…" Bartok's broken whisper was nearly inaudible.

She pressed closer to him, his blood smearing her hands as she pressed his right hand between hers. "I love you," she murmured. "Stay with me. Keep breathing."

"I love y—" he gasped. He groaned on the next breath, louder and stronger.

Owen's song in her heart rose, wild and pure. It was defiance and submission, love and obedience and trust, glittering like sunlight on water.

She prayed, with all her heart, with feeling that went far beyond words.

Owen's shoulders slumped. Still he sang, and still she prayed.

Bartok's breathing steadied. "Are you all right?" he whispered. "Aria?" His hand clenched on hers.

Owen gasped, his breathing ragged. He sat back, his chest heaving and his eyes closed. He swayed, nearly falling into Aria before he straightened.

Aria whispered, "Is he…"

"He'll live. I can't replace the lost blood, but the damage is healed." Owen blinked and shook his head, as if shaking away dizziness. He glanced up and around at the others, then focused on Aria and Bartok again. "What happened? We meant to lure them away."

Bartok grunted with effort as he tried to sit up. Owen and Aria supported him as he leaned back on his elbows. He took several deep breaths to steady himself. "They started toward her. They were going to attack Aria. I couldn't let them," he whispered. He blinked as if trying to focus. "The second one leaped… You healed me." He met Owen's eyes. "Thank you."

Owen's slight smile broadened. "It was my honor." He turned to Aria. His pale skin was even paler, and his hands trembled. "They turned on you?"

"Yes." Hysteria burbled up. *Bartok is alive.* Aria swallowed her fear and found herself shaking and nauseated as adrenaline flooded her veins. "I thought maybe they realized I was Fae, at least a little bit. I didn't want them to hurt anyone else, so I tried to get a little distance between me and the others. One of them leapt at me, and Bartok shot it.

But the other one attacked him, just because he was in the way. It wanted me, but..." Her voice cracked. "It just shook him..." She caught her breath on a sob. *His arms and legs broke on the concrete. His skull cracked against the floor. Blood and bone, broken bits and pieces.*

She bent down again, her cheek against Bartok's chest. His ribs and sternum moved beneath her, solid and whole, his breaths steady and reassuring, though perhaps faster than they should have been. He put one hand on her hair, fingers entwined until his nails scratched softly against her scalp.

"I'm all right," he whispered. "Thank God. And Owen."

Owen murmured, "But what made it stop?"

Aria looked up him. Blood from Bartok's shirt smeared her cheek, sticky now in the cool air. "What do you mean?"

"A vertril would not leave its prey voluntarily. Why did it not kill him and then attack you?"

Aria blinked. "I... shouted at it. When it looked up, Colonel Grenidor shot it." Belatedly she looked for him, standing a few feet away. "Thank you."

He nodded, his eyes flicking away and then back. "Glad to help," he said gruffly.

"You shouted at it?" Owen frowned.

Aria felt her breath quickening again with remembered terror. "I told it to leave him alone and go away." She frowned. "Are vertril animals? I mean, they're engineered, you said, but they're animals, aren't they?"

Owen blinked. "Yes. What else would they be?" He turned to look at her, blue eyes holding her gaze for long heartbeats. Then his lips parted

317

in a slow, triumphant smile. His eyes gleamed. "I thank you, Aria."

He stood, blinked a little dizzily, and then stalked to Gabriel. "Give me your radio. I left mine with Cillian."

Gabriel handed it over without question.

Owen thumbed it on. "Bring the vertril back. All of them."

CHAPTER 30

"WHAT?" GABRIEL GASPED. "Bring them back?"

Owen looked over his shoulder for an instant, blue eyes bright and wild. He grinned, white teeth catching the light.

Then the Fae were sprinting toward him, blades flashing, faster than Aria would have thought possible. A month ago, it would have been faster than her eyesight could register. Now, it felt as though time slowed around her.

"Behind me!" Owen shouted.

They obeyed, though not without obvious hesitation. Cillian stopped before him, breathing hard, pale cheeks slightly flushed. "My lord brother, you risk…"

"Behind me," Owen murmured. He smiled, and from behind Owen's shoulder Aria saw Cillian's eyes widen in shock, perhaps horror.

Yet he obeyed.

Then the beasts poured into the room, too many, filling it up, jostling with each other, so many that some could not force their way into the open space and remained in the tunnels, growling and snapping at each other in their eagerness to lunge forward.

Owen sang, his arms outstretched. The light cast his shadow over the growling vertril, the shadow taller and leaner than Owen himself, arms spread like wings. *Or like a cross.* The beasts panted, their breaths fogging in the icy air. Owen's voice was impossibly beautiful, pure and perfect and joyous.

Aria fell to her knees. She couldn't sing with Owen, but her heart soared with his voice.

The vertril pressed themselves to the floor, flattening their bodies. One shimmied closer to him, the motion like a puppy eager to please its master.

Owen let his song fade, watching the creatures. "Now," he turned to them, white teeth flashing in a feral grin. "That's better."

WITH A GESTURE, Owen commanded the vertril to depart. They bounded away through the tunnels in all directions.

One of the women sank to her knees, her eyes closed. "Oh God."

Owen offered her a hand. "El has shown us his favor. Will you join us as we sing?"

Her hand trembled, and he smiled reassuringly.

"Who are you?" she whispered.

"A servant of El, whom you also serve."

CHAPTER 31

HOURS LATER, at the basilica, Aria found Bartok in a quiet corner. She handed him a cup of hot water. "I was going to make tea but I think we're out. At least this is warm."

"Thanks." His voice was a little rough with fatigue, but he smiled up at her from where he leaned against the wall.

She sat down beside him, shoulder to shoulder. "Thanks, Bartok." Her voice shook, and she cleared her throat. "For in the tunnel, I mean."

He wrapped his long fingers around the mug. "You're welcome." He glanced at her; then he leaned to press his shoulder against hers for a moment before straightening again. "You can call me Toby."

"Oh." Aria glanced at him, trying to read his expression in the dim light. "Everyone calls you Bartok. I thought you preferred it."

He shrugged. "It's my name; I don't dislike it. But I think that got started because Gabriel was angry when I first joined the group. He called me by my last name to maintain distance. Maybe keep me as an outsider."

She drew back and frowned. "Really?" *I would have thought better of Gabriel.*

"Well, I never asked him, but that's what I assumed since I'd introduced myself as Toby. He doesn't mean anything by it now; it's just habit. But…" The corners of his mouth twitched upward. "I'd prefer it if you weren't as distanced."

"All right. Toby then."

The warmth in his eyes made her blush.

"How do you feel?" she asked.

"Tired." He sagged lower against the wall. "Hypovolemic shock is far from trivial. Lord Owen said he can't replace the blood I lost, so I should be dead, regardless of the other healing. He must have supported my life somehow with megdhonia. So I feel thoroughly alive and yet… incredibly tired." He smiled, leaned his head back against the wall, and closed his eyes. "God is good," he murmured. His left hand rested on his leg, and he turned it palm up, as if inviting her to place her hand in his.

Aria hesitated. Then ever so gently, she slipped her hand into his, letting their fingers entwine.

The corners of Toby's mouth lifted in a faint smile as he drifted into slumber.

THAT EVENING, Toby Bartok was reading the Bible when a group of Fae approached. He looked up in surprise to find Owen sitting cross-legged just in front of him, the other Fae ranged out behind him in silence.

"You said once that there was no mention of Fae in your Bible. Does it explain how humans came to exist?" Cillian asked from just behind Owen.

"Yes. It's right at the beginning." Toby flipped back to Genesis. He read the account of creation: light; water; land; plants; stars, the moon, and the sun; living creatures of all kinds; and mankind. "'So God created mankind in his own image, in the image of God he created them; male and female he created them. God blessed them and said to them, 'Be fruitful and increase in number; fill the earth and subdue it. Rule over the fish in the sea and the birds in the sky and over every living thing that moves on the ground.' Then God said, 'I give you every seed-bearing plant on the face of the whole earth and every tree that has fruit with seed in it. They will be yours for food.' There's more detail later, about how God created man first, then made woman to be a fitting companion to him." He flipped forward and scanned the page, looking for the verses.

"Wait," Owen said. He caught Toby's gaze. "What does that mean, 'in the image of God'?" His voice had a weight to it that made Bartok's eyes widen.

"Um…" Toby rarely stumbled over his words, but he did now, momentarily rattled by Owen's intensity. "We know some of what it means, but I don't think anyone fully comprehends all the glory of that description. But I've been studying it, and this is what I've found."

He took a deep breath, as if steadying himself for a difficult conversation. "Humans are unique among God's creatures in the way we love. Animals like dogs can love, for lack of a better word, but not as a conscious choice. We are creative, as God is. No animal is creative; I've heard of animals being trained to paint, but they don't have the creative urge or the ability and desire to perfect their work to standards they set for themselves. We are creatures of spirit; though we live in physical bodies, we have souls, and our souls are ultimately more important than our bodies, which perish. Our souls will find eternal joy or eternal suffering based on the spiritual decisions we make in a physical reality."

Toby frowned as he thought. "We communicate; we have a desire to be understood by others and to understand others. We use symbolic language; we write, we make art, and we ascribe meanings to culture and tradition that other creatures do not. We are intelligent; animals can be clever, but not intelligent in the way we are, thinking of the future and shaping the world around us. We are relational; we form families and societies not because we have to, but because it is our nature to find richness in community. And we are moral; we make decisions based on a sense of right and wrong. Even when our sense of morality is warped, that sense helps guide us."

Niamh, sitting beside Owen, had grown preternaturally still, every line of her face and body taut. "And what are we, then? Not animal. We create. We are intelligent. We communicate. We find richness in family and community. We are moral."

Her lips twisted a little at that. "What are we, then?"

Owen made a movement with one hand so subtle that Aria nearly missed it. Niamh sat up straighter and bowed, her nostrils flaring with subdued anger.

Owen and Toby locked eyes, and Toby swallowed. Owen gave a slight nod, his lips barely lifting in a smile. "Speak, Dr. Bartok. I think I agree with your answer. What are we?"

Toby licked his lips and looked down at the Bible. "I think..." He sounded a little breathless, as if the idea had caught him by surprise. "I think you're human. Human in every way that matters."

Niamh blinked. "What?"

Owen's faint smile widened. "I agree."

Cillian's voice was quiet but shocked, as if he could not fathom that he had heard correctly. "Lord Owen, what have you said?"

Owen did not look away from Toby. "As Dr. Bartok has explained, humans are like us in every way that matters. In every defining characteristic, they are like us. Or we are like them. Even our ability to touch megdhonia is explained by a minor genetic difference, no greater than that of color blindness, and years of training. If they are made in the image of God, then we must be as well. Turned Fae can return to communion with El in the same way humans can. We are not animals. We are not even cousins to humans. *We are humans.*"

"THAT CANNOT BE TRUE. Can it?" Cillian breathed. "We are so different."

325

Toby scrubbed his hands through his hair, leaving it sticking up. He leaned forward, his voice intense. "Have you ever seen an Ethiopian? A Norwegian? A Vietnamese?" He bounced one lean leg with excitement as he talked. "I've examined Lord Owen, remember. Fae must be humans! Your bodies are supported and maintained by magic, excuse me, megdhonia, your lives are extended by megdhonia, but you are like us! Your teeth are exactly like ours, except you have no cavities and perfect alignment."

Owen nodded. "Go on." His eyes were alight with affection and pleasure at Toby's excitement.

How did I not see that at first? He loves Toby like a son and a brother and a father and a friend all at once.

"If Fae split off from humans, the split occurred so recently there has been very little genetic drift. Anyone in our group is as closely related to you as a native Polynesian is related to a Swede! We're the same species, with different upbringing and a few minor genetic differences. Ethiopians will have black skin and hair, Swedes may be blond and blue-eyed, and Vietnamese will have almond-shaped eyes and brown skin. But these are superficial differences... biologically they mean almost nothing.

"Race among humans is a social construct more than anything. There are minor physiological differences; some African groups have a slightly higher incidence of sickle cell anemia. A greater percentage of Asians are lactose intolerant. But those differences are insignificant at a species level; these tiny details serve only to highlight how very similar we are." He ran his hands through his hair again. "Remember when I told you about the rods and cones in our eyes? Tetrachromats, people who have an extra type of cones in their eyes, are rare, perhaps one in ten thousand humans. But for many of them, it has no effect; learning how to use the extra cone, to see additional colors, requires training and practice. Only one in millions actually fully uses the capability they were born with! Others have the capability, but never notice it and don't exercise it enough to utilize it.

"What if the megdhonia gene is like that? Perhaps a few humans get it, a very few. Fewer still figure out how to do anything at all with it. The gene is recessive, so unless both parents carry the gene, the child won't express the gene, although they might carry it on to future generations. Perhaps the beginnings of the Fae were when two parents who had the gene and figured out how to use it, at least a little, had children and taught them how to use megdhonia from birth. These children would have become much better at it than their parents. Perhaps that was from training... or maybe God taught them how. Anyway, those who had the ability naturally chose spouses who also had the ability, if possible." Bartok's eyes widened and he added, "And perhaps the normal population tended to suppress magic, either the expression of the gene or deliberate training, by burning and driving out 'witches'."

Owen's subtle smile faded at this addition. "It is a good theory. I cannot tell if it is correct. Our histories, for all our long memories, have been lost in time. I have wondered, at times, whose doing this was."

Niamh's eyes were steady on his face. "You think the dark ones did it?"

327

Owen gave a slight shrug. "Perhaps. Or the Fae themselves did it, for reasons I cannot guess. Perhaps they meant to save us, their descendants, some pain or question they thought would be detrimental to us. Perhaps some turned over the decision, or perhaps it was permitted by El."

Niall's glowing words appeared in the air before them. *Or perhaps the dark ones reveled in our separation from our human brothers and sisters.*

Silence fell, and the Fae seemed lost in the thought.

Finally, Owen said softly, "One thing is clear. We were given power for a purpose."

The Fae looked up at him as one, blue eyes clear and bright on his face.

Bartok drew a soft breath. "Yes. God does not ever act without purpose."

Owen's voice remained soft, but its power cut through the darkness like a brilliant ray of sunlight; his words shook the dust from the distant concrete walls. "If God's purpose is to bring light and life to humanity, we were not given power so that we could hide away in the darkness, keeping ourselves safe.

"Why were we made? To serve El, to sing to him and bring him pleasure in our obedience. To love him, as we have not understood love until now. But what is love? Obedience. What is obedience? Love.

"And what is the purpose of power? To serve El in obedience and love."

Cillian breathed, "What are you saying, Lord Owen? Are we to fully enter the human world?"

Owen sighed softly, his expression troubled. "I don't know. I must spend time with El. I do know

328

that we cannot isolate ourselves so thoroughly. We have much to learn of El, but we know one thing: El loves humans." He looked up, holding Cillian's gaze with his own. "We must also."

NIALL SAT IN FRONT OF OWEN. *I have chosen my heir. Is my choice acceptable to you?* Niall's face looked a little tense, as if he were unsure but hopeful.

Owen raised his eyebrows. Perhaps Niall spoke directly into Owen's mind because Owen smiled a moment later.

"It is."

Is the decision to be formalized now?

"No. Only your decision is necessary now."

Niall bowed his head. Then, as if relaxing after a difficult exam, he scooted forward and wrapped his arms around Owen's neck. Owen returned the embrace, strong arms engulfing Niall's thin body. His cheek rested against Niall's dark hair, and he closed his eyes.

CHAPTER 32

ARIA SAT SOME DISTANCE from the rest of the humans, ready to begin her megdhonia exercises. She'd been doing them nearly every day, if only for a few minutes, whenever Owen caught her eye and indicated he was ready.

As usual, the Fae were hidden, so she appeared to be alone to the "normal" humans. They were getting used to her regularly meditating, or praying, in private and left her in peace. No one yet had any idea that she was sitting in a group of Fae, learning to use her latent abilities—"magic"— and the Fae agreed with her that it was probably best that way for now.

He sat a few feet from her as she closed her eyes. By now she could immediately feel his presence as well as detect the other Fae individually and as a group, even with her eyes closed.

She drew in a breath and let it out slowly, trying to clear her mind of the events of the last few days. El did not change. He was eternal. He was good.

Owen's familiar restrained kindness guided her into the exercise. He never actually spoke into her mind, though she knew he could. Perhaps he viewed it as invasive, or perhaps he merely didn't want to distract her. Then his mental touch pulled back, leaving her confused for a second.

"May I speak with you a moment, Aria?"

Bartok's voice startled her, and she blinked up at him blankly for a moment.

"Of course."

He knelt in front of her. Owen narrowly avoided being sat on. The Fae were still hidden. They silently and smoothly shifted to make room for Owen to move out of Bartok's way. *They're probably trying to avoid startling him, now that he's right in the middle of them.*

Bartok looked a little pale, and she frowned at him. "Are you all right?"

He swallowed. "Yes, just a little nervous." He gave her a quick smile and licked his lips. "I wanted to ask you a question." He stopped again and cleared his throat before saying, "Aria, would you marry me?"

Light glinted on a blue stone set in a white metal ring held between his thumb and forefinger.

There is nothing I want more.

Looking into his kind brown eyes, she answered, "Yes."

Time stopped.

331

Petro stood a few feet away. He was twice Aria's height and so bright that merely looking at him hurt her eyes. His brilliance cast no shadows.

No one reacted to him. No one moved at all, and in fact, the sound of her *yes* was still hanging in the air. Bartok's warm eyes were on her face, his expression of embarrassed joy catching at her heart. Owen's face was frozen in an expression of amused affection as he stood some distance behind Bartok, his hand making some motion toward the Fae around them.

Petro's voice rumbled like distant thunder. "I have been temporarily granted more authority than usual in order to correct a situation I set up through my previous interference. I had hoped this need would not arise, but it has."

"What?" Aria's voice rang with frustration.

He turned his eyes toward her.

Aria cried out in fear, stumbling backward. His glowing green gaze made her feel like a mouse frozen before a cobra ready to strike. He was alien and terrible, a shining star no human could comprehend.

Yet she felt no malice from him; it was more a sense of smallness, insignificance, and powerlessness that made her heart beat wildly.

"Do not be afraid," Petro said.

"What?"

"Do not be afraid of me. I am not going to harm you," Petro's voice rumbled again.

"You've never minded us being afraid before."

Petro blinked slowly and nodded once. "Perhaps I should have."

Was that an apology?

"I wish to do this as justly as possible. Therefore, you need to understand things more fully. I
will provide you with some information, and then
you must make a choice."

Aria swallowed. *That sounds dangerous.*

"As you may have suspected, I had some part
in the fact that you were raised human. I did not
instigate the killing of your parents. However, I
interfered slightly by assisting your brother in hiding, and in protecting you from being killed."

Her thoughts spun for a moment. "I didn't
know that. Why? I thought you didn't care about
our deaths."

Petro inclined his head in acknowledgment.
"Correct. I did not. Death does not mean much to
me now either, but I understand a little more than I
did then. I interfered then because I wanted to understand more about love and redemption. I hoped
that the information I required could be ascer-
tained by observing two intermediary stages, a Fae
who developed for a time in isolation after parent-
ing barely sufficient to establish him as Fae, and a
closely related Fae, who, having the fully expressed genetic capacity to be Fae, was raised entirely human.

"Understand, I interfered minimally to accomplish this. If I had done nothing at all, both you
and your brother would have died with the rest of
your family group.

"I did not expect the Fae under Owen to provide such surprising additional data. This complicated things much more than I had anticipated. It
confused me."

Aria felt the displeasure in his words. *He is not often confused, and he doesn't like it at all. Well, neither do I.*

"In my confusion, I was tempted. I nearly made serious errors, but grace was given to me to allow me to step back from the precipice I faced." Petro's voice rumbled deep enough to shake the ground.

"What precipice was that?" she asked.

He blinked at her, the glowing eyes highlighting the inhuman beauty of his massive features. "Two, actually. I tell you this for the glory of El. Not because you ask it or because it is required of me, but because I wish to attest to the grace of El, who created us both. The first was when you rescued Owen. My interference would have resulted in your death before your appointed salvation; it is not permitted to interfere in a way that compromises a human's free will. If you had died as an infant, you would have done so under the grace of the covenant El established with your people. By causing you to be raised human, I jeopardized your soul. Yet it was appointed that you were to be saved, and though El permitted my interference, he would not allow you to suffer eternal consequences for my... curiosity."

Aria swallowed a sour taste in her mouth. "El is to be praised."

"Indeed. The second was when Colonel Grenidor was instructed by a demon to call upon the demon's power to banish me and the power of El from his presence. He was also instructed to use bullets covered in the blood of a martyr. If he had done these things, I would have been tempted to react in anger, and in my anger, I might not have remained righteous. I had been tempted by the same being, and I was… dangerously close to believing his lies, or perhaps reacting against them in an unrighteous way, which would have had the same result. I am not sure which he actually intended."

"He did what?" Aria wasn't entirely sure whether she was referring to Grenidor or to the demon, but Petro did not answer the question anyway.

"The continuing developments resulting from my interference are about to create another problem. You and Bartok wish to marry. This would have been permitted if you had been raised fully human and had no knowledge of Fae or megdhonia. Yet this is not the case. I am not permitted to reveal to you how much or how little your abilities might develop, but they have unmistakably begun to develop. You need to understand that even partially functioning Fae are not permitted to marry humans who lack such inborn ability. Too many issues arise when spouses are so unequally yoked for this to be permitted. If you had been raised Fae, you would know this. You did not know because of my interference. This is a problem."

"I thought…" She frowned. "Niall said once that a human and a Fae had a child. Why is it a problem now?"

Petro tilted his head as if puzzled by the question. "Fae history is not flawless, but I believe he was referring to a relationship between a Fae and a human with a partially expressed genetic ability to control megdhonia, though it was not recognized by either humans or Fae at the time. Even that was highly unusual, and not exactly analogous to your situation. Also, the genetic expression of megdhonia in Fae has strengthened somewhat since then, while in humanity it has become so rare as to be essentially nonexistent. Humanity and Fae have become more distinct from each other since then. You are still one species, but the covenants under which you operate have been made less fluid, and there is less room for commingling of blood.

"The problem must be resolved. The simplest way would be for you to renounce the marriage."

Her expression must have made it clear that that was not an option.

"Another way would be to undo what I did, and allow both you and your brother to be killed, as would have happened naturally. You would have died under the Fae covenant, and your souls would not be forfeited. Yet El has used the situation I created for good, and to undo that would be… less than ideal.

"Additionally, I have learned. I wish to set things right as much as possible, not merely remove the problem." He stopped and stared at her for a moment.

Aria was startled to realize that he was now apparently the same size as a regular human, though she hadn't perceived when or how he changed. He stood with unutterable stillness, his gaze on her face. The whiteness of his clothes burned into her eyes; his face was even brighter. She squinted as she looked at him. Then she looked at Bartok, still kneeling in front of her. The ring in his fingers glittered in the dazzling light.

She licked her lips. "Would it be possible to remove the gene from me? Would that solve the problem? Then we could marry, right?"

"This is the reason I have come." His voice reverberated, softer now, but filled with power. "Removing the gene from you would be permitted, and would be a superior solution. However, to correct the inequity in this way would require... more. It is more than simply a gene in your body. The essence of megdhonia is that some of you extends beyond the plane of human existence, and thus, is not constrained by the physical laws of this universe. Humans call it a soul, though your understanding of it is limited. All humans have a soul, and all souls have eternal significance. Megdhonia, through both genetic expression and training, means that your soul extends past the confines of this universe. It does not mean that your soul is fundamentally altered... it is merely stretched and partially located elsewhere. It also means that Fae can maintain some kind of control over their soul, as humans maintain some control over their breathing.

"The gene gives you the potential to do this, but only the potential. The control you are learning now means that more of your soul moves beyond this plane of existence. In essence, more of you is elsewhere. It is this movement of your soul, if you will, that creates the issue.

"You would have to be forced back into this plane alone for the rest of your life, until death frees you from this constraint, as it does for all other humans.

337

"However, I cannot force your soul back to this plane, even the slight distance it has already extended, without your express consent."

Aria frowned and thought.

Petro waited, his face expressionless but his eyes glowing with intensity.

Then she said slowly, "I want to marry Bartok." She glanced at Owen's expression again, feeling the familiar surge of love and affection and gratitude for everything he was, and everything he had given her. Then back at Bartok, his smile that was almost shy, at the suggestion of tears gathering in his eyes as he heard her say *yes*. "I am a Christian. Bartok is a godly man, and I love him. He loves me. I can't imagine that I need to fear for my soul, no matter what happens in this lifetime. I'm willing to give up megdhonia for him."

He still gazed at her without blinking, his gaze sharp and perceptive.

"Just..." she took a deep breath. "Just promise to fix things the best way possible."

Petro blinked then, a startled look on his face. *I've never seen him look startled before.*

"You would trust me to make such decisions on your behalf after what I have told you about myself and my manipulations?" he asked.

"If you will promise that you are fully committed to working within God's plans, then... Yes. I will."

Petro's face broke into a brilliant smile, glittering and joyous. "Done." He vanished, and the world restarted.

The sound of her "yes" faded, and Bartok's smiled widened. He slipped the ring onto her finger, folding his hand around hers as he did so.

Then he glanced around with a puzzled expression and asked, "Where did all the Fae come from?"

Aria looked at him blankly for a second, then looked around the circle. The Fae were hidden, and their expressions said they were stunned at his question.

She laughed out loud for the first time in a very long time.

AFTERWORD

Thank you for purchasing this book. If you enjoyed it, please leave a review! This story is continued in A Long-Forgotten Song Book 4 (coming soon).

C. J. Brightley lives in Northern Virginia with her husband and young children. She holds degrees from Clemson University and Texas A&M. You can find more of C. J. Brightley's books at www.CJBrightley.com, including the epic fantasy series Erdemen Honor, which begins with *The King's Sword* and continues in *A Cold Wind* and *Honor's Heir*. You can also find C. J. Brightley on Facebook and Google+.

THE KING'S SWORD

ONE

I crossed his tracks not far outside of Stone-haven, and I followed them out of curiosity, nothing more. They were uneven, as if he were stumbling. It was bitterly cold, a stiff wind keeping the hilltops mostly free of the snow that formed deep drifts in every depression. By the irregularity of his trail, I imagined he was some foolish city boy caught out in the cold and that he might want some help.

It was the winter of 368, a few weeks before the new year. I was on my way to the garrison at Kesterlin just north of the capital, but I was in no hurry. I had a little money in my pack and I was happy enough alone.

In less than a league, I found him lying face-down in the snow. I nudged him with my toe before I knelt to turn him over, but he didn't respond. He was young, and something about him seemed oddly familiar. He wasn't hurt, at least not in a way I could see, but he was nearly frozen. He wore a thin shirt, well-made breeches, and expensive boots, but nothing else. He had no sword, no tunic over his shirt, no cloak, no horse. I had no horse because I didn't have the gold for one, but judging by his boots he could have bought one easily. There was a bag of coins inside his shirt, but I didn't investigate that further. His breathing was slow, his hands icy. It was death to be out in such weather so unprepared.

He was either a fool or he was running from something, but in either case I couldn't let him freeze. I strode to the top of the hill to look for pursuit. A group of riders was moving away to the south, but I couldn't identify them. Anyway, they wouldn't cross his path going that direction.

I wrapped him in my cloak and hoisted him over my shoulder. The forest wasn't too far away and it would provide shelter and firewood. I wore a shirt and a thick winter tunic over it, but even so, I was shivering badly by the time we made it to the trees. The wind was bitter cold, and I sweated enough carrying him to chill myself thoroughly. I built a fire in front of a rock face that would reflect the heat back upon us. I let myself warm a little before opening my pack and pulling out some carrots and a little dried venison to make a late lunch.

I rubbed the boy's hands so he wouldn't lose his fingers. His boots were wet, so I pulled them off and set them close to the fire. There was a knife in his right boot, and I slipped it out to examine it.

You can tell a lot about a man by the weapons he carries. His had a good blade, though it was a bit small. The hilt was finished with a green gemstone, smoothly polished and beautiful. Around it was a thin gold band, and ribbons of gold were inlaid in the polished bone hilt. It was a fine piece that hadn't seen much use, obviously made for a nobleman. I kept the knife well out of his reach while I warmed my cold feet. If he panicked when he woke, I wanted him unarmed.

I felt his eyes on me not long before the soup was ready. He'd be frightened of me, no doubt, so for several minutes I pretended I hadn't noticed he was awake to give him time to study me. I'm a Dari, and there are so few of us in Erdem that most people fear me at first.

"I believe that's mine." His voice had a distinct tremor, and he must have realized it because he lifted his chin a little defiantly, eyes wide.

I handed the knife back to him hilt-first. "It is. It's nicely made."

He took it cautiously, as if he wasn't sure I was really going to give it back to him. He shivered and pulled my cloak closer around his shoulders, keeping the knife in hand.

"Here. Can you eat this?"

He reached for the bowl with one hand, and seemed to debate a moment before resting the knife on the ground by his knee. "Thank you." He kept his eyes on me as he dug in.

I chewed on a bit of dried meat as I watched him. He looked better with some warm food in him and the heat of the fire on his face. "Do you want another bowl?"

"If there's enough." He smiled cautiously.

We studied each other while the soup cooked. He was maybe seventeen or so, much younger than I. Slim, pretty, with a pink mouth like a girl's. Typical Tuyet coloring; blond hair, blue eyes, pale skin. Slender hands like an artist or scribe.

"Thank you." He smiled again, nervous but gaining confidence. He did look familiar, especially in his nose and the line of his cheekbones. I tried to place him among the young nobles I'd seen last time I'd visited Stonehaven.

"What's your name?"

"Hak-" he stopped and his eyes widened. "Mikar. My name is Mikar."

Hakan.

Hakan Ithel. The prince!

He looked a bit like his father the king. It wasn't hard to guess why he was fleeing out into the winter snow. Rumors of Nekane Vidar's intent to seize power had been making their way through the army and the mercenary groups for some months.

"You're Hakan Ithel, aren't you?"

His shoulders slumped a little. He looked at the ground and nodded slightly.

He had no real reason to trust me. Vidar's men would be on his trail soon enough. No wonder he was frightened.

"My name is Kemen Sendoa. Call me Kemen." I stood to bow formally to him. "I'm honored to make your acquaintance. Is anyone following you?"

His eyes widened even more. "I don't know. Probably."

"Then we'd best cover your tracks. Are you going anywhere in particular?"

"No."

I stamped out the fire and kicked a bit of snow over it. Of course, anyone could find it easily enough, but I'd cover our trail better once we were on our way. A quick wipe with some snow cleaned the bowl and it went back in my pack.

He stood wrapped in my cloak, looking very young, and I felt a little sorry for him.

"Right then. Follow me." I slung my pack over my shoulder and started off. I set a pace quick enough to keep myself from freezing and he followed, stumbling sometimes in the thick snow. The wind wasn't quite as strong in the trees, though the air was quite cold.

I took him west to the Purling River as if we were heading for the Ralksin Ferry. The walk took a few hours; the boy was slow, partly because he was weak and pampered and partly because I don't think he understood the danger. At any moment I expected to hear hounds singing on our trail, but we reached the bank of the Purling with no sign of pursuit.

"Give me your knife."

He gave it to me without protest. He was pale and shivering, holding my cloak close to his chest. I waded into the water up to my ankles and walked downstream, then threw the knife a bit further downstream where it clattered onto the rockslining the bank. Whoever pursued him would know or guess it was his, and though the dogs would lose his trail in the water, they might continue downstream west toward the Ferry.

"Walk in the water. Keep the cloak dry and don't touch dry ground."

"Why?" His voice wavered a bit, almost a whine.

I felt my jaw tighten in irritation. "In case they use dogs." I wondered whether I was being absurdly cautious, whether they would bother to use dogs at all.

He still looked confused, dazed, and I pushed him into the water ahead of me. I kept one hand firm on his shoulder and steered him up the river. Ankle-deep, the water was painfully cold as it seeped through the seams in my boots. The boy stumbled several times and would have stopped, but I pushed him on.

We'd gone perhaps half a league upriver when I heard the first faint bay of hounds. They were behind us, already approaching the riverbank, and the baying rapidly grew louder. I took my hand from the boy's shoulder to curl my fingers around the hilt of my sword. As if my sword would do much. If they wanted him dead, they'd have archers. I was turning our few options over in my mind and trying to determine whether the hounds had turned upriver or were merely spreading out along the bank, when the boy stopped abruptly.

"Dogs."

"Keep walking."

He shook his head. "They're my dogs. They won't hurt me."

I grabbed the collar of his shirt and shoved him forward, hissing into his ear, "Fear the hunters, not the dogs! You're the fox. Don't forget that."

Made in the USA
Middletown, DE
22 May 2016